SANDSTORM

Joyce Yarrow

D. X. VAROS

Published by:
D. X. Varos, Ltd
7665 E. Eastman Ave. #B101
Denver, CO 80231

Book cover design and layout by
D. X. Varos, Ltd using art
©SelfPubBookCovers.com/DesignzbyDanielle

ISBN
978-1-955065-00-9 (paperback)
978-1-955065-01-6 (ebook)

Dedicated to Daria Price,
my first storytelling friend.

1. Runaway Train

I still remember Leon's curly black hair bouncing off his shoulders as he strode through the cavernous Chicago station, where we were changing trains for the southern route. I'd seen him yesterday, on the *Lake Shore Limited*, passing between cars on his way to the snack bar. He'd leaned against the sliding door on the other side of the coupling, looking down at me—he must have been at least six-foot-three. A ray of sunshine penetrated the grime on the window, glancing off his sheepish grin at having been caught smoking. His thick lips had drawn attention to the thinness of his face and I'd felt an urge to kiss him.

After we boarded the *Texas Eagle*, Leon passed by my seat and nodded in my direction. I wasn't surprised. I'd put my hair up, which made me look older.

He waited 'til the night before we were due in El Paso to introduce himself and invite me to join him in the dining car. I guess there's no danger of entanglement when your goodbye is scheduled and printed for all to see. I felt an instant connection with him and loved the way his thick Boston accent stretched vowels to the breaking point.

Leon told me he played flute and was in a jazz orchestra, but I knew how easy it was to lie to strangers. I did it myself. I told Leon I was eighteen.

"I thought you were younger. You wouldn't lie about that, would you?"

I couldn't tell if he was joking or asking for real. I was about to confess to being sixteen, one year older than my real age of fifteen, when the waiter came to take our order.

"Ever had vichyssoise? It tastes a lot better than it sounds."

"I'll take your word for it," I said.

"Then I'll take your word about your age. I'm only two years older than you."

I was glad Leon had bought my story and even happier when the food arrived and my empty stomach let out a growl that made him laugh. As we ate, the sunset floated by like a giant napkin streaked with shades of mustard and ketchup.

"It must be hard for you, Sandie," Leon said. "How are you holding up?"

What could he mean? How could he know the purpose of my trip?

"I hate riding coach for long distances," he explained. "It throws my back out."

Relieved that my new friend could not read minds, I dug into the creamy rice mixed with saffron and mushrooms. The bland taste reminded me of the last meal I'd eaten at Aunt Stella's, hyper-conscious of my packed suitcase under the bed just a room away. It contained some money I'd pilfered from her purse plus the pittance I'd saved from working at her bridal boutique. After buying my train ticket, my roll of bills was as thin as the cinnamon-sprinkled crepes that Leon treated me to for dessert.

"Whither bound?" he asked.

Young as I was, I spotted the phrase as a ploy to make himself seem worldly. *He's a charmer*, I thought.

"I'm on my way to Tucson. Spending the summer with my dad, like I do every year." I wanted the falsehood to be true and who knows — if I stuck with it maybe my wish would come true.

I'd never felt so comfortable with anyone as I did with Leon. Being with him was like diving into a pool where the water perfectly matches your body temperature. He claimed to be 20, on his way home to El Paso after two years of college in New York, but his way of looking at commonplace things, as if seeing them for the first time, made him seem closer to my age.

"See the way that woman grips her spoon? It's like there's an ogre in her soup she's afraid will steal it." Later, as we sped past neatly kept farms and fields outlined by stone walls, he asked, "Why rectangles? If acres were measured in circles civilization might have turned out different."

It was crazy but I understood exactly what he meant.

After dinner Leon took me to the observation car and we made out under the star-filled glass roof. He wasn't clumsy or rough but he wasn't overly smooth either. There were hesitations, looks that asked permission, and I was pretty sure that if I turned down Leon's offer to share his sleeping compartment he wouldn't get pushy. That's why I accepted, in spite of suspecting he'd planned it all along.

It was a good thing Aunt Stella had put me on the pill as soon as Aunt Flo came visiting. "I don't care if you wait 'til you're forty to have sex kiddo, you're not going unprotected on my watch." Probably the most thoughtful thing she'd ever said.

I was relieved to see Leon put on a condom and careful not to let him know it was my first time. *Sex is like putting a tampon in, only bigger,* my one friend at the high school in Queens had told me.

As Leon moved inside me, I felt my heart speed up, sending pulsations through my body keeping time with the rumbling train. I let these new sensations carry me away, feeling the tension grow, not knowing where it would lead or how it would be released, until I felt him shudder and withdraw. Leon rolled off and pulled me back against him on the narrow bunk, so that my head lay against his shoulder as he stroked my hair. I was wide awake, possessed by a strange mixture of rapture and disappointment.

3

"Tell me something about yourself." Leon had sensed my distance and wanted to bring me back.

I pretended to be asleep, not wanting to spoil whatever nice illusions he had about me by answering dumb questions.

Leon shook my shoulder, insisting. "Sandie, when I first saw you, I thought you could be the conductor's daughter, walking around the train like you'd seen it all before."

"My dad's no hardworking railroad man."

"What's he like, then?" My pesky bunkmate used his free hand to turn my face toward him, like he wanted to catch every word.

Honesty was not a habit with me but neither was sharing a narrow bed on a train. Maybe that's why I gave in and told Leon how my father—who since I was old enough to talk had insisted I call him Frank—was really a child himself.

"What makes you think that?"

"There's lots of examples. When he has a job, which is not often, he quits after a few weeks for no reason and plays checkers in the park with his buddies. And his ideas about right and wrong are completely elastic. It's okay to keep things you found on the bus or subway instead of turning them in to the lost and found because 'when people value things they don't lose them.' But it's not okay to cheat at cards. Frank says it's not a crime to shoplift as long as you have a real need for something. According to him, bragging about anything real I might accomplish is gonna give me a 'swelled head,' but lying is no problem, as long as I'm 'creative.'"

"He sounds like a real creep."

"Not really," I said, springing to Frank's defense just like I did at Mom's memorial service, when I overheard my Aunt Stella gossiping with her friends. I told Leon how Stella said people like her brother were "just born irresponsible" and I had yelled "Fuck you! Don't talk about my dad that way!" slapping her face twice before anyone could stop me.

4

Leon propped his head up on an elbow and looked me in the eye. "So you're the only one allowed to criticize your dad?"

"Damn right. Maybe he didn't like holding my hand or hugging me but he did teach me to love the ocean. When the weather turned warm he'd pick me up at school in Yonkers and we'd ride the bus all the way from Yonkers to Orchard Beach in the Bronx. I think admission at the main entrance was free but we always used the shortcut through the chain link fence near the bus stop. Frank called it The Hole in the Fence, like it was an actual place.

"He had to widen the gap so we could wiggle through without getting scratched by the jagged wires. Once we were through, he'd pull the pieces of metal back together. I have to admit, his lessons in fence-closing have come in handy now that I've got my own reasons for making a clean getaway."

Leon stopped stroking my hair and I could tell his interest had moved up another notch. That's when I changed my mind about telling him how I'd ended up on the train. If Leon was really 20 like he said, I didn't want him getting into trouble for hanging out with a teen runaway. Talking about the beach was safer.

"Frank always followed the same routine but that didn't make me any less afraid. I used to wait on the army blanket and ask myself what I'd do, if instead of swimming the length of the beach he got caught in the undertow and the ocean dragged him away forever. Sometimes I cried but usually I held on until I spotted him on the way back, his head bobbing from side to side with every breath. He'd pop out of the water and plow through the sand with that little shuffle he tries to hide. Frank had polio as a kid and one of his legs is little bit shorter than the other."

Leon closed his eyes and I stopped talking. "I'm not asleep," he said. "I'm totally into your story. Please, go on."

"Okay. There's not much to it. After Frank took a break it was my turn to swim alongside him. He never slowed down, so I did my best to keep up. Just when my legs felt too weak to kick, he'd stop and yell over the sound of the surf, 'Had enough, Sandie?' Then, like always, he'd keep swimming."

"Not how I'd treat my kid," Leon said.

"Well he did make a strong swimmer out of me. When we were ready to go home, he'd ask, 'do you want to take the bus?' and I'd say, 'not on my life,' my way of giving him permission to spend our bus fare on ice cream for me and a beer for him. Hitching a ride was easy. Who could resist a little girl sitting on an overstuffed backpack by the side of the road?"

"Especially a little girl who grew up to be as pretty as you," Leon murmured as he drifted off to dreamland, missing the saddest part of the story.

What I never told him was that after Mom died, Frank tried parenting me on his own and failed miserably. One scorching August afternoon I came home from school to find a note on the kitchen table. *Stella will pick you up tomorrow morning. I promise I'll send for you. Love, Dad.*

I knew where he'd gone. Lately that was all he'd talked about. Moving out west and starting a new life in Arizona on his friend Devan's ranch. In between the deep sobs shaking my pillow that night, I had tried to listen to the voice in my head saying he was thinking of me when he made his decision to go it alone. That it would have been selfish to pull me out of school just a year short of graduating junior high and drag me into the unknown. That he'd never desert me.

***

We reached El Paso at 3 a.m. and I matched strides with Leon from inside the train as he strode down the platform across the tracks. I waved when he reached the exit, sad that I'd never see him again and wishing him well.

Returning to Car G, I found my seat, empty and waiting. Leon had asked for my phone number and I'd made one up, guessing that 408 was the right area code for Arizona. I liked him but the future he looked forward to had nothing to do with me.

Eight hours later, I detrained in Tucson, welcomed by a blast of hot air that suffocated my anxiety about seeing Frank more than any of my classmate's pills or even a shot stolen from Aunt Stella's whiskey carafe. By the time I located the closest exit to the street, the thin sleeves of my cotton pullover were saturated with sweat and pinned to my underarms.

I hadn't given much thought to what Tucson would be like and as I walked through the heat-soaked neighborhood I was surprised to see adobe bungalows that looked authentic, not like the ticky-tacky ones I'd seen in western movies.

In a park near the train station, old men huddled on the barely shaded benches, their angular profiles sending a shiver of ancient history up my spine. Unsure how far the Cuban Spanish I'd picked up in New York would stretch, I walked a few blocks before stopping to ask directions from a blond teenager in a tilted beret and shortened black pants, his calves bulging with snake tattoos. His eyes darted behind me as if looking for someone else. "Tanque Verde Road is way on the other side of town. You can walk up Fourth Avenue and get a bus on Speedway."

The AC on the bus re-awakened my doubts. Would Frank be glad to see me in spite of my arriving uninvited? If he asked me what I wanted — why I'd come all the way to Tucson — how could I translate the hope mixed with dread I was feeling into words he'd understand? *You won't have to take care of me — I won't be a burden. Yes, I've got to finish high school but I can work on the weekends and I don't eat much. I've grown up — more than you know — and I'm not the kid I was when you left. I'm good company.* I imagined his eyes, cold rocks of green-gold agate warming as he listened and filling with moisture when at last I got through to him. "You're my daughter," he'd say, "I thought I was doing what was best for you but now I see we're meant to be together."

7

2. Desert Quest

The bus was crowded with college students, some talkative, some tuned into their phones, most of them getting off before my stop on the east side of town. Walking up Tanque Verde Boulevard in the blazing sun, I paused to pull a headscarf out of my suitcase and admire the curved outlines of the foothills to the north.

A pair of giant cacti stood guard at the entrance to Mediterranean Village, their stiff arms pointing skyward, spines at the ready. Brown stucco, three-story buildings with red tile roofs sprawled over acres of parking lots connected by patches of strange plants with puffy leaves. If all the apartments here were piled on top of each other, they'd form one giant high-rise. At least then they'd offer a view of the mountains, instead of soggy swimwear and towels flung over balcony railings.

The front door of building G was covered with cracked inlays of desert flowers and unlocked, with no sign of an intercom or any security devices. In the lobby, a cheap reproduction of a cowboy dancing midair above a bucking bronco, doomed to remain aloft forever, was mounted over an even cheaper looking chair. Under the mailbox for 2D, white letters punched into a black plastic strip read *F. Donovan*.

I walked up the stairs as slowly as I could, all at once wishing I was someone, anyone, else.

The man who opened the door was a browner and leaner version of Dad but the sideways hug he gave me after an endless moment of hesitation was familiar. Since Mom's death, Frank had avoided body contact with me more than ever.

"Come on in. Let's find a place for you to sit."

Cardboard boxes occupied every available space in the living room, which was furnished with a sad yellow couch, a TV on a metal stand and some plastic patio chairs. "It's amazing what you can accumulate in a year's time," he said, clearing a pile of clothes off the couch to make room and handing me a tall glass of water. "You gotta' stay hydrated, kid."

"I thought you were staying at Devan's ranch."

Frank and Devan had met in the children's ward of a Catholic hospital in New Jersey, where in the late nineteen sixties they'd shared the honor of being two of the last few hundred American kids to contract polio after the vaccine came along. The boys were inseparable as teenagers and I'd listened to many stories of their adventures, which ended with Devan being sent to "Juvie" for torching the classic '70 Impala owned by his rival for Annie Slowalski's affections.

After his rehabilitation, Devan moved with his parents to a ranch they'd bought in Arizona. Donkey's years later, as Mom would have put it, Devan's parents died and he inherited the spread. Frank read his friend's letters out loud to his little daughter, promising to take me with him when at last he "was in a position" to accept Devan's frequent invitations to visit.

"What the bastard never told me," Frank now said, "was that he and his wife had converted the place into a resort for spoiled rich kids. I hung in there for a few weeks but after taking those brats on forced marches and teaching them the fine points of shoveling shit and combing the nags they've got stabled out there, I quit. I need a job that doesn't involve unblocking toilets."

10

He continued his usual list of excuses while I looked around at the cardboard boxes. "Have you just arrived or are you moving somewhere?"

"One more day and you'd never have found me." He said this with a touch of sadness that made me wonder if he was glad I had. "Don't worry," he added, having caught my look. "I would have left you a note. Stella called a few day ago. You're not her favorite person right now. I thought I taught you better than to steal from the hand that feeds you."

I ignored the bait. "Where are you moving?"

"It's complicated. Are you hungry?"

Over tuna fish sandwiches, mine washed down with milk and his with Tuborg, we warily exchanged information, like spies from different countries forced to work together.

"If you'd phoned ahead I would have picked you up at the airport."

"I took the train — and your number isn't listed. Stella chose to keep your whereabouts a secret."

"She has her ways," he said with a grimace, implying that his disappearance from my life was a misunderstanding we could blame on his temperamental sister.

"Why did you run away from Astoria?" he asked.

"It's complicated."

"Okay, okay. I'm sorry I ran out on you. I thought Stella would be a better caretaker."

"She's not and I don't need one. Why can't I live with you?"

"Believe me, I'd like nothing better." He cleared the table and had his back to me when he said, "Trouble is, there's room for just one where I'm going."

"And who would that be?"

I waited while he forced himself to look at me. "I met someone. She's got a small house out in the desert. When I lost my job she suggested I move in, just 'til I get back on my feet. I suppose, now that you're here, I could try..." He looked around helplessly and I asked myself what this woman could possibly find so attractive. *He needs a mother more than I do.*

Suddenly I was very tired. "Do you mind if I lie down for a bit. Then I'll see if I can find a cheap hotel."

"There's no need for that — the hotel I mean. At least not yet. The rent's paid up for two more weeks." He pushed aside some boxes, clearing the way to the bedroom. "Here's a clean towel. You can take a shower when you wake up."

Lying on his bed, which smelled faintly of nicotine and something else I didn't want to think about, I thought I couldn't blame him, not really. He barely had his own head above water. Any extra weight was sure to pull him under. My dad wasn't the swimmer he used to be. I started to doze off and images from my two years living with Aunt Stella floated through my head.

***

At an age when I was outgrowing my clothes every six months, my main goal had been to make myself small enough not to be much trouble. I tried hard to convince myself Stella believed she was playing my dead mom's role. But when she confiscated the tube top I'd worn to the beach on so many happy outings with Frank, saying "I can't let my you run around looking like a hooker," I felt her ripping the last remnants of better days right out of my life. Later that night, I snuck into my aunt's bathroom and carefully inserted tiny grains of red pepper in her lipstick tube. The howls of distress coming from her room the next morning gave me enormous satisfaction.

"I'll sue those mother fuckers! I'll take every dime they've got!" Stella ranted in the car, squirting aloe vera from a tube onto her swollen, red wax candy lips. We were on our way to *Tessa's Trousseau*, a bridal shop Stella had bought with the insurance money left by her dead husband Clark. I'd already spent most of the summer ironing dresses in the stifling back room.

12

Stella claimed owning a bridal shop was the perfect cure for the pain of having gone through three divorces. "It's like I'm a recovering alcoholic working in a bar. Every time a young fool drunk on dreams of her perfect union comes into the shop it strengthens my resolve never to marry again."

On the way home in the car, Stella asked, "Did you do something to my lipstick?" in that *I'm a patient person who's about to lose it* tone she specialized in.

"Must've been a child worker in China getting her revenge," I said, pleased with my own cleverness in spite of the inevitable repercussions.

My aunt said nothing, but she piled on the ironing and when I got my paycheck there was a note attached. *You're not in China but if you ever do harm to me again you will be.*

I clung to hope in the form of Frank's weekly postcards. The messages were brief. *I miss you. See you in June. Be good. Love Dad.* I loved the mythical jackalopes, with giant floppy rabbit ears making a joke of their antelope legs and the photos of one-story wooden buildings squatting on Main Street against a backdrop of vast open space totally alien to my life in Queens. I pinned the cards on the wall above my bed, arranging them in the shape of an arrow pointing westward, out the door of my room to the road I'd soon be traveling. I wanted to write Frank back, but none of the cards included a return address.

I might have toughed it out at Stella's until my high school graduation if my cousin Giles hadn't come home after graduating from college to find his room occupied. Stella stage-whispered to him in the kitchen, "You should pity the girl instead of being angry. She's got no place else to go." He seemed to calm down after that, but I sensed trouble in the way he looked at me when he made up the fold-out couch in the living room. Sure enough, Giles developed a habit of barging into his/my room, wearing nothing but a towel wrapped around his waist. He made a big show of rummaging through the tall-boy dresser, searching for something to wear. It was a ridiculous charade, because all the garments that fit him were in the Navy duffle bag he'd dumped in the hallway.

It was only a matter of time until Giles dropped that towel. When he did, I snatched a handful of plush velour off the floor and with one well-aimed snap sent him howling out of the room.

A week later, looking through Stella's purse for some loose change for the laundry room, I discovered a letter in Frank's handwriting. *I'm not fit for fatherhood, never was. Cash the check and let her buy something nice. Then break the bad news.* The letter was more than a year old and Stella had kept every cent of the money. I'd copied the return address in Tucson onto the back of my hand.

***

I woke up in Frank's room with a splitting headache and a bad case of fish breath. His voice was a low murmur in the other room. I cracked the door so I could hear him on the phone.

"I called the Runaway Hotline. They have a Home Free program — they'll put her on a bus at their expense and send her back. Please Stella — you're my only hope."

I couldn't hear Stella's answer but I knew what she'd say.

"Okay, okay — I get it," Frank responded. "She's my responsibility."

I retreated to the bathroom, standing under the slow lukewarm dribble in the shower stall as I considered what to do next. One thing I crossed off the list was crawling back to New York and begging Aunt Stella for forgiveness, even if it were offered, which was extremely unlikely. Maybe it was just Frank's panic talking and he'd get used to having me around.

He'd hung up the phone by the time I emerged in clean jeans, drying my hair with a towel I was afraid would disintegrate if I rubbed my head too hard.

"Let's go for a drive. I'd like you to see Devan's place."

14

"Are you still on speaking terms after you quit?"

He was halfway out the door and I had to follow him outside to hear his answer. "Of course. My friendship with Dev bounced back quicker than a cowboy runs through chewin' tobacco."

The western twang in his voice didn't surprise me. Dad was a chameleon. And the Recovery Ranch stencil on the side of his pickup seemed to support his statement.

We listened to a plaintive singer on the Spanish radio station, which oddly enough made me homesick for New York, as Frank drove west and then into the foothills, past quarter-acre subdivisions packed with particle board houses as suited to the landscape as grass huts would be in Manhattan.

When the blacktop turned to dirt I got my first glimpse of the desert *au natural* against the backdrop of the Santa Catalina Mountains. The giant saguaro cacti I'd seen near Mediterranean Village were here in the thousands, some of them blooming with deep red flowers that according to Frank were distilled into ceremonial wine by the Indians. "Never tried it myself but I hear it packs a wallop."

We drove by the ruins of a square adobe house, minus its roof, walls covered with scaffolding. "A hundred years ago this was a station on the Pony Express route, a piece of living history. In a few weeks all that's left of it will be a plaque in the ground next to some lawyer's condo." His anger sounded genuine. Maybe Frank had absorbed more than the lingo from his new environment.

The ruts in the dusty road slowed the truck to what seemed like an endless bouncy crawl. *Just one more bump and my lower back's crippled for life*, I thought. At last we rolled onto a smooth macadam surface.

"Devan's folks kept some cattle," Frank said, getting out to open a bright red metal gate connected to an electric fence. I was getting a sense of the perimeter of Recovery Ranch and it wasn't small.

The narrow black road continued to cut through the desert with knife-like precision. Frank turned off the AC and rolled down the windows. "Take a deep breath."

Although the smells coming in from all sides were new to me and not unpleasant, chicory and something like licorice — anise Frank said — the aromatherapy wasn't enough to quell my unease.

I strained for a glimpse of the ranch house. It didn't appear for another ten minutes, and then only as a black spec in the distance. Minute by minute the spec grew larger against the limitless sky, ultimately expanding into a massive hacienda, rocks embedded in its thick clay walls. Behind the Spanish style house a featureless concrete building towered over the small bunkhouses surrounding it.

"Are you sure this isn't a Russian prison?"

Frank laughed unconvincingly. "I doubt they had horses."

He pulled up next to a group of teens who were unloading bales of hay from a truck and loading them into a two-story barn. "Speaking of horses, why don't you go have a look? I need to talk some business with Devan up at the house."

***

I heard the snort before my eyes adjusted to the dim light in the barn. One was ebony black with a white blaze under his forelock, the other a speckled bay mare. I stroked the black's nose, soft as the foreskin I'd been shocked to feel on Leon's penis. The comparison made me giggle.

"Prince doesn't like to be laughed at." Over my shoulder I saw the owner of the voice, a dark-haired girl in an army fatigue shirt that was either the real thing or a great imitation.

"Hi. I'm Danielle. Where's your stuff?"

I stood there looking at her, so Danielle explained, "I'm in charge of new arrivals, getting you set up in your bunkhouse, orientation, that kinda' stuff."

16

"Not necessary. I'm just visiting with my dad." It felt strange saying *my dad* after such a long time.

Danielle looked over at the house through the open barn door and then back at me. "He say he was gonna' talk some business with Devan?"

"They're old friends."

"Sure. Old as money changin' hands."

It took me two seconds to get the gist of these words and then I was off and running. Halfway up the porch steps I heard an engine start behind me. Frank would have beat me out the driveway if a group of kids hadn't chosen that moment to drag some piles of firewood across the path of his truck.

I tugged at the door handle on the passenger side but by then he'd locked himself in. I jumped on the floorboard and leveraged myself onto the front fender and then the hood. A group of residents had gathered to watch the fun.

Frank got out of the truck and dragged me off the hood, hustling me over to a grove of scrub oaks where he could deal with my behavior in private. His voice was a low hiss. "You're gonna' stay here and from what Devan's told me you'll start to like it. The kids learn real life skills and he's been generous enough to offer you a job that will cover the cost of your room and board."

"Like the one shoveling shit that you were too good for?"

"I knew there'd be no talking to ya'." That obnoxious drawl was earning its keep.

"So you decided to abandon me — it's what you do best."

"You stole from your own flesh and blood and gave my sister no respect. It's better you catch on that there are consequences." Self-righteousness coming from the likes of him stunned me into silence as he continued blabbering. "This place is a lot better than a foster home and you'll learn to obey the rules." As if he hadn't taught me that 'rules are for fools.'

17

"Sandie, you'll come out of here with some appreciation of what freedom means — you have to earn it. If you behave yourself, maybe in a few months, when I get on my feet..."

"No. Not you. You'll never stand up like a normal person. You're gonna creep around on all fours for life, like a whipped dog complaining about how unfair life is while you slink from alley to alley. And one day you're gonna wake up in a flop house in some sorry city, wondering if anyone at all knows you're alive. And you'll try to find me so you'll have somebody to hold your stinkin' hand when you die but it won't do you no good 'cause by then I'll have forgotten your name and when this stranger calls, I'll hang up the phone and that'll be your last memory of me — a big, fat, *click*."

I didn't choose these words, they chose me, as if a ventriloquist had replaced my voice with a stranger's, filled with hatred and a vocabulary to go with it.

"I'll send your stuff over tomorrow." Frank's back was straight as he walked away. I'd given him the out he needed.

I sat on the ground and banged my hands against the sharp pebbles in the dirt 'til the palms bled. I pictured myself wandering out into the desert, losing my way, drying up into a stack of bleached bones and the thought brought with it a strange comfort. If things got too bad, I knew what I would do.

3. Breakout

A year into my stay at Recovery Ranch, the fantasy that Frank would be back to fetch me any day had been replaced by the dull, angry ache of acceptance. I'd seen dozens of residents come and go, returned to their parents while I continued to replay my last conversation with my father in a hopeless loop of despair. Not a day passed when I failed to wonder how he could have dumped all that blame on me for stealing the train fare from New York, when he was the one who was a thief. He'd stolen my mother's energy and life and it was his own heartless desertion combined with Stella's greed that had pushed me over the edge.

The bunkhouse I shared with five other girls was spotlessly clean and permeated with a smell that early on I recognized as fear. On my first night, one of the newbies, an anorexic-looking girl I later came to know as Tiffany, sobbed continuously into her pillow.

Although I had little pity to spare for anyone, for some reason I felt protective toward Tiffany. I'd gotten a glimpse of her thick halo of platinum hair prior to her initiation, which made it doubly painful to see her walking around like a starved POW with a shaved head and oversized eyes. My own hair had been spared, I assumed because Devan had me working in the front office and didn't need a bald receptionist frightening parents already skittish about signing their kids' freedom away.

Recovery Ranch did not cater to sissies. The Outdoor Intensive, a series of endless, Herculean tasks assigned by the staff at whim, was guaranteed to turn the most hardened juvenile delinquent into a slab of quivering Jell-O. The goal was to push everyone beyond their endurance and that no one had died during my stay was a small miracle and not the result of any compassion shown by our counselors during the forced marches though the desert, military style calisthenics, and meaningless hard labor we "clients" endured.

I soon figured out that resistance was no use and I was better off embracing the challenges. After weeks of daily rock climbing, I discovered muscles in my arms and thighs I'd never known existed. I also spent as much time as possible with the horses. Their large quiet eyes provided the only patience and receptivity allowed to exist on the Ranch. However, any positive side effects from being close to nature were canceled out by the brutality of the group therapy sessions.

"We've got to break you down before we can build you up," was the pathetic excuse given by the counselors, who showed us every day how much better they were at breaking than building. Those in the "sharing circle" were encouraged to "be honest," which Tiffany said was code for dishing out abuse to your peers.

At first, I refused to participate and sat in stony silence. The staff were experts at dealing with "intractables" like me. They punished the others in the group for "alienating a member," withholding food and petty privileges to force the group to apply pressure, harassing the "non-participant" from all directions. I tried inventing stories to share, complete with crocodile tears shed over supposedly heart-rending traumas—in one version I lost my little brother under a speeding subway train—but my fellow inmates saw right through me. At best they were indifferent, and the worst ones wanted the truth about my life to use as

20

ammunition. Everywhere I went, relentless eyes tried to peer into my soul, refusing to give me peace, driving me to confess crimes of which I had no knowledge. Every day I witnessed another underage resident crumble into a groveling heap, willing to say or do anything to please his or her tormentors and be allowed to go home.

Tiffany carried herself like a piece of delicate glass manufactured by her namesake and stared so hard at the ground when you spoke to her you thought she'd set fire to her shoes. The Activity Director viewed her charge's thin arms and stick-like legs as a personal affront. "We're gonna bulk you up so the next time somebody offers you some crank you'll have the strength to say no!" Lettie barked when she dragged Tiff out of bed for calisthenics.

We all tried faking it, turning jumping jacks into bunny hops when Lettie's back was turned, but it was Tiffany who the AD forced to do extra pushups when she was caught.

"Can't you see she's gonna collapse?" I blurted out one morning.

"Fine," said Lettie. "You can take her place and give me fifty."

"Next time don't do me no favors," Tiffany scolded me later, as we waited on the lunch line for our meager portions of mashed potatoes and dried up chicken nuggets. "They're gonna think I'm a weakling and lay it on even thicker."

The crybaby had some spunk after all.

"If that's how you react when someone tries to help, I'd hate to see you when you're riled up," I said.

Tiffany responded with a laugh—a sound so rarely heard in the cafeteria that heads turned.

After that, we hung out together during what little free time we had. Along with most of the kids at the Ranch, Tiffany had witnessed my arrival and humiliation by Frank.

"Isn't your mom around? How come she doesn't come and get you?" she asked.

"Because when I was thirteen she started coughing nonstop and missing days at work. She said it was a cold she couldn't shake. I knew a lie when I heard one and I asked my dad what was wrong. Frank told me, 'Brenda's got emphysema,' in an angry voice, like my asking the question made the disease worse. Inside a month my mom's yellow pantsuit jackets were flapping off her thin arms like flags of distress."

"That's so sad." Tiff lit up a joint and when she shared the precious contraband with me, I could tell she meant what she said.

"Even now, I can't stand the smell of raspberry-filled chocolate cupcakes," I told her. "All during her illness, Mom's co-workers from the Breckendale Catalog Company brought her pastries from the donut shop across the street. They'd sit at her bedside, their eyes on the goodies calling to them from the table, probably wondering if she'd devour the cupcakes after they left or throw them out. She packed them in my lunch bags instead. After Mom died, I felt guilty for missing those treats. It took me a long time to remember that when I was small she used to call me 'cupcake.' Those raspberry-filled circles were a lot more real and nourishing than the wheezing skeleton she became. They were our last and only connection."

"My mom's gone too," Tiff said. "Nobody knows where she is and I don't wanna talk about it."

***

Our favorite meeting place was behind a giant rock unearthed during construction of a new bunkhouse. We'd consume our supply of smokes and exchange warnings about which of the more gung-ho counselors had to be avoided. By Ranch standards, we were friends. In spite of which, it took Tiff almost six months to trust me with some basic facts about her life.

"My dad's a bush pilot in Alaska."

"Sure, and mine's the King of England."

Tiffany glared at me. "I bet you don't know how to cook over an open fire or dress an Elk. Pop taught me how to survive in the wild. One of these days he'll land his twin engine Otter in the baseball field and take me home."

"Sure he will." I knew way better than to try to dislodge my touchy friend's belief in the miraculous. "I heard you're a jail-dodger who got sent here by a judge. What were you busted for?"

She snorted. "It's big time—I stole Sudafed from a drug store so me and my boyfriend Todd could make our own powder, maybe sell some on the side. He already had the equipment we needed and the iodine crystals and RP."

"What's RP? Rotten potatoes?"

"Red phosphorous—you get it off the strike pad on a matchbook."

"Todd sounds like a real chemist."

"He was and it killed him. He thought he knew how to cook meth but the stuff he made kicked his ass off this earth and almost killed me too. Not that I cared. I was so messed up I would have snorted my own poop if I thought it would take the pain away. Speaking of which, how would you like to get drunk?"

Tiff's scheme was simple. She was friends with one of the boys, who knew how to make wine out of saguaro fruit. "Tash's father is a member of the Tohono O'odham tribe," she said. "His mother's a white woman from one of the wealthier families in Tucson. Tash ended up at this hellhole they call a ranch after he ran away from her house in the suburbs to the San Xavier Reservation so many times the police called him the Eighteen Mile Kid."

According to Tiffany, Tash snuck out of the Ranch at night and used a long pole to harvest the saguaro fruit. "All we need is an alcohol stove to cook the pulp. He says it turns into syrup. You let it sit for a few days and that's it."

"Where are you hiding all this paraphernalia? If Devan finds out, he'll march us into the desert to dig our own graves."

"Not a problem. Remember how they boarded up the hot box after the people from Children's Services came?

After they left, Tash loosened up a few panels and now it's his secret hideaway."

The wine got us so sloshed we didn't mind the disorientation, nausea, and dry heaves. Tash was a sweet boy and when he was drunk enough, he sang what he called, "magic songs that take me far away from this terrible place." One night he told us a story about the coyote who envied the bluebird's bright blue feathers so much that he bathed in the lake where the bird got its color and dyed his own fur a brilliant blue.

"As he ran, the coyote looked to see if his shadow had also turned blue. He paid no attention to where he was going and crashed into a stump so forcefully he was thrown to the ground. When he got up, he was covered with dirt and that's why coyotes' coats are the color of dusty earth."

Tash took a long swig of saguaro wine and continued. "My mother was the bluebird and my father the coyote who sadly thought he could be just like her. He was mistaken. After their divorce, my mom refused to let him visit me, so I went and found him on my own. He's not someone who could survive life in a split-level house with an Astroturf lawn, but he taught me to love the beauty of my own skin."

The next day Devan tore down the hot box. Enraged by his discovery of the rotten saguaro fruit, he cut rations for everyone in half, sure that some hungry soul would give up the wine makers. When that didn't work, he assigned a newly hired Counselor Mike, to interrogate us individually.

Rumor had it Mike had been fired from his job as a State Prison guard for practicing excessive brutality. He commandeered one of the boys' bunkhouses and forced the inmates to sleep out in the open so he could question suspects at any time of day or night. He made no secret of his distaste for Indians and quickly zeroed in on Tash as his main target.

That afternoon, Tiffany and I were hiding in the brush beneath the bunkhouse's only window, listening in anguish to our friend's screams as he was beaten. We were sure Tash would never talk and terrified that Mike would get carried away and stomp the slightly built boy to death.

Tash's yowls of pain stopped for a while and when they started up again, I'd heard enough. "Stay here," I told Tiff, who was too frail to be of any use in a fight. I snagged a two-by-four left over from the demolished hotbox—Lettie would have been proud—and rushed inside.

Mike stood over Tash, his fists raised, preparing to deliver another rage-filled blow. At the last second he hesitated—had he heard my footsteps approaching? When he spun around to face me, I swung the lumber straight at his head. The so-called counselor propelled his arms upward and pushed the plank over and down, smashing the full weight and force of my attack onto Tash's terrified, upturned face.

We shared one moment of stupefied silence. I stood frozen in horror, giving Mike time enough to recover himself and imprison my arm in a vise-like grip.

"Your fingerprints are on the delivery end of that board. You killed him to keep him from spouting off about your misdeeds. I did my best to stop you," he said, exulting in the lie. "I'm turning you in to the police."

Keeping hold of my arm, he yanked his cell phone out of his back pocket. I kicked him hard in the shins and when his grip loosened, struggled free. As I ran, his mocking voice followed: "You won't get far!"

I flew out of the bunkhouse and Tiffany, who had seen everything through the window, joined me in flight. We got as far as the giant woodpile behind the admin building and crouched down behind it.

"I killed Tash, I killed Tash..." I murmured over and over.

"It wasn't your fault. I saw that bastard slam down your arm. He set the whole thing up."

I wondered why the emergency bell, an eardrum-breaking cross between a jackhammer and a siren, was silent. The answer lay in the fancy SUV with California plates parked in the carport in front of the office. They were

25

offloading a new arrival plus gear. Poor kid. She looked tough in her lumberjack shirt, which would only make things worse.

The unsuspecting girl and her parents followed Devan inside. He would hurry them through the paperwork and as soon as her folks left, he'd initiate a lockdown and a search. The last place he'd be looking for a runaway would be right in front of him.

"Give me a sec," Tiff whispered.

She strolled over to the far side of the van and motioned me over. Someone had left the sliding door open.

I crawled in halfway and turned to face her. "I hope I see you again," was all I could think to say.

"Whatever you do, don't get out before you cross the border into California. That should take four or five hours. Then head for Los Angeles. This guy Russell owes me a favor and he'll take you in." Tiff handed me a candy-wrapper with an address and phone number scrawled on it. "You can keep it. I have it memorized. Good luck," she said and slid the door closed. Barely breathing and flattening my body into the floorboards behind the back seat, I waited for the sound of ignition and the rumbling of wheels.

4. All that Glitters...

It was a miracle I didn't pee myself during that unending ride. I stuck it out all the way to San Diego, hidden from the pair of misfits in the front seat who, like my deadbeat dad, had found the perfect place to dump their unwanted child. Not a charitable thought. Not a charitable world. At times, their voices rose above the country music blaring from the speaker level with my ear and I could make out a few choice words: "Damn! Why did she make us do this!" from the Mom and "She's got to learn the hard way, just like I did," from the dad. What a pair.

We pulled into the driveway of their faux adobe house with its fake, rubber tile roof and fancy curtains. Stella would have loved it. After they'd carried everything inside, I crawled out of the van. The woman came to the window, sensing some movement, and I was tempted to reveal myself. It was almost worth the risk to see the surprise on her face.

I had no cell phone, no money, and no food. The keys were still in the ignition but only an idiot would steal an SUV while being wanted by the police in the next state over.

It was a short walk from *bed-aburbia* to the beach, where I said a quick "hello-goodbye" to the Pacific and took a deep breath of sea air to sustain me. Hiking north on Highway One, I felt conspicuous in my sweaty, torn t-shirt, the only one I had, and nervous about the kind of person who would pick up an obvious stray like me.

A beat-up, red station wagon skidded to a halt a few yards in front of me, backed up, and pulled over to the curb. A pair of elderly hippies wearing bright colors much too young for their age got out and looked me over. They introduced themselves as Rachel and Stanley, like this was the normal thing to do when picking up a hitchhiker. I gave my name as Sandie. No need to lie to these hipsters, who looked like they'd accept anyone at face value who wasn't a serial killer.

"We're on our way to Santa Barbara, Rachel said. "How about you?"

When I told them Malibu, Stanley looked doubtful. "You'd need a boob job and a Gucci purse to get admitted to the food market up there, much less an actual house."

Rachel bumped his arm, as if she was used to their sharing a perpetual joke. "For all you know she's a movie star's daughter."

From my seat behind her in the car, I got a good view of the lady's dyed-blonde, bird's-nest hairdo, from which I wouldn't have been surprised to hear a few chirps. They had good taste in music though, and Michael Jackson serenaded our drive through the beach towns along Pacific Coast Highway. When the road dipped down toward the water, I could see the bobbing heads of surfers clinging to their boards. The salt air was nice, until it took on a chemical smell.

"That's the stink from the Long Beach oil fields," Stanley said.

An hour later we turned up Malibu Canyon and they let me off at an ultra-modern building that resembled a library designed to look like a UFO. In the distance, a speck of ocean was visible between the sleek steel columns supporting the circular structure.

Could this possibly be where Russell lived? Tiffany had never mentioned him during our nightlong, drunken talks. Maybe he was special to her and she'd wanted to keep him for herself. Which was too bad, since when he came out to meet me at the gate, I was immediately attracted to Russell's muscular physique and his short, reddish-gold beard gleaming in the Southern California sun.

"You must've had some good rides. Tiffany called and told me what happened. From what she said, I didn't expect you to get here so soon."

He put his hands on my shoulders and held me at arm's length, like he wanted to make sure I was real. "You've got good bone structure, like J. Lo, only your nose is turned up. Are you hungry? I hope you like Chinese."

I couldn't believe he'd ordered take-out and was celebrating my arrival, like I was a friend he hadn't seen in a while. But that's the way Russell was. He didn't do things by halves. He took me in like a stray lamb and treated me like a queen.

It took a week of living in luxury, with my own room and bath and no pressure from Russell to do anything but sleep, for me to work up the nerve to ask him, "What kind of business are you in?"

His eyes flared and he crossed his arms like a genie who'd been asked to reveal the source of his powers.

"Oh, come on, Rusty. I come in peace. You know that."

I'd made up the nickname on the spot. Russell liked it, because he said, "I'll show you," and I followed him down the stairs into his workshop for the first time.

I stared in fascination at what I would soon come to recognize as the tools of Russel's trade: platinum crucibles filled with flux solutions he later explained were heated in the furnace to more than 2,200° F to force rubies to grow, the burnout kiln and centrifugal casting machine, and sets of pliers, tweezers, and files that shared a table with a jeweler's saw and calipers, along with the all-important polishing brush.

"I make replica antique jewelry and I grow and sell synthetic gems—sapphires, emeralds, and spinel, but mainly rubies. There are lots of synthetic jewels floating around out there but my customers prefer paying top dollar for what looks the most genuine."

"You make gems that can pass for the real thing?"

"Listen baby, my fakes are way better than the Chinese. I use the flux method. It's complicated and hard to explain. There's one dealer who buys everything I can produce. I know all the latest tests for authenticity and how to get around them."

I didn't like being called baby, or 'broad' or any of the other outdated slang words he loved to use. When I complained, Russell said he'd picked these expressions up from movies I was too young to have seen.

"Life's got a right to imitate art." That was the line he stuck to and I didn't make a big deal out of it. He was sensitive in other ways that mattered, like when I woke up, covered with sweat and agitated by recurring nightmares of Tash's death and he'd bring me lemon tea, laced with whiskey and sit with me while I fell back to sleep. Russell taught me how to survive, even thrive, despite being one of the hunted.

No wonder Tiff had put us together.

"She was a freshman in high school when I was a senior," Russell said when I asked how they'd met. "Quite precocious, I might add." He put on a British accent for this last bit, in an offhand way that painted a picture of him hanging out in a castle with friends. Not surprising, since Russell came from money and knew how to fit in with the upper crust.

His house in Malibu Canyon was two miles from the beach where he went surfing at dawn. Once I thought I saw Leonardo DiCaprio riding the curl of a wave right behind him but Russell never said a word about it.

On the surface we were a typical California *Nouveau riche* couple. Except that one of us was a jewelry forger and the other was wanted for murder and lived under an assumed name, frequently changing her appearance. Occasionally, I'd go online to hunt for news reports about what happened at the Ranch. When I couldn't find any, I presumed Devan and his cronies had managed to hush everything up. Still, the police didn't give up easily on a homicide and would be searching for me on the quiet.

Whenever he had a bit too much to drink, Russell would go on a rant about how much he'd admired his father, until he discovered the family business in downtown Los Angeles was trafficking in blood diamonds. How he'd bided his time and learned everything he could about the trade. How his first big thrill came from fooling his father with a copy of one of his dad's own pieces — a giant emerald in a twenty-four-carat gold setting. The first time he told me all this, he ended the tirade with, "So now you know. I'm a Bard graduate who majored in political science and like most politicians, devotes himself to the science of fakery."

Russell saw us as kindred spirits living outside the law and the financial system he despised. I was too young to know better and adopted many of his ways, just like I'd absorbed my dad's.

Most of all I loved watching him practice his alchemy. I was the only person with whom Russell shared the secrets of his craft and this contributed to his mystique. That, and the fact that he was the first person I'd met who created beauty with his hands.

With the same precision he applied to his craft, he constructed a new identify for me as Sandra Storm. This was a takeoff on Sandstorm, his nickname for me when I got into one of my angrily depressed moods. He put Sandie Donovan to rest, delivering a touching funeral oration at the Stand-Up Bar in Santa Monica. "You have that rare chance, a second life. Enjoy it!" he shouted.

At first I was glad to be free of the weight of bad memories associated with my family name. But the thought that this camouflage might be permanent—that the Tucson Police had entered my name in the FBI database as a wanted felon and I might never be able to call myself a Donovan again—was depressing. Especially when I thought about Brenda. If Frank was the one who played fast and loose with the truth, Mom was the kind of person who, when she found coins on the sidewalk, saved them in a jar to return them, "just in case."

Sensing my mood, Russell pulled me close and after more than a month of living together like brother and sister, we shared out first kiss. It was worth the wait.

He booked us a vacation to St. Croix and it was under the full moon, on a red and black embroidered Mexican blanket spread out next to a palm tree fronting the beach, that we first had sex. I told him it was my second time, the first happening on a train and not amounting to much. He laughed and gave me a pink tablet imprinted with a bunny rabbit. Rolling on waves of Ecstasy, it felt like when we caressed each other we were touching everything and everyone in the world. He called me "Sandstorm, my whirling beauty" and we drove each other crazy.

Russell took me snorkeling for the first time, showing off his encyclopedic knowledge of tropical fish and dazzling me with sayings like, "thieves are the only people honest enough to admit we own nothing on God's earth."

Even on St. Croix, he kept the business going via WhatsApp and would disappear into his own world, changing from my relaxed, playful Rusty into a person I thought of as Russell the Pretend Gangster Guy.

On our last day on the island, he presented me with a bracelet inlaid with emeralds surrounded by small diamonds. "Green, for your eyes, the real thing, not one of my fancy tricks."

Back in LA, I told him I wanted to be his "apprentice." I put it that way so he wouldn't refuse. What I really wanted

32

was to be his partner. At first he gave me the grunt work of buying supplies, mainly stainless steel, and cheap gold plating he used for making fake gold chains to sell in Inglewood.

When I voiced my disappointment, he said, "You've got to learn patience, Sandie. It takes up to a year to grow a crop of rubies in the solution. In the meantime, I sell chains to tide me over. Everyone wants them and mine easily pass the acid test for eighteen carats."

Gradually he let me help him with the more complex processes, right up to the day when I was able to create my first original Art Deco sapphire ring in the style of Raymond Templier, a famous French jewelry designer from the nineteen-twenties. The sapphire needed work, he said, but Russell was pleased with the ridges I'd carved on the setting, following his instructions on how to convincingly age the silver.

"A few more tries and you might make something we can pass as the real thing."

"You're just being nice," I said, secretly rejoicing. When it came to his craft, Russell made no compromises. The most money he'd ever made from counterfeiting was a hundred grand for an emerald necklace he told me was auctioned off by the buyer for twice that much.

Russell taught me everything he knew about forging Deco jewelry, except how to deal with the fences and other shady characters who dropped in at all hours. He didn't have to explain that without these risky transactions we could never afford our fancy lifestyle. He'd shoo me away before opening the back door, unapologetically banishing me.

"It's too dangerous, Sandstorm. And you're too precious to risk."

This was the closest he ever came to saying he loved me and for a long time it's all I needed.

After 'Sandra Storm' became the first in my family to get a GED, I registered for acting classes at Santa Monica College. Russell was amused. "Everybody wants to be in show biz but most of them end up on the business side of a horse."

I winced at the scorn in his voice but stood my ground and eventually he reversed course. "You've reinvented yourself in real life so why not on stage or in the movies?"

I was relieved to hear him say this but not surprised when he added, "Don't even think about bringing any of your new friends to the house, babe."

***

I walked into my first drama class with no clue what to expect. I was late, having gotten lost on campus. The instructor flashed me a quick smile and introduced himself as Darshon Alexander. His burnt-cocoa face showed no lines, making it hard to tell how old he was.

The students were paired off and in the middle of an exercise in sharing secrets. Darshon reassigned his partner to me, a large woman named Pamela whose soft voice I first took for a sign of weakness. Pamela and I were supposed to confide things in each other that we'd never shared with anyone. No reactions or follow-up questions allowed. When my turn came, I thought about all the crap buried in my life. Without thinking, I said, "My father abandoned me at a boot camp in the desert."

Pamela met my eyes in silent sympathy. I could practically see the words, one by one, as they strained to exit her throat. "My husband doesn't know I had an abortion five years ago."

"Did you think he'd leave you if you told him?" I blurted, forgetting Darshon's instructions. "Sorry, I'm an idiot."

"That's OK. I figure I spared him a lot of pain and may have saved our marriage. He's a Catholic."

During the weeks that followed, I learned a lot about acting in Darshon's class but there was something else that kept bringing me back. Every time he asked us to draw on our own experiences to create characters, I was forced to

34

admit how much I had in common with my fellow students. Although most of them seemed to live charmed lives and to take their future successes for granted, they'd also had big doses of the pain life inflicts on all of us. When it came down to the nitty gritty, these were my people.

It was in Darshon's class that I learned how imaginary feelings can be the most genuine, especially for people like me who hate showing our emotions. He bluntly told me that as an actor who started out on the minus side of life, I had the advantage.

"You're good at playing the underdog."

"I'm also damn good at theatrical make-up," I said. "Have used it for years to disguise my identity. To be honest, I'm a born liar."

"Then if you're telling me the truth, who's speaking?" Darshon asked.

"Aren't we *all* pretenders?" I was shining him on but when I took his question home it triggered a bunch of others. Would it hurt Russell if I quit the jewelry business and went to school full time? And if I worked hard enough, could I graduate from a college playhouse to a professional stage in the "real world" south of Malibu?

On the day I finished my Level Two acting class in the Theatre Arts Program, Russell disappeared. He'd gone to the Wreck Room, a pool joint on Hawthorne Boulevard where he sold white gold chains that were basically made of stainless steel. I woke up alone in bed at 4 am. When he didn't answer his phone, the worry kicked in and I started calling him every half hour. I could feel myself turning into the panicked child at the beach, watching the ocean for Frank to swim back to me.

At five that afternoon, after calling around to a few emergency rooms to make sure he hadn't been in an accident, I drove to Inglewood and asked the bartender if Russell had come in the previous night.

"Yeah. He was here for a while and then he went out the back alley with some guy. Looked like they had serious business. Left his drink on the bar. Not like him."

"What did the guy look like?"

"Youngish, white, with a crew cut."

I paid Russell's tab and drove back to Malibu. A million scenarios competed in my head. I imagined a sale gone bad and Russell's body dumped in the wetlands south of Marina del Rey.

The front door to our house in the Canyon was wide open, with two police cars parked in the driveway, static squawking from their radios. If they'd come to tell me Russell was in a car crash there'd be no need for all this. I drove past the house slowly, eyes straight ahead and made a discreet U-turn, using the backroads to get to the coast road.

In Ventura, I stocked up on fast food and whiskey and checked into a motel with corridors that smelled like wet sox overlayed with Lysol. At least I had my own credit card in the name of Sandra Storm, thanks to Russell. He'd taken good care of me, but we'd never discussed the risks he was taking. How naive I'd been to let him shut me out of the day-to-day business. I put my cell phone on the bedside table and turned on the TV for some much-needed anesthetic.

Sleep finally came in the middle of an infomercial. An hour later I woke with a start, desperation springing from my subconscious like a fiend, taking control of body and mind. I curled up under the thin coverlet and tried to think good thoughts and visualize fluffy clouds, the way Russell had taught me when I had panic attacks during our early days together. He had a tender side that sometimes overrode his secretiveness and short temper. Yet after all this time, I barely knew what made him tick.

How could someone amass a fortune — ill-gotten, yes, but created from scratch with the artistry of his hands — and lose it in less time than it took to rack up a pool table? All I could do was pray that Russell was okay and had a backup plan.

I didn't hear from him for two interminable days. Feverish with anxiety, I took a call from an unknown number. "I've made bail. Where are you?"

No apology for having worried me, his voice as dull as unpolished silver. I told him the Horseshoe Motel.

"Good. Wait for me and be ready to leave."

He showed up driving a car I'd never seen and looking like a beaten dog. Two nights in jail will do that to a man, especially if he's used to sleeping under silk sheets.

"What happened?"

"Fucking guy offered me twice what the chain was worth. I should have listened to my gut and turned him down. Right after I stuffed the money in my wallet, him and his fraud squad pals cuffed me, threw me in a cruiser and drove to the house, where they executed their all-powerful search warrant. I'm toast, Sandie. Totally cleaned out. Bank accounts frozen too. Good thing I had cash to post my bond, although it's a total loss now."

"You're jumping bail?"

"What do you think? Get in the car."

5. ...Isn't Gold

It was hard to swallow that after three years of living with someone who granted my every wish without asking much in return, I was forced to do whatever it took to get us by — con jobs in shopping malls, questionable modeling gigs, more questionable videos. I got damn good at scamming department stores by faking high-priced returns. A cut above posing naked in the movies. But not by much.

Although Russell had to know how I felt, he was trapped inside his own blues. He'd grown up in comfort and wasn't used to hard times. Instead of seeing poverty as a challenge to overcome he saw it as proof of failure. I watched his ego crumble like a cracker disintegrating in a hot cup of soup.

He'd always hated dope — said it fogged up his mind — but since his arrest and our flight from Los Angeles, the "new Russell" indulged in anything he could swallow. I kept an eye out for needles and thanked my lucky stars I didn't find any.

My strategy was to keep a good distance from him and squirrel away as much money as I could. There was no use in complaining or asking Russell to cool his jets. The meth made him paranoid enough as it was. The slightest criticism of his commitment to self-destruction would result in exile.

And despite my fears, I was attached to him emotionally and at times ached for him physically.

We celebrated my twentieth birthday by taking a short break in a state park north of San Francisco. Our campsite was in the middle of a redwood forest and would have been heavenly if it hadn't been surrounded by what looked and sounded like a biker's convention. Not my idea of relaxing. We headed back to the rooming house in the Lower Haight a full day ahead of our plans.

An ageless black man was standing beneath the overhang of the old Victorian's entryway, sheltering himself from the rain. Tall and thin, he appraised us through rheumy eyes and bummed a smoke, fingers shaking so badly Russell had to light the Marlboro for him.

"Much obliged. I go by Curtis, he said." His voice was the steadiest thing about him.

Russell invited Curtis in. During our travels, he'd begun to adopt strays over whom he could feel superior. He offered our guest the best seat in the house, a plywood rocking chair with a splintery wooden frame, the cushion ripped to shreds by a former tenant whose mental state I hated to think about.

After a delicious dinner of canned Spaghetti-o's in tomato sauce and fried Spam, Curtis focused his one good eye on me, the other one totally clouded by a cataract.

"You know how to play?"

Curtis had noticed the guitar Russell said he'd stolen, "to keep you out of trouble." The gift was more a claim of ownership than an act of love. The new Russell's kindnesses came with an edge.

"I strum a little," I told Curtis.

Brenda had saved up to buy me a beginner's guitar with strings so high above the fretboard I could only pick out a few tunes. The instrument had disappeared after she died and I still wondered if Frank had hocked it.

"You play Train Runnin'?" Curtis asked.

40

"No, but I'll bet *you* do." I offered him the Gibson. He shook his head sadly and held up his trembling hands. "Not anymore."

I played House of the Rising Sun, the only song I knew by heart. Curtis listened intently, as if I was Bessie Smith or something.

"I like the way you sing," he told me. "It makes me feel good."

Russell had once told me the same thing, but lately he was so strung out he wouldn't know a song from an audio hallucination. I was glad when Curtis decided to stick around.

***

It was late June and Haight Street was populated by wide-eyed tourists as well as a few phantoms who looked like pictures I'd seen of San Francisco flower children, perpetually stalled at a stop sign in the City of Love. At night, I was grateful for the loud music thumping through the thin walls of our room. It drowned out the intimate animal sounds made by the neighbors. Curtis had put his sleeping bag in the alcove next to the bay windows, an architectural flourish left over from grander days. He knew how to blend into the woodwork and joined us only for hit-or-miss meals or a smoke when asked. Even so, lying next to Russell on the mattress we shared, I was acutely aware of the other man in the room sharing the darkness, relieved that Russell was too wasted to climb on top of me.

Whenever I got paid by what Russell euphemistically called my "photographer friends," I'd stop and pick up a bottle of Curtis' favorite whiskey on the way home.

"You've got a thing for that old man, don't you?" Russell would half-kid me, talking like Curtis wasn't in the room at all.

"She's a sweet woman, and I know you mean to treat her right," Curtis invariably said, walking the fine line, careful not to antagonize his host.

One afternoon, when Russell was out doing God knows what, Curtis asked, "You play chess?"

"My dad used to play, so I know the moves, but that's about it."

Curtis dug into the canvas bag where he kept his pipe and some other treasures and pulled out a small metal box with a chessboard painted on the lid. "I don't see all that well," he said. "Can you set it up?"

I removed the tiny magnetic pieces and dropped them onto their appointed squares. "Like I said, I'm not very good."

"All you gotta' do is look ahead a few moves."

"Not my strength, although sometimes I wish it was." We both knew I was talking about more than chess.

"He's lucky to have you, but it don't seem to cut both ways. You're not afraid of him?"

"You don't know Russell like I do. He's just having a hard time."

"No doubt," Curtis said. "But like Guitar Shorty tells it, 'ain't the fall that kills 'ya. It's when you hit the ground.'"

"Don't you worry about me. I've got my own plans."

"No doubt," Curtis said. His eyesight was so bad that whenever his turn came he had to hold the tiny board up near his face to study it. A couple of times I surprised us both by boxing in his pawns with my knight, but I could tell he was cooking up some sneaky moves. It was a little frustrating but worth it to hear his triumphant cackle when he checkmated me.

"Not everybody picks this game up as fast as you did," he said.

"Picks what up?" It was Russell, come back to the nest for a "lie down."

"Nothing," I said, quickly sweeping the pieces back into the box. I didn't want Russell challenging Curtis to a game because I was sure he'd lose, and Russell being thwarted at anything wasn't a pretty sight—something I'd discovered when he threw a full-blown tantrum after being tricked into accepting counterfeit money from one of his clients.

***

As we limped across the country in a beater that burned a quart of oil every two hundred miles, I was acutely aware of the deteriorating condition of the passenger in the back seat. Russell served up some horseshit about getting Curtis medical treatment in New York for his Parkinson's. I knew we'd never get that far.

The car died in Wichita. Afraid the cops would arrive and check his fake ID against one of their databases, Russell decided to abandon the rust bucket in the middle of North Hillside Street. Curtis, who could barely walk, was having trouble keeping up and I expected Russell to jettison his "charity case" at any moment.

After we checked into a Hawaiian-style motel, I summoned a cab to take me and Curtis to the Wesley Medical Center. The driver, a jittery cowboy wannabe dressed in carved boots, jeans, and a red checked cotton shirt, watched me guide Curtis into the taxi but made no offer to help. During the ride, he continually popped up his clip-on sunglasses, having angled the rear-view mirror so he could monitor his suspicious looking passengers. I deliberately met his gaze and after our eyes had collided several times, he refocused his attention on the road. I paid the fare with precious money taken from my getaway stash.

By the time I led Curtis through the sliding doors into Emergency reception, he'd retreated deep into himself and was barely aware of his surroundings. I was planning to talk with a doctor first, to share what little I knew about my friend's condition, but the sight of all the authority figures I'd have to deal with—the intake workers and security guards—changed my mind.

I led Curtis to a seat on a bench near the window. He was trembling even more than usual, but he did manage a vague smile when I planted a kiss on his check. "You'll be alright," I said, futilely attempting to infuse the words with some conviction.

As I walked away, I told myself repeatedly that I had no choice. But there was no getting round the fact that I was leaving the one human being I had grown close to during the chaotic months on the road—the one person who, sick as he was, had doggedly tried to make me smile—to sit alone in a waiting room until the state decided what to do with him. *Like father, like daughter.* I dug my fingernails into the palms of my hands and toughed it out. *What else could I have done? It's my own fault for getting attached to the fucker.*

***

Over the next few weeks we crossed the country, leaving a trail of bad paper on our way east. When we arrived in New York City, Russell took me to a party in the West Village—lots of designer drugs and alcohol, but little food. We were met at the door by a waif-like apparition smoking a clove cigarette and leaning on a cane with a silver handle. I was impressed by our hostess's upscale wardrobe and how her self-confidence gave her an undeniable air of entitlement. "This is Andrea," Russell said. "Best paper mover in the business."

"So you're Russell's new sidekick." Andrea examined me closely, like a pawnbroker fingering a newly arrived string of pearls. After pouring us drinks, she took a break from entertaining her guests to check out the credit cards Russell had brought. She specialized in creating fake IDs for stolen plastic. Her service had to be quick since her clients were usually in town for the length of one billing cycle. We purchased enough ID's (at $350 each) to cover us for a month.

Russell used some phony plastic to book us into the Regency on Park Avenue, more than a few steps up from the motels we'd bunked in on our cross-country "tour," as he called it.

The entire time we were in New York I felt uneasy. I was afraid of running into someone I knew from my time living with Aunt Stella and having to explain myself.

A week later we rented a car and headed west again. As Russell's newly acquired addictions combined with his delusions of invincibility, things went steadily downhill.

"I hate when you drive stoned. You're scaring me," I said.

"Am I now, really?" he teased, swerving the car across the white line and back again like a crazy person. "Where's your sense of adventure, Sandstorm? Seen too many sights already? Stick with me and we'll get to that pot of gold."

Trouble was, I'd lost sight of the rainbow and fantasized about having a plush apartment like Andrea's, with lots of friends and a business that didn't require zigzagging across state lines.

***

We were holed up in the Quality Suites on the outskirts of Kansas City, Kansas, KCK as the locals dubbed it. I was on the couch, watching TV, trying not to think about where or when we'd make our next move. Russell was lounging in the bathtub, stoned on whatever it was he'd scored in Indianapolis. I mentioned going for a walk and he wouldn't have any of it.

"You've got a rep now. You're not some low-profile broad," he croaked, knowing how steamed I got when he called me that.

On top of whatever drugs he'd taken, Russell had ingested a dose of cold syrup and liked the woozy effect so much he swallowed half a bottle. His head was resting precariously on the edge of the tub and, afraid he'd pass out

45

and drown, I went and tucked a pillow under his head. I could hardly believe this was the same man who'd taught me how to drive a car and shoot a gun. I wouldn't have trusted him with either. A wreck of a boat lost in a fog of his own making.

His face relaxed into a goofy grin, like a kid playing hard one minute and falling asleep on the floor the next. Crazy, but I felt close to him at that moment.

"There's something I forgot," he mumbled.

I peered down at him, steam from the hot bath rising in my face. "What?"

"That girl you were friends with in Arizona, on that ranch... the one who gave you my address in Malibu..."

"You mean Tiffany?" I was sure Tiff had either died or gone to prison. She'd made that one call years ago to tell Russell I was on my way and I'd never heard from her again.

"She phoned when you were out." Russell started to drift off.

I nudged his shoulder, none too gently. "Rusty. Tell me. How long ago was this?"

"Not sure. A few years maybe."

I stayed calm, determined to weasel out the rest.

"What did she say?"

"Who?"

"Tiffany! Think! It's important!"

Russell paused, his head starting to slip off the pillow. He righted himself, still refusing to make eye contact.

"Out with it, Russell."

"She told me she ran into Tash."

I must be hearing things, I thought. "That's not possible. Tash is dead."

"Tiffany saw him in the supermarket in San Francisco. He asked for you. She said she thought you'd like to know."

The shock of comprehension washed over me, and then bit by bit my power of reason returned, and with it a torrent of anger. How could Russell have deceived me so totally? I'd been running from the law for no reason.

46

"Damn you, Russel! Why did you keep me in the dark for so long!?"

He tried to focus, his eyelids drooping. "I'm sorry. I didn't want you to leave me."

The full weight of his deception and how pathetically selfish he'd been started to sink in.

"At least tell me where Tiffany is!"

I gave up when I saw his eyes were screwed shut and he'd slid down in the bath, his nose barely above the water.

My deceitful partner had left his phone on the sink and when I was sure he was unconscious, I gently dried off his wet thumb and placed it on the home button. He grunted but didn't move. It took a few seconds to locate Tiffany's info in his address book. She'd had no cell at the Ranch and idiot me had swallowed Russell's lie about her disconnecting the number she'd called him from. Three-four-seven, a New York City area code.

I was now in as much of a hurry as Tiff had been when she scribbled Russell's address on the Mars Bar wrapper. Using my eyebrow pencil to write her number on a doubled-up scrap of toilet paper, I grabbed a bunch of toiletries from the medicine cabinet and strode into the bedroom. Pent up frustration sang in my veins. I was leaving. It didn't matter that my emergency fund was down to a hundred bucks and I had no idea where I'd get the bus fare to New York. All I could think of was finding Tiffany and the amazing fact that Tash was alive!

Reflected in the mirror on the wall above the dresser, my face had a newly determined look. I pulled a close-fitting nylon cap over my caramel, sun-streaked hair and slipped on a wig with a mass of dark curls. Then the thought came: *They're not looking for you, not for murder anyway. Maybe assault, which means you'd better keep playing it safe.*

I completed the makeover by donning a pair of rhinestone eyeglasses, my idea of Midwestern chic. Anyone I encountered would see an ordinary girl-woman in her

47

early twenties, crammed into hip-hugging jeans that flaunted her slim build. I was ready to go out on my own.

Retrieving my emergency fund from its hiding place, I wiggled the stack of bills into my front pocket. It wasn't going to get me far. The genuine diamond bracelet Russell had given me was long gone. I packed a suitcase and turned to the "treasure trove" of fakes that Russell had left in plain sight on the bedside table. This evidence of his trust brought on the guilts and I made sure to take only my fair share of what we'd fabricated during our chaotic time on the road. There was one ring I didn't recognize. It looked old as the hills and maybe as valuable. I hesitated and then grabbed it. *You owe me this one for being such a liar.*

The sound of draining bathwater alerted me. Russell was alive and awake enough to have pulled the plug. Until that moment I'd intended to say goodbye, to give us at least one last moment to remember. But he was stronger than me and had changed into someone capable of violence when he was crossed. I quickly hid the suitcase under the table near the front door.

A few seconds later, naked as a jaybird, he blocked my way out. "Where do you think you're going?"

"Out for some fresh air. Do you want something from the store?"

"How much money have you got on you?" He reached for my purse, something he would never have done when we lived in Malibu.

I pulled out a twenty and gave it to him, willing myself not to look at the suitcase just like I'd done years ago at Aunt Stella's. Some things never change. "Twenty's all I got."

Russell stood there until I gave him another ten. "I need the rest to buy tampons and soda," I said as casually as I could and walked out the door. Too bad about the suitcase.

I walked close to the buildings, hugging myself in the thin, grey sweatshirt that was all I had to stave off the chilly breeze, unusual for a summer evening in Kansas. Damn him, I'd made up my mind. I was sick of the hit-and-run lifestyle that kept me from exploring the dozens of towns and cities we powered through. It was past nine and getting dark. My next step was a total mystery but anything would be better than riding around in circles in Russell's lost caravan.

6. Crossing the Line

About a half-mile from the motel, I came upon a small business district left over from the days before giant malls and Amazon must have crushed the city center. Most of the stores in the low-slung brick buildings were closed for the night but the sign above the back door of Little Jim's Pawn Shop was lit. I needed some travel money fast.

I crossed the narrow alley just as the pawn shop went dark. A small, wiry man was bolting the backdoor, bank bag tucked protectively under his arm, a golf cap on his head. I walked over as casually as I could. "Excuse me, but I have some jewelry I need to sell."

"Sorry my dear, we're closed. We open tomorrow at 11, come by then."

I showed him what I had, holding it under the security light, hoping he'd decide it was easier to lowball me than try to drive me off.

"I don't know where you got these," he said with a resigned sigh. "You can leave them with me on consignment, but I'll have to authenticate their provenance and that may take a few days."

What does he think this is, Christie's? In a split second beyond thought, the elegant pearl-handled revolver Russell had given me on Christmas Eve and taught me how to use came out of my purse and pointed itself at the shop owner's head. Stiffening with fear, he unlocked the security bag and handed it over, eyes trained over my head, not daring to look me in the face. His whole body trembled.

I want to get this over with as much as you do. "If you turn around and keep your eyes on that door handle while you count to one hundred you won't regret it." I'd pitched my normally husky voice as low as it would go.

The terrified man nodded his head vigorously, and I slipped away, fighting the urge to run, forcing my feet to move slowly while my mind raced. I had numbed my mind and body while committing the robbery and now my nerves woke in a sorry state. Anxiety constricted my chest, reducing my breath to short wheezes. Dots danced in front of my eyes. The outlines of the buildings shifted and blended like the shapes in the scenery of a college play I'd performed in during another lifetime.

I made it as far as the Texaco mini-mart and locked myself in the foul-smelling bathroom. Breathing as shallowly as possible, I moved the gun from my purse to the waist of my jeans, making it easier to toss the weapon down a sewer or into an empty lot. I shed my glasses and wig, then combed out my hair. My tresses were not the only twisted things in my life. I'd crossed a line I'd always meant to stay clear of, had done it out of desperation, after sinking so low I'd forgotten what it was like to look up. I told myself I'd never have used the gun if the old man resisted, but the police had no way of knowing that. I'd executed an armed assault. There was no fix for any of it.

Unzipping the money bag, I was surprised to find an unexpected bonus mixed in with the cash, three gold rings— one set with a diamond that looked like the real thing. Quickly, I reached under my sweatshirt and slipped the jewelry into the small pouch sewn into my bra. The little sack housed the emergency fake ID that Russell had so thoughtfully provided, along with my mother's wedding band, engagement ring, and cameo brooch. It felt like sacrilege to mix the stolen articles with the only relics I had left from my Mom's life, but safety came first. After counting them, I stashed the wad of wrinkled bills in my purse. My plan was to hop on the next bus going east and use what was left of the twelve hundred dollars to make a fresh start in New York.

Just a few steps outside the bathroom, I spotted the policeman. There was no way to backtrack without calling attention to myself. He was chatting with the clerk and seemed relaxed, feeding my hope that he was merely on a break and here to pick up a sandwich. But then, behind and to the left of the cop, I saw the short man in the golf cap. The jewelry store owner tugged on the officer's sleeve and pointed at me.

In the split second it took to calculate the officer's distance from both the front and side doors compared to my own, I got my legs moving. I need to jam out of there, yet it felt like I was running in slow motion, my feet strapped to iron weights.

"Stop!"

I ignored the command, picking up speed and snaking through the cars in the strip-mall parking lot like a character in a video game, trying to make myself a difficult target while counting on the cop being reluctant to shoot a woman in the back. I glimpsed a stand of trees in the distance. If I could make it that far... My shoulder bag caught on a side-view mirror and the thin strap snapped, sending the purse in one direction and me in another. Helplessly I watched my bag disappear under a low-slung sedan. *Shit!* I kept running.

I'd covered another ten yards when the pop of gunfire sent shockwaves through my body, top to bottom. I skidded to a stop and turned around.

My pursuer was a healthy twenty yards off, but he'd convinced me the game was up. I raised my arms in surrender, just as an Apple Market ten-wheeler loaded with groceries turned into the shopping center. The squeal of airbrakes signaled the driver had seen the policeman's frantic signals and was trying to stop. Physics said otherwise. By the time the truck shuddered to a halt it was directly between me and the equally winded officer, momentarily cutting off pursuit.

This was all the edge I needed. With a burst of speed, I gained the cover of the trees, only to find what I'd mistaken for a large tract of undeveloped land was a thin greenbelt running along the freeway. I searched frantically for a place to hide. A few sickly pines and nothing on the other side but speeding cars. I risked a look over my shoulder and nearly stumbled over a tree root.

Jumping over a fallen log, I landed awkwardly on the frontage road, twisting my right ankle, ignoring the throbbing pain as I raced along the roadway. My lungs were bursting and I was losing ground. By now the backup units would be on their way and the way my luck was going I'd run straight into a police car.

Vehicles zoomed by on the highway on the other side of the fence. A red Do Not Enter sign came up on my left. I swerved across the road and jogged up the exit ramp against oncoming traffic, jumping on the curb to let the cars pass.

Grateful for the lack of LED lamps lighting the shoulder of the highway, I climbed over the metal railing and into the darkness. I was safe for the time being, treading through low brush, favoring my ankle as best I could. A car rounded a curve on the frontage road, brushing me with a ray of light. The driver might call 911 but I was more concerned about a smaller beam tracking toward me, sweeping the area in a methodical pattern. I scrambled backward, out of range, and froze.

The glow from the flashlight was moving in the same direction as the traffic. I waited for it to pass my location, then loped the opposite way through the greenery. After the short rest, my ankle felt a little better and I picked up the pace.

Directly ahead of me, a line of cars was lined up on the ramp leading onto the freeway. Injected one-by-one into the right-hand lane as if from a syringe, they accelerated to match the speed of ongoing traffic. On impulse, I broke off a branch from a shrub and scraped the jagged edge along my bare arm, scratching deeply enough to draw blood. Although the stinging pain was not as bad as expected, I was sure I'd feel it later. Wincing, I tugged at the edges of the wound to get the blood to flow freely, smearing it over my face.

The sound of approaching sirens grew louder, careening up and down the scale.

When a vehicle entered the ramp with no cars directly behind it, I dashed onto the V-shaped island painted on the blacktop between the busy highway and the merge lane. I waved my arms wildly, pulling down the hood of my sweatshirt to make my bloody face clearly visible. The driver stomped on his brakes.

I sprinted to the car. He rolled down the window and I pulled out the gun stashed in the waist of my jeans and pointed it at his head. "Out of the car. Now!"

He reached for the key to turn off the ignition.

"Leave it running! Out — now!"

I trained the gun on him as he opened the door and stepped out. He was young, not much older than me, with a buzz haircut and fleshy face. "Be my guest," he said, refusing to cower despite the fear that claimed his eyes.

"Shut up and lie down on the ground. Over there!" I gripped the gun tightly and pointed to the edge of the road. He obeyed me without question, having no way of knowing I'd never stoop to shooting an innocent person.

I slid behind the steering wheel, jerking the gear lever into drive, and hitting the accelerator. With a squeal of tires I was on the highway and swerving over into the fast lane. Behind me, the sirens stopped with a "whoop!" and in the rearview mirror I saw the blue and red lights pull off the road at the place where I'd jacked the car. A few more seconds and I'd have been cornered. I allowed myself a yelp of relief before decelerating to the legal speed limit, which I kept to from that point on.

55

When my heartbeat slowed enough for me to think, I considered what to do with the car. It was an older Toyota Corolla, lacking a GPS tracking device, which was good, and running low on gas, not so good. Any second now the Highway Patrol would catch me up. Too bad there'd been no time to smash the lightbulb over the rear license plate.

The signs on the Turnpike pointed the way to Kansas City's namesake in Missouri. Maybe the police would call it quits at the state line. That was okay with me, except I remembered Russell saying that if you commit a felony in one state and cross into another, the Feds jump in and circulate your description all over the country. I was better off getting rid of the Toyota in KCK. I would phone Russell when I got there. He'd have connections, would be able to find a chop shop. He may have lied to keep me with him, but he'd never lifted a hand against me. And maybe he'd forgive my disloyalty if he ended up profiting from the deal.

Out of habit, I reached to get my cell from my purse. With a jolt I remembered that my phone, wallet, ID, and all the money I'd stolen were lying on the ground in a parking lot miles behind. If the police got hold of my things they might get my fingerprints off my fake California driver's license. Although Russell had altered my appearance in the picture, making it highly unlikely they'd ever connect Sandra Storm with the Sandie Donovan who ran away from Recovery Ranch four years ago and had wounded a fellow resident so badly she thought she'd killed him.

I took the next exit off I-70, which put me on South Seventh Street, after which I turned onto Kansas Avenue and scouted the neighborhood. Lots of Mexican restaurants and a barbecue place that made my stomach growl. Only 10 pm and hardly a soul on the street.

South Mill rose gradually to become a viaduct, passing over what looked like a train yard. I swung a U-turn, drove back, and turned onto a small road running at street level next to the elevated roadway. I hadn't driven far when I saw what I was looking for, a patch of ground sheltered by the concrete structure overhead, already home to a nest of abandoned cars. It was a perfect, out of the way spot to spend the night, which made me nervous because other transients might know about the place. I drove in a circle, using the headlights to check for sleeping bags thrown on the ground or other signs of human habitation. Nothing but a few trash bags, not even a beer bottle. I parked the Toyota in the deepest shadows I could find. Looked like I'd have this hellhole to myself.

Lucky for me that my treasure pouch was intact and safely hidden inside my bra. I fingered the emergency ID Russell had created for me. I was about to become Sandie Doyle.

"Pretty cool, using a fake ID as cover for your *real* fake ID. Keep it handy, you never know when you might need it," he had joked. "There's even a usable social security number to go with it."

It would take some getting used to but *Russell, I'm no longer your Sandstorm.*

I devoured the half-melted energy bar in the glove box with gratitude. I wanted to explore the car further but couldn't without turning on the roof light. I sat in the dark, breathing deep and fighting back a panic attack. I'd never been in as tight a spot as this. Committing an armed robbery and a car-jacking guaranteed prison time.

Look on the positive side, I told myself. You got away from Russell, scored some cash, outwitted the police, and discovered an ideal hiding place. Never mind that the area is so isolated you could be attacked by a serial killer and no one would hear you scream. I repressed this ugly thought and moved into the passenger seat, reclining it as far as it would go.

***

I was diving, had plunged deep below the surface of the sea before remembering that there was no air tank on my back. My arms ached with effort as I swam toward the entrance to a cave, desperate to find an air pocket. The weak sunlight filtering through the water was suddenly blocked by something large and menacing, a monster looming above. I somersaulted in terror, trying to hide.

A car horn blared on the roadway above and I sat up with a start, trying to shake off one bad dream as I awoke to another.

I used my saliva and the back of my hand to clean the dried blood off my face and left arm, feeling more like a stray alley cat every minute. Then I got busy searching the car for anything useful. There was a sun visor on the back seat, and next to it a canvas shopping bag—looked like I'd ripped off an eco-friendly driver. Both items would come in handy. The papers in the glove box were disappointing but there was a prize awaiting me in the trunk—a navy blue over-sized sweater that I pulled over the grey sweatshirt bound to be included in the description of me circulated by the police. I would have to do something about my hair too.

I was sure that if I left the car with its doors unlocked and the keys under the seat, someone would come along and steal it, creating a nice diversion for the cops. But I was also sure I wouldn't get far on foot, with hardly any money to get my ass out of town. I fired up the Corolla. Risky as it was, my best chance was to sell it for parts at a junkyard.

Back on Kansas Avenue, I drove through the neighborhood, noticing how different it looked in the daylight. I was surprised to see some decent looking California bungalow-style houses sprinkled among the cinderblock garages. The sight of a body shop on the corner was an encouraging sign.

I turned north and drove a few blocks, then explored the side streets looking for a junk yard. The fuel gauge was deep into reserve and the car threatening to stall by the time

58

I parked in the driveway of Junk Begone. I waited, growing more nervous as the sky grew lighter. The police would be out and about.

At seven-thirty, a Ford pickup turned in. "You're an early bird—I'll be right with you," the driver called to me in lightly accented English. He got out to unlock the main gate, then hopped back in and entered the yard. I coaxed the Toyota to life and followed.

The cramped office occupied a tin-roofed shack, an oasis of tidiness compared to the chaos in the lot, where car parts were strewn everywhere and a dozen or so wrecks waited like corpses for their organs to be removed.

"What can you give me for the car?"

"Do you have the title?" he asked.

"No, I don't."

"Well, well. You've got some nerve, I'll give you that." He seemed amused by this disheveled woman who'd brought him a stolen car. From my end, he looked well put together, almost suave for a junkman, down to his Timberland boots and reddish brown Izod shirt, a nice match for his skin tone. After some half-hearted negotiation—I knew I didn't stand a chance of getting a better price—I left the salvage yard with a hundred and fifty bucks plus the fifty I'd salvaged from my rainy-day fund in my pocket. Two hundred seemed like a fortune and then I remembered how Russell had once spent twice that amount on a pair of Neiman Marcus gloves for my birthday.

I strolled down South Twelfth, the canvas bag dangling from my arm, trying to look like an early morning shopper. Traffic picked up, and a few drivers honked at me, one making lewd gestures and snidely offering me a ride. I was ravenous and the moment I turned the corner onto Kansas Avenue, I scouted out a place to have breakfast.

Seated at the counter inside Manuel's Taqueria, I greedily consumed an order of huevos rancheros and a glass of orange juice expensive as liquid gold. Over coffee, I assessed my situation. I needed transportation funds and it was too risky to take jewelry so recently stolen to a pawn shop. A plan formed in my mind as I paid the check.

I followed the waitress's directions to the Cross Lines Thrift Store on Shawnee Avenue. The place was well stocked. The clothes weren't stylish, but they were cheap and didn't smell like someone's dead relatives. And the stock of wigs was impressive. I bought a carry-all with working wheels and a brown, alligator-leather purse to put the finishing touches on my respectability.

***

At one pm, a redhead wearing a low-cut yellow sundress and high-heeled sandals exited a Metro bus in downtown Kansas City, Missouri. The smile this woman wore as she walked along, straining her neck to look up at the tall buildings on either side, was not the goofy grin of a tourist—it was the newly confident expression of someone who felt at home for the first time in weeks. This was a real city. I could get what I needed, hopefully without seriously hurting anyone, and then get lost.

I passed several hotels, looking them over. None seemed right for my purpose. Until, directly across the freeway, I noticed a marquee covered with giant black letters—Welcome Sprint Sales Force.

Welcome and then some.

I walked across the overpass, running my plan through my head.

From the lobby, I took the escalator to the mezzanine and hid my carry-all behind an upholstered chair outside the sports bar. Four guys at a table were on their fourth or fifth beers from the sound of it, their raucous cheers and boos accompanying the game between the Royals and the Twins.

I sat at the bar and ordered a Perrier with ice to make it look good. A pale green chiffon scarf was draped over my shoulders, left open to emphasize the cleavage created by the tight-fitting sundress. Thirty seconds max before someone propositioned me. It was more like twenty.

"Buy you another one?" He looked around fifty, cocky for his age but seasoned, like an aging rock star.

"Another what?" I asked, turning toward him on the stool and slowly crossing my legs. "Is something missing?"

"Actually, not a thing. My name's Trev. What's yours?"

"Delores." I granted him a slight smile, which he eagerly returned. "If you *were* in need of something, how much would it cost?" Trev asked.

"Two-fifty."

"There's an ATM in the lobby. Don't go anywhere. I'll be right back."

***

As soon as we entered the room, I sat down on the bed and held out my hand, palm upward. "You have to pay in advance."

He gave me the cash with no protest, but when he made a move to join me I shook my head. "I'm sure you'll understand if I insist you take a shower first."

When I heard the water running, I went through his wallet, helping myself to another hundred and a credit card. Quickly, I let myself out, running down the hallway and using the stairs to exit the hotel through the basement.

This guy Trev was no baby, but he'd let me take a big chunk of his candy.

I now had four-hundred fifty dollars. I preferred to travel by train, but ID was required when you bought a ticket. A bus was the only option, although not necessarily a safe one since ICE agents were known to board them.

A few blocks from the Greyhound terminal, I wiped the Lady Colt clean and disposed of it in a dumpster. Walking away, my sense of relief quickly faded. I'd thrown away my protection. If only I could have taken it on the bus.

7. Re-entry

I awoke in time to see the window next to my seat swap its view of the late afternoon sun for total darkness. For a moment I was back on that ill-fated, westbound train coming out of Grand Central more than six years ago. Rubbing the crick in my back and shaking my grogginess, I placed myself firmly in the present, aboard a bus inside a tunnel leading to New York City's Port Authority terminal.

To pass time on the Greyhound, I'd regaled my ever-changing seatmates with several versions of my life story. I especially liked the one in which I was an actress from Wichita on my way to audition for a role in an off-off-Broadway play. "The director's one I worked with in Los Angeles." I added this telling detail to give my lie the ring of truth and did my best to ignore the real yearning it aroused in me.

We pulled up to a loading platform, where a young woman strapped into an enormous backpack patiently listened to her parents' last-minute instructions. Her silver earrings twinkled in the dim light and the precisely cut bangs gave her a neat, collegiate look. *That could have been me. All of it.* I brushed off this useless thought.

Despite its highly touted renovations, Port Authority called to mind a reupholstered couch smelling of stale beer.

Walking past the late-night population of ladies hawking their wares and bleary-eyed students who couldn't afford to fly, I concentrated on finding a working pay phone. A good thing I'd saved Tiffany's number on that candy wrapper. If I'd transferred her info to my phone it would be lying alongside my purse in a Kansas City parking lot and I'd have no way of finding her. Tiff and I had been tight as two steel guitar strings and I didn't even know her last name.

The number went directly to voice mail. With no cell of my own to take a callback, there was no use leaving a message. I waited a few minutes and tried again. *Damn.*

The bus fare and meals had gobbled up most of my cash. On my way toward the exit, I passed several men who looked me over, some of them so hungrily it gave me the creeps. I had no desire to participate in what they had in mind and had never sold myself—unless you counted a camera lens as a john or my pretending to be a hooker in Kansas City.

Near the information booth, a well-dressed woman— Coach Bag, expensive haircut, an air of privilege—stuck out like a tropical bird slumming among the sparrows. This lady didn't bother to hide her interest, as, hips tilting, purse swaying, she walked over and came to the point. "Would you care to join me for a drink at my hotel?" Her voice was liquid caramel and an aroma of desperation cut through the expensive perfume.

For a moment, I allowed myself a glimpse of a luxurious bed at the Hyatt Regency, room service, champagne, the works. But the price was too high.

"Sorry. There's someone meeting me." I wished to God this were true.

Walking through the maze of passageways leading from the bus terminal to the 42nd Street subway station, I passed a series of mosaic murals. The colorful glass orbs floating around like lost souls caught my eye—art intended for passersby like me, stressed out and struggling to make it through the night. Headlights roared out of the darkness, announcing the arrival of the E train, which I took to 14th Street.

By the time I reached Union Square, twilight had surrendered to inky blackness. Skateboarders zoomed in and out of sight, most of them teenagers, all confident in their ownership of the park after dark. A few well-heeled tourists had bravely ventured from nearby hotels to watch the fun—exactly the sort of people I could pitch.

I scanned the ground for some paper or cardboard to use for a sign but changed my mind after considering my own negative reactions to people who advertise their plight. I decided to circulate through the crowd and approach only the well, or at least adequately, dressed. "I'm a few dollars shy of getting a room," was the line I used most often.

Three hours later I had what I needed. Plus a wealth of insensitive comments I'd endured in silence while keeping my eye on the prize.

My reward was a night in the dorm of the International Hostel downtown, a chance to squirm around on a meager slab of foam in search of a comfortable position while listening to European and African students chattering in every language but English—a club of world travelers with low budgets and high enthusiasm.

I kept my clothes on and fell asleep craving a hot shower. An hour after lights out, I jerked awake, eyes and ears alert, sensing something was wrong. The only sounds were the snores and snorts of the heavy sleepers. It took a few seconds for me to comprehend that someone with broad shoulders and an enormous head was sitting at the end of my mattress.

"Hey! Get off!" I yelled, wishing I had some pepper spray.

A boyish, male voice pierced the darkness. "Henry! Get the fuck out of here. Leave the lady alone!"

The menace at the foot of my bed jumped up and ran toward the exit. Backlit in the doorway, my rescuer let the behemoth pass.

By now I was on my feet. "Thank you."

I followed him into the common room to get a better look at my Sir Galahad. Like me, he had freckles widely spaced on a pale face, with hair the color of wet straw. Unlike me, he was short, maybe five foot two.

"You're just a kid."

"I'm Griffin, and Henry's my best friend. I don't wanna' see him getting into trouble. He's curious, is all."

"He's not a house cat, Griffin. He's a confused person who needs help."

"Yeah, I know. But please don't say anything to the night supervisor. She'll eighty-six him."

I guessed Griffin was no older than fifteen. Two years older than I was when my mom died. "Shouldn't you be playing video games and smoking pot in your parent's basement?"

"Not possible," he said matter-of-factly. "There's a guy in Brooklyn who looks after me when he's in town. He'll be back next week. He needs talent. I can hook you up if you catch my drift."

I was afraid I did and saddened by how young he was and how easy it was for him to pigeonhole me as one of his tribe. "I handle my own business. Thanks for saving me from the clutches of gentle Henry."

Griffin smiled. There was something about him, a kind of sad wisdom.

"Where are you from?"

"Utah, and I don't wanna' blabber about it. Understand?"

"I understand perfectly. I know what it's like to be dependent on people you can't trust."

"Don't look so worried. I've got my life here now. I'll wager I'm better read than you are. And then, there's my looks." He flexed his biceps and twisted his upper body like an exhibition boxer.

The kid was on the downhill path and where he was going could get pretty dark. Even darker than it had been for me.

"Look, do you have a phone? Maybe we could stay in touch. My name is Sandie." *A generous offer from someone who had to panhandle her first night's rent in the city.*

Griffin shook his head in a thanks but no thanks way. "I've got a cell but the guy who gave it to me scopes out every number I call. I guess you could say he's paranoid. And since he's my ticket... I'm sorry. I'd better get goin' now."

I didn't need him to spell it out — to say if it was drugs or sex he was selling for this guy. It didn't matter.

"Take care, Griffin."

"You too, Sandie."

Groggy from lack of sleep, I walked from the hostel to the corner drug store and spent half my remaining cash on a pre-paid phone. Fingers crossed, I made the call.

"Hello?" I could hardly believe I was hearing Tiff's voice.

"It's me, Sandie."

A few beats passed. "Russell said you skipped out on him. Did you?"

It wasn't enough to be a goddam liar. He had to try and poison my friendship with Tiff too.

"It wasn't like that. He's not the sweet guy he was when we met and he never told me you called or that Tash is actually alive."

There was another pause. I heard voices and the clatter of dishes in the background.

"That sucks. He should have told you about Tash. Carrying around that kind of guilt can kill you." This was a different Tiff. She'd always turned up her nose at what she called the "stink of psychobabble."

"Where are you, Sandie?"

I told her and she gave me the address of the café in Washington Heights where she was waitressing. "You can

67

have a late breakfast and then we'll go over to my place. See you in an hour."

***

Half blinded by the sudden appearance of the sun, I walked down West 181st Street. The low-slung buildings and shoppers on the street gave it a small-town feel. The café would have been called a luncheonette in Mom's day, with booths along the wall and a long counter where you could get quick service. I chose a table near the window.

"Care for a glass of Saguaro red? I hear it's got a kick to it." Tiffany looked nothing like the waif I remembered from Recovery Ranch. I doubted I'd have recognized her if we'd run into each other on the street. Her face was round where it should have been concave, sallow cheeks now rosy, the feathery shock of platinum hair neatly tamed into a shoulder-length cut. Her eyes, which Tash once described as "wistfully sarcastic," had softened, along with her body, suggesting that she'd traded in her taste for speed for a healthier appetite.

"Where are your leg shackles?" I asked, only half joking. We'd shared a bunkhouse that was more like a prison block and seen each other demeaned on a daily basis. It felt awkward to be interacting on the outside.

Tiff's manic laugh hadn't changed one bit. "I can't believe it. The other day I was thinking about our time in Arizona and now here you are."

"Lucky you," I said, but I was pleased. Riding up here on the subway, I'd had an attack of paranoia, imagining how easy it would be for Russell to drive a wedge between Tiff and me. She'd never said how they met and I'd shied away from asking, honoring our code of *lay off unless I ask you to ask me.*

Tiff brought me a cup of coffee and a sandwich and after an impatient customer paid his bill, she pulled her quilted

68

jacket off a hook on the wall. "I've got a couple of hours before the noon rush. Let's get out of here."

As we walked past the stone gates at the entrance to Fort Tyron Park, Tiff told me she lived nearby and up 'til recently had been sharing her apartment with someone named Marigold. "We came east together. She turns tricks and makes more money in one night than I do waitressing for a week. Last month she moved to Long Island. I don't know the particulars. I imagine a john set her up."

"You get weekly visitation rights but you better call first." I said this like I was the one negotiating the deal and Tiffany cracked up.

She turned serious when I asked about Tash. "Russell said you ran into him."

"It was in San Francisco and he didn't look too good, Sandie. No scars on him though, at least not the kind you can see. He didn't seem interested in staying in touch, maybe the memories were too painful for him to revisit. We wished each other well and continued shopping. It was weird."

Tiff and I climbed a set of marble-specked stairs and entered the courtyard of a u-shaped apartment building on the skids, its walls missing more than a few bricks. Inside the elevator, dim light barely penetrated the tiny, barred window and I was relieved to see a recent inspection date behind the glass of the framed certificate.

Tiff's third-floor apartment verged on depressing, with dark cream walls and a boarded-up fireplace. The glowing pink globe suspended from the ceiling failed to cheer the place up and a cold draft of air made me shiver.

"Sorry!" she said and hurried into the kitchen to light the oven. "Fucking landlord shuts off the heat from nine to five, when most people are out working. He won't turn it on again 'til tonight, the cheap bastard."

Tiff wheeled my carry-all into a decent-sized bedroom down the hall.

"Marigold paid up through the end of the month so you can start paying your share on the first. Here's your key. It'll be refreshing to have somebody here who doesn't walk around with a price tag hanging from her cha-cha."

She'd rightly assumed I had no place else to go.

"What's the rent?" I asked.

"It's $1,200 including utilities. Maybe you can sell some of the jewelry Russ said you confiscated."

"I only took my share! For God's sake, Tiff, I left with only the shirt on my back!"

"Okay, okay. I believe you."

I unpacked the thrift-store clothes I'd bought in KCK and we chatted about the classes Tiff was taking at night school. "I'm working on a digital arts degree. Turns out I've got a knack for html."

She'd really gotten her life together. It was hard not to compare this with my own poor showing so far.

"I've got to get back to work now, Sandie. You can use my laptop to look through the want ads on Craig's List."

That would come later. I wasn't sure how Tiffany was paying her share of the rent on a waitress's salary. But I did know it would be impossible to hold up my end unless I unloaded what I'd taken from the old man in Kansas City first.

***

I was there at 9:30 am, in time to watch the custodian unlock the security doors to a nondescript building on West 47th Street. Golden West was squirreled away at the end of a long corridor on the fourth floor, the premises deliberately low-key, almost shabby. But who knew better than me what appearances could hide?

There was only one window open for business, thick enough to be bulletproof and manned by an elderly gent with a limp bow tie and disheveled, red hair. "What can I do you for?" The folksiness was phony, thin icing on a cheap cake.

I withdrew each piece of jewelry from the black velvet pouch as if it were a significant part of my personal history—all except the two items of actual sentimental value—my mother's wedding and engagement rings. I needn't have bothered with the show. Red had seen it all. He squinted through his jeweler's loupe at my offerings, ignoring the line of sellers queueing up behind me. He murmured something I couldn't make out and then took a sip of coffee from a mug that looked like it was rinsed out annually, if at all.

"I can purchase the rings for the scrap rate—you keep the diamond—I don't deal in them. The cameo is worth something, but you'll have to take it elsewhere."

He placed the thick gold rings on the scale and punched some numbers into his calculator. "You've got 15 grams at 18 karat quality, adds up to $560 less our commission. Let's make it a round five-hundred."

"You're kidding—they would appraise for much more."

"If you can find a buyer, be my guest. We deal in scrap. Everything else is too risky."

"Make it five-fifty."

"Five twenty-five, last offer."

A second dealer materialized out of the back room and opened a window to accommodate the rush. His salt and pepper hair was expensively cut and the thick gold chain around his neck reminiscent of an '80s movie. He looked me over, raven-black eyes transmitting a practiced come-hither look, the expert on the prowl.

Red tapped on the computer keyboard, recording the purchase, and then opened a checkbook ledger. "To whom should I make this out?"

"Cash."

He glanced up at me like he was going to say something, then thought better of it.

That's right, it's *none of your damn business.* "Can you recommend a place to sell the cameo?" I asked.

71

"We're not a referral service."

The dealer who had plugged into me spoke up. "I've got some business at Navid's. Give me a few minutes and I'll walk you over."

I took a seat in one of '50's style black vinyl chairs lined up against the colorless wall. I must have watched Red raise the loupe to his eye, load up the scale and make his best offer at least a dozen times before his co-worker (or co-owner) closed his window and came out to join me. He carried a hard-cover attaché case with a combination lock.

"I'm Kip," he said. My initial impression of carefree playboy was contradicted by an up-close view of the deep furrows in his forehead.

"Sandie Doyle." I stressed my last name. According to Russell this was the quickest way to gain respectability in a stranger's eyes. "Thanks for helping me out."

Kip bypassed my offer to shake hands and instead cupped my elbow in his palm and guided me towards the door. It was a technique both formal and sexy and I could easily see him perfecting it in front of a mirror. As we left, I caught a look from Red that said *he's at it again.*

***

Navid turned out to be an Iranian with a lovely, crooked smile who ran an antique jewelry business on Lexington. He offered me four hundred for the cameo and I held out for four-fifty, to which he reluctantly agreed. At auction it would be worth three times that much but a girl's gotta eat. Navid made out a check to Cash without a second thought.

"That's a nice little nest egg you're accumulating," Kip commented.

Off the cuff I told him I'd come to New York to work on a film and had been stiffed by the producer. "The director lent me some money to cover my bill at the Regency. After I pay him back, I'm hoping he'll throw some work my way." This reinvention of myself was becoming a habit. It was as if being released from Russell's almost constant supervision, a horde of identities inside me were clamoring to get out.

When I'd finished my transaction, Kip asked, "Anything for me?" The Iranian nodded and ducked down to search for something in the glass case. He bobbed up again to present a velvet-lined tray filled with gold jewelry. "I can take some of these on consignment," Kip said. "Not much cash floating around."

"It's okay. You're a regular customer."

Kip picked out a platinum bracelet and some rings, then fiddled with the lock on his briefcase. I looked away, feigning noninterest. By the time I looked back, the case was closed and Kip had it handcuffed to his wrist.

"Can't be too careful these days," he said. Then, when we were back on Lexington, "After I drop this stuff at my office, how about coming over to my place? I'll cook you a scrumptious lunch."

Interesting how "careful" didn't extend to strange women he saw as attractive. Either that, or risky behavior turned him on. "Don't you have to work today?" I asked.

He grinned. "I set my own schedule. I'm usually out selling on the road. Buying scrap is just a sideline."

I declined Kip's invitation, saying I'd be busy moving into another hotel. Attractive as Kip was, Russell was still in my blood. Maybe it was the difference between collecting and selling what others produced and being a creator of jewelry that tipped the balance. "Tell you what," I said. "Give me your number and I'll call you when I'm free."

"Sure. Anytime is good. I get up early but I wouldn't mind staying up late with you." To bring his point home, Kip pulled me into an embrace and gave me a full kiss on the lips before walking away.

I felt a sudden attack of loneliness and resisting my efforts to keep them at bay, images of happier days with Russell broke through. The more ordinary, the better—shopping at the Topanga Mall for dishes and board games (Russell loved anything that wasn't on a computer)—him

73

reading the *LA Times* over breakfast while I paged through *Elle*—the two of us wheeling a jam-packed grocery cart through the supermarket, a carton of eggs balanced precariously on top. Russell had taught me a lot and made me feel loved and important until he lost his business and then his mind.

One month's rent covered and not a thing owed to anyone. On the way back to Tiff's place I bought a bottle of wine to celebrate.

8. Don't Quit Your Day Job

It was Tiffany who suggested I apply for a gig as a cosmetics consultant in a department store. "You've got a lot of experience changing your own appearance. Why not share your talent with others?" She meant well but the way she put it made me cringe.

"You should think about it, Sandie. A friend of mine works for Naturel and I hear that after six months as a trainee you get full benefits. You could apply on the web."

I submitted my resume online under the name of Sandie Doyle and was shocked to get an e-mail from Naturel two hours later, scheduling a phone interview for the same day. When the call came, the woman who interviewed me enunciated every word as if her life depended on it. In answer to, "Why do you think you're right for this job?" I delivered the lines I'd rehearsed, talking a bit too fast but with conviction.

"I know faces and what they need to look their best. Most women use makeup to hide blemishes or create an impression—I know how to use it to enhance someone's personality or to create an entirely new identity. I'm the one you want."

"From your resume, I gather you've had no sales experience."

"Once you convince somebody you can make them beautiful, pushing product isn't a problem, is it?"

The interviewer paused. "I like your honesty and hope you have the talent to back it up. We've got a seminar starting tomorrow. I'll send you the details."

***

Vacuum-packed in the downtown A train, I came close to falling asleep on my feet and almost missed my connection with the E train. I got off at Fifth Avenue & 53rd and ran up the stairs. Not a good first impression, being late for the first day of training.

Judging from the level of excitement in the air, the women (I didn't see any male candidates) who showed up at the Hilton Hotel near Rockefeller Center might have been competing in a Miss Universe pageant or auditioning for American Idol. *Why make such a big deal out of smearing face cream on wrinkled shoppers?* When I learned what the starting pay was, it seemed I'd be better off tending bar and wrangling big tips. Too bad I had no experience mixing cocktails.

My fellow trainees were mainly actress-slash-singer-slash-reality show contestant types, many of them new to New York, likeable but it seemed to me, naïve. It was true the food was first class and the skin physiology class fascinating, but didn't they get it that after getting the star treatment we would all be turned loose in the city to try to survive on less than $90 a day?

As I discovered, Naturel had high expectations. Aspiring make-up consultants were not only required to memorize the entire product line in two days, but also to demonstrate instant expertise on the qualities and benefits of each grain of face powder, each drop of foundation, blush, or mascara and every globule of the seemingly endless parade of moisturizing creams.

I did my homework, and when the time came for hands-on practice, my experience gave me an advantage over the other wannabes. It was easy to make the switch from the

76

dramatic make-up I'd worked with in theatre school in California to the subtle shades that enhance a woman's natural skin tone. One week after I completed the seminar, they placed me in the mid-town Macy's as a paid trainee.

My counter coach, Ingrid, was a likeable girl with dyed jet-black hair that lent a vampirish look to her pale Scandinavian face. Our supervisor, Marla, wore high-button shoes and high-neck blouses that made her look the part. She held the team strictly to the clock, monitoring the cash register like it contained her personal fortune. To her credit, Marla was also compulsively fair about splitting tips, regardless of who sold the most product.

We were all trained to make eye contact as soon as a shopper entered the store. This wasn't hard since the Naturel booth was located to the left of Macy's front entrance. Decorated in multiple shades of pink and beige, the demonstration area was an enticing, perfumed oasis, projecting an air of opulence and lit with table lamps that flattered the least glamorous of customers.

I came to appreciate my well-heeled clientele, most of whom were glad to take my advice and treat me like an equal. There were exceptions. One irritable woman with a bad complexion requested a mountain of pore-clogging foundation and became abusive when I suggested a lighter application. I wanted to tell this harridan that wearing a mask was fine if you were in the Mardi Gras parade. Mindful of my bread and butter, I patiently applied more blush.

My first take-home paycheck came as a splash of cold water. So much money went for taxes and then half of what remained was already earmarked for my share of rent and utilities. It looked like a working woman's financial life was as precarious as the dicey schemes that crossed my mind on a daily basis and that, so far, I had resisted.

Tiffany agreed when I told her I thought surviving in New York was "as tough in its way as our days at the Ranch."

"If you're interested, Sandie, there's someone I know who can get you a credit card skimmer," she told me. "That place where you work is a potential goldmine."

How much? I stopped myself from asking, knowing I'd never steal from Naturel's customers. First, they trusted me. And second, my honest employment was threatening to make an honest woman of me. Too bad it paid less than I could live on.

My other option was to scour Craigslist and a few other sites for adult film gigs. *Being squeamish is a luxury you can't afford.* There were a few ads for what I'd forced myself to do when on the road with Russell, all of them easy to decipher.

One of them caught my eye. *Wanted, uninhibited model. No interaction required.* Trying not to overthink it, I placed the call.

"Daisy Studios," a bored-sounding voice answered.

"I'm calling about your ad on Craigslist."

"Have you got some experience?" He sounded like he couldn't care less.

"Yes, and I haven't had any complaints so far."

"There's a three o'clock slot open. You should plan to be here for at least an hour and a half." What he meant was that if I passed inspection, the camera would roll and I'd get paid.

***

Located a few short blocks from the Bedford Avenue subway station, Daisy Productions occupied the entire third floor of a rundown industrial building, one of the few in Williamsburg that hadn't been demolished or gutted and remodeled during the gentrification craze. I rode up in the freight elevator and was greeted by a paunchy, middle-aged man with wisps of excited grey brillo behind his ears. "So, you're Lauren," he said. "Have you thought about changing your name to something more exotic?"

I chuckled inwardly but didn't share the joke. Lauren Bacall was Mom's favorite actress and here I was, taking her name in vain.

"If you don't mind, I'll call you Yellow Rose. I like that dirty blonde hair of yours. I'm Monty, by the way."

Since neither of us offered to shake hands there was an awkward pause during which Monty caught me staring at his pinky rings and immaculately groomed nails. "Palmolive liquid soap commercial, 2002. That's where you've seen them."

What could I say? I followed him inside. Although he looked harmless enough, I made a mental note of the exact location of the pepper spray I'd kept in my purse ever since that night in the hostel.

We passed through a video editing suite packed with computers and into a living area with a bare, industrial look—a couch covered with fluffy shag pillows that looked like movie props, the coffee table littered with porno magazines, no surprise there. However, the half-eaten pizza and partially filled paper cups suggested that the *No interaction required* line in the ad had been misleading. My suspicions were confirmed when we reached the other side of the loft, where a nude, muscle-bound stud illuminated by a key light was practicing poses in front of the window, his bare chest smooth as a wax doll's. He nodded at me and his erect member gave a short salute.

"Like I told you on the phone, I only work solo," I told Monty, the shrillness in my voice resisting any efforts to control it.

"Don't blow a fuse before we get started or you won't have any energy left for the camera," Monty advised me with forced patience. "That guy's auditioning for a feature we're putting together. You're in Studio B." He pointed to an open doorway off to the side, beyond which waited an empty, brightly lit, king-sized four-poster.

"Nice color coordination," Monty pointed to the purple velveteen coverlet. "It's an exact match with the color of your skirt. We can work that in. Make yourself comfortable. I'll be back in a minute. You'll find some toys and a few refreshments on the nightstand."

The bedroom walls were painted a light saffron, tastelessly suggesting a Buddhist temple or yoga studio. Red tassels dangled from the corners of the canopy over the bed and a pair of handcuffs was fastened to the bottom end of the bedpost. Reaching into the pile of sex toys on the night table, I picked up a dildo. It smelled faintly of cleaning fluid and I put it down quickly in disgust. The bottle of whiskey was more appealing, as well as the miniature water pipe, its bowl conveniently loaded with a sliver of hashish. Monty knew how to keep his "stars" happy.

I poured myself a shot of booze and downed it quickly, then hunted around in the drawer for a book of matches. The hash smelled pungently sweet and after the second inhale I floated into a detached state, my mind free of inhibitions, my muscles loose and relaxed.

I stripped to my bra and panties and slid under the dark green silk sheets.

"Do I have to use the gadgets?" I asked first thing when Monty returned.

"No, not if you can make it look interesting without them." He got busy adjusting the lights and focusing the camera. "Show us what arouses you," he directed, as clinical as any doctor surrounded by medical students.

While preparing to pleasure myself for the camera, I felt my self-assurance slip a notch or two. Last year, when I'd made some videos for gas money, Russell had been less than secretly pleased about having a woman who could generate "that kind of cheese in an hour without letting anyone touch her." The setup was unsavory then and even more humiliating now.

"Ready, Yellow Rose?" Monty asked. "Don't forget to arch your back and wipe that sour look off your face. I'm not paying you to turn off my viewers."

80

Sometimes you don't realize you've had enough, and then you do. I reached for my clothes, causing Monty to groan and replace the lens cap on the camera. I was out of there before he could say a word.

On the way to the elevator, I opened an unmarked door that I thought led to the stairs. And there they were, two boys, hurriedly getting dressed. The youngest looked no older than twelve. He glanced in my direction and his gaze passed through me, as if he lived in a world of ghosts on the other side. It took a moment for me to place the second boy. It was Griffin, my teenage friend from the hostel downtown. When he didn't respond to my nod, I backed out into the hallway. *You're not a social worker. It's none of your business.* I walked away, hoping the ripple of guilt in my gut wouldn't turn into a wave.

"Is something off?" the stud asked. He was waiting by the lift. Dressed, he seemed a lot less threatening, his long hair being his most prominent feature instead of the oversized cock. The fisherman's cap and granny glasses were a surprise. On the ride down, we stood awkwardly side by side.

"This isn't my kind of gig," I said. "I prefer legit theatre when I can get it."

"Right." His tone said he assumed I was lying.

"All the best with your career," I said when we got outside. He looked at me in surprise and a small smile broke through his sulky countenance.

"Look. I've got a friend in Park Slope who produces indie films, the real deal. If you're interested, his name is Sloan Malloy. Here's his card. Tell him Roy sent you. One of his female cast members quit at the last minute. I think you might have the kind of face he's looking for."

I accepted the card with thanks. It seemed that by wishing good fortune on Roy I might have created some of my own.

***

81

Walking to the subway, my mental picture of the two boys, the younger one wiping lipstick off his mouth, the garish red smeared all over his chin, replayed in my head. And then I was back in the days of my own childhood, hitchhiking home from the beach with Frank.

Frank had set me in my usual place by the side of the road. It was not our lucky day. A half hour passed before a maroon station wagon pulled up and the passenger door swung open. "Get in, honey," I heard a kindly voice say. The driver wore a suit, thin straw hair neatly combed, and I was overheated and impatient enough to forget my father's strict instructions never to get into a car by myself.

I heard Frank call, "wait a minute!" and then the fetid smell of the man's breath overwhelmed me as he reached across my body and pulled the passenger door shut. Realizing my mistake, I pulled at the door handle but not quick enough to beat the click from the driver's side. I was locked in.

"Be a good girl and I won't hurt you," he said, pulling away from the curb. I turned to look through the back window, but there was no sign of Frank. Then a loud thump on the front of the wagon whipped my head around and there he was, banging on the windshield with a tree branch, big green leaves flying off each time he delivered a solid whack.

The driver veered and accelerated, and I watched, first in horror as Frank fell off the hood, and then in amazement as he tucked himself into a ball, rolling on the ground and then jumping back to his feet and chasing the car. Traffic slowed and in the rear-view mirror the driver saw his nemesis—as Brenda would have said—fast approaching. Barely slowing down, he unlocked my door and gave me a shove.

The next thing I knew I was in Frank's arms, crying my heart out. "I'm sorry. I'm sorry," he kept repeating, as he carried me to where the backpack lay on the sidewalk, cursing himself out loud for having forgotten the mini first aid kit that Brenda nagged him to bring to the beach.

Frank had dug through his pockets, miraculously finding enough coins for us to take the bus. He gripped my hand tightly on the ride home. When we got there, the apartment was empty. Brenda was due back from work any minute. "She'll want to know how you got that bruise," he prompted me.

"Don't worry. I'll tell her I took a dive off my bike," I said. He smiled at me then, one of the few times his little girl felt he was truly proud of her.

***

The memory of my close call and Frank's heroics was vivid enough to make me turn around and walk back to Daisy Studios. Griffin was out front and not pleased to see me.

"Monty set me up to meet someone. If this guy Stu sees me yackin' with you —"

"I've got my own place now." I scribbled my cell number and address on the back of an envelope that I folded and slid into his back pocket, just as a gold Lexus station wagon pulled up. The passenger door opened, and Griffin disappeared inside, swallowed whole.

I stepped off the pavement to cross the street, making a show of adjusting my purse-strap while stealing a quick glance at the driver. Silver-haired, in his 50's I guessed, and would have looked patrician if not for the loose, pouty lips that spoiled his profile. Maybe I wasn't brave enough to throw myself on the hood of the car and rescue Griffin, but at least I could memorize this creep's features. I would have snagged his license plate too if he hadn't turned his head and forced me to duck out of sight.

9. Action/Camera

I stood outside Daisy Studios, staring at the beat-up business card that Roy had given me. Maybe it was time to explore some new, more legit possibilities. After seeing Griffin and his buddy looking like their faces should be plastered on a billboard for missing children, I felt disgusted with the underground film world and more than ready for a change. What did I have to lose? I called Sloan Malloy.

"Roy at Daisy Studios suggested I contact you. He said my face is what you're looking for."

"I didn't think Monty and his crew cared much about faces."

"That's not my fault," I said. "Can I audition?"

There was an awkward silence on the line, followed by a sigh. "Your timing's good, I'll give you that. How soon can you get here?"

Here turned out to be a classic Brownstone on President Street, in Park Slope, an area I hadn't visited since Brenda took me to the Brooklyn Museum ages ago.

The chichi cafes had multiplied, eating up their own neighborhood and forcing out the corner groceries. No more sticks of the brown licorice Mom once told me were sold from jars when she was a kid.

Sloan came to the door dressed in designer army fatigues and boots to match. He locked his gaze on mine, like a hunter challenging his prey to convince him it should be allowed to live. His uncompromising manner brought back a Stella Adler quote I'd seen on Darshon's classroom wall— *Actors need a kind of aggression, an inner force. Don't be only one-sided, sweet, nice, good. Get rid of being average. Find the killer.*

I followed Sloan through a wide hallway carpeted in a traditional dark green that failed to tame the silver and black velveteen patterns on the wallpaper. It was hard to guess his age—maybe early thirties—because as soon as he launched into a non-stop description of the film, he became an excited teenager.

"There are a lot of sight gags in the script but it's not really a comedy, more like an anti-love story," he said. "Although in the end they get together." I tried to remember all the cinematic terms he used—*allegory*, *mockumentary*, *character color coding*—planning to look them up later. He was an inch or two shorter than me but his bursts of energy and enthusiasm made him seem taller. Sloan was Monty the pornographer's exact opposite. It was hard to believe I'd met them both on the same day.

"I'll get you something to drink and then you can tell me about yourself," he at last drew a breath to say.

While Sloan was gone I tried to cook up some bullshit story about touring with a summer stock company but I was out of my depth and knew it. When he came back, I took a deep draught of the Jones Soda he handed me and told him the truth. "Although I've taken some classes, I'm not a professional. The one thing I *do* know about acting is how to put myself into someone else's skin."

He handed me some pages. "Your name is Janine and you're a tattoo artist."

"Give me a minute."

I read the direction notes at the top of the page. *Theo, who lives in the suburbs, is infatuated with a Goth girl from*

Brooklyn who won't give him the time of day. He decides the only way he can win her love is by covering his body with tattoos.

Theo enters the tattoo parlor where Janine, dressed in a skirt and headscarf, is sweeping the floor of a room filled with cardboard boxes. The walls are bare except for a poster of a naked woman with stalks of bamboo tattooed on her lower back.

JANINE: Sorry we're closed.

THEO: I can pay you to work overtime.

JANINE: You don't understand. I've sold the business. Come back next week and you can join the health club that's moving in. Much better choice.

THEO: See this as your opportunity to create a masterpiece. I want you to create a full body rendition of The Scream. You know, the painting by that German artist, the one that was stolen.

JANINE: Edward Munch was Norwegian. And they recovered the painting.

THEO: What if I told you I need this tattoo so the person of my dreams will decide to love me.

JANINE: Look kid, a few years from now you'll wonder if she was worth it and believe me you won't want to go through the agony of having the ink removed. Consider it the hand of fate that I'm closing up shop, better yet, the hand of Allah.

THEO: I don't understand.

JANINE: I'm returning to my roots in Islam. We don't believe in defacing bodies.

THEO: But it's okay to blow them up?

Refusing to rise to the bait, Janine picks up a box and carries it outside.

***

I took my purse into the bathroom down the hall. I had only a make-up kit and a hairbrush but this was my area of

87

expertise and I knew what was needed. Janine would have fuller lips than mine—an effect I achieved by applying both deep and light shades of vermillion—and dark, dramatic eyes outlined in kohl, the upper lashes thickened with liquid liner. I pulled my hair back from my forehead to accentuate my cheekbones and tightened the straps on my bra to generate some cleavage above my lace-trimmed tank top.

Finding my character's voice without any direction or rehearsal was a challenge, but Darshon had shared some cool tricks in class. I looked in the mirror and asked Janine, "What's your greatest fear?"

How could you begin to understand? You've never been the target of ethnic cleansing. I let that sink in a little bit. Then I made my entry and Sloan and I read the lines.

"Nice characterization but the thing is..." he said, and I braced for the splash of cold water.

"You've got the character's external mannerisms down pat but I don't get the feeling this woman is caught up in the throes of making a huge decision. She's in the process of changing her entire way of life and doesn't know how it'll go. You've got to dig deeper and let us know what's cooking underneath all that bravado. I'll give you a hint. Most likely it's a world of pain."

I tried again, doing my best to make the lines sparkle, but I'd run out of ideas and the scene fell flatter than a day-old Pepsi.

"Sorry — you do have some raw talent. I simply don't have time to coach a beginner. We start shooting in three days."

What could I tell him? That I was good at conning people and making them see what they wanted to see? That my 'stage' was real life and my survival often depended on the believability of my performance?

"How about a call-back for tomorrow? I know I can play this part."

Sloan laughed. "I like your chutzpa." The card he gave me showed an address in Chelsea. "We're rehearsing at the producer's apartment tomorrow night. Be there promptly at seven and I'll give you one more chance."

On the train ride from Brooklyn back to Manhattan, I wondered if Sloan was right. I was good at portraying appearances and mannerisms but when the time came to dive down to where the big fish lived, could I take the pressure?

After consuming a reheated calzone that Tiff had abandoned in the fridge, I wiped the crumbs off the kitchen counter and picked up the script for *Careless Love*. It was easy to commit Janine's lines to memory. The tough part was breathing life into them. This was my first audition outside of school, in the real world and if I nailed it, maybe next time there'd be some real money.

I poured myself a glass of wine and reminded myself of all the stories Darshon told his students to discourage us from engaging in "rookie fantasies." No way I was going to embarrass myself with daydreams about an acting career.

Or was I? I woke in the middle of the night, tugging at the edge of a rapidly dissipating dream. A woman in a bikini stood at the edge of a blue-green pool in the courtyard of an elegant mansion, drink in hand, admiring the sunset. For a moment I gazed at the world from the perspective of a successful movie star. Then someone knocked the martini out of my hand and the image faded.

***

Never go into a job cold. You've got to have a plan and be ready to handle whatever comes up. Russell and I had prepared meticulously and as a result, I'd been able to hold my anxiety in check when walking into a bank in Kansas City or Columbus, whether I was cashing a single forged check or cleaning out an entire account. Today was different. My chest felt tight and my thoughts were uneasy. Because what I wanted most could not be stolen. It had to be earned.

On the way from the subway to the producer's address on West 28th, I stopped briefly to inhale the fragrance of a bucketful of white lilies displayed in front of a storefront sandwiched between two newly constructed glass towers. It was depressing to see Manhattan's Flower District, an oasis of green and growing plants, was being sacrificed to the gods of development.

My mood was not improved by the sight of my destination, a grey metal door smeared with graffiti. *Maybe I should drop the whole deal. Why pin my hopes on an impoverished indie filmmaker who can't afford to rent a decent rehearsal space?* I was struggling to make up my mind when the door opened and Sloan came out. He'd substituted Nikes, sweatpants, and a tight-fitting blue t-shirt for the fatigues he'd worn in Brooklyn.

"Go on up to the second floor. I've got to run an errand. Be right back." I watched him hurry down the street, *One-Take Wonder* printed in block letters on the back of his shirt.

Like the front door, the building's grimy lobby and hallway were sub-par and left me completely unprepared, when the elevator door opened, to find myself on the threshold of a luxury loft with twenty-foot ceilings, complete with a décor copied straight from some house beautiful magazine.

A tall, gawky woman in jeans and a Rousseau-blue velvet jacket darted across the room to greet me. Her short black hair was combed behind her ears to set off shoulder-length silver earrings.

"Welcome, Sandie. I'm Leslie Ann, Executive Producer of *Careless Love.*"

I was embarrassed to have assumed the producer was a man. I was also fascinated by a large painting of four primitively drawn flowers, centered on the wall behind an antique couch upholstered in gold brocade and itself a work of art.

"That Andy Warhol silkscreen is the only real art we have left," Leslie Ann said. "And as much as I love Sloan's latest project, I've told him this is one piece that will never go near the auction block."

I envisioned her coming home to find a dark rectangle where the frame had been, my fence suitably impressed, money changing hands—all in the second it took me to draw breath and say, "It's beautiful."

How incorrigible I was, for someone who had a steady day job and whose lawless days were supposedly behind her.

Leslie Ann escorted me into the rehearsal space, where floor-to-ceiling bookshelves lined the walls and four actors looked up at her from their seats around a glass-covered library table. Their faces were partially illuminated by rays of sun streaming from the skylight. It could have been a professionally lit set.

"I see you're dressed for the part," commented a rectangular-faced person with intensely cerulean eyes. "I'm Chris and I go by the pronoun 'they.' I'm playing Theo.

"Pleasure to meet you, Chris," I said, ignoring the comment on my appearance. I'd made myself up as Janine, my hair hidden under a dark green silk hijab and now, seeing the casual attire of my fellow actors, realized my mistake. I took off the headscarf and draped it over the back of my chair, taking a seat at the table.

Chris introduced Estevan, who radiated intensity and Nicki, who was playing Theo's judgmental girlfriend, her reddish hair swept up like a giant raspberry.

Sloan hurried in and as soon as his ass hit the chair we started the read-through. None of us struck me as being especially good, except for Estevan, who played Theo's best friend, a screenwriter who commits suicide after his lover is killed in Iraq. Chris and Nicki delivered their lines like the living dead, yet Sloan failed to put the screws on. Since he'd worked with all of them before, I suspected he knew they were saving what they had for the camera. When my turn

91

came to play the scene with Chris, Sloan told us to stand up and "give it some legs."

I was doing fine until I lost concentration while delivering the line, 'Consider it the hand of fate that I'm closing up the shop.' It just didn't jive with the independent, in-your-face person Janine was supposed to be. Otherwise, I thought I did a decent job portraying a street-smart businesswoman with a manner as prickly as the tattoo needles she used to earn her living.

Sloan waited until I was seated to give me his notes. "You're slipping in and out of character like a schizophrenic on steroids. Try using a 'what if' to trigger your responses."

What if. I cast myself as a minister's wife, delivering hot meals to the sick. I smiled and Sloan picked up on it. "Ready?"

This time I tried on how it felt to morph from an uninhibited tattoo artist into a demure Muslim woman. I let my body language connect to the images behind my eyes and the dialog took on new meaning. When I said, "We don't believe in defacing bodies," and looked down at my own, Chris gave me a once-over that made me blush. *This is the difference between acting and putting on an act.*

Up to that point I hadn't know that Sloan could smile. "Nice work, Sandie" he said, "but you can do better. Your scene is scheduled to be shot on Thursday. I want to see Janine's whole life flashing before my eyes before she gets to open her mouth."

How the hell am I going to do that? Then the implications of his words sunk in—I had landed the part.

"What's the pay?" I asked after the others had left.

"Scale."

"How much is that?"

"Two-fifty a day."

"Any chance of three-hundred?"

Sloan arched his eyebrows in disbelief. "Need I remind you that a typical newbie would be grateful to work for free

92

just to have a film on their resume? Wait here a sec and I'll get a W-9 for you to fill out."

We completed our business, and on my way out I couldn't resist taking another look at the Warhol in the living room. From force of habit, I also made a mental note of the Brinks keypad mounted near the front door. A crudely camouflaged sensor was mounted on the windowsill overlooking the fire escape, which meant that this was a conventionally hard-wired system. I had no inkling how to disarm the thing. *It's just as well you don't,* said one of the two Sandies inside me, the newly minted honest one.

Estevan was waiting for me out front. "Don't let it bring you down. Sloan wouldn't have been so hard on you if he didn't think you had talent."

"It takes more than a little criticism to crush me."

"Being crushed isn't such a bad thing for an actor. Look at it this way. We're the grapes and the director's the wine maker. Being smashed to a pulp is part of the job. Me and my partner Neal are throwing a party on Friday night. You're welcome to come, Sandie. Bring a friend if you like."

"Thanks, I'll check my date book." I inwardly snickered at this fiction.

I've been invited to a social gathering by a fellow actor, the words echoed in my head as I walked back to the subway. It had been so long since someone I thought of as normal reached out to me, I had trouble believing it was real.

Tiffany was home and from the way she reacted to my good news, I may have been a bit too bubbly and full of myself. After all, I'd landed a paying acting gig in New York. An occurrence that Estevan had told me was "as rare as a taxi driver stopping to pick up a tall Black man on the street at three a.m."

"I'm happy for you, really I am," Tiff said. "And I'll be relieved when the check that guy cuts for you doesn't bounce. Theatre folk are notorious for mismanaging their money."

If this remark was meant as a wet blanket, it came off dry as King Tutt's bones.

"You don't understand, Tiff. We rehearsed at the producer's loft on West 28th. She's got money and knows how to spend it. There's a real Warhol hanging on the wall, like it was nothing. The street door is covered with graffiti, so you'd never guess the elevator opens to a luxury loft on the second floor."

"I hope they've got insurance."

"I'm sure they do, judging from the state-of-the-art Brinks security system. Not that a pro would find it much of a challenge."

My roommate looked at me with enough interest to make me realize I'd said too much. "Are you planning a heist?"

"Forget it, Tiff. That's not my thing, not anymore."

"I understand. You followed Russell down the garden path and now that he's not around to give you cover, you've decided to change your ways."

This wasn't true and it hurt that she'd think I wasn't up to making my own choices.

"Believe whatever you want," I said. "I've got a 4 p.m. call for tomorrow, so I'd better study up on my lines."

10. Ben

Sloan had rented The Tarot Reader at the corner of Prince Street and Sullivan and hired a set builder named Jeffrey Vega to transform the tiny storefront into a tattoo parlor. Heavy-set, with a raspy voice and enough keys dangling from his belt to unlock a state prison, Jeffrey doubled as a props master and was a wizard at crafting authenticity out of nothing.

"This guy painted a fake de Kooning for me that was every bit as good as the counterfeits they sold at the Knoebler Gallery a few years back," Sloan said when he introduced me to Jeff.

The props master told me he created everything from airplane models to the tiny straw-roofed huts that were used in aerial shots of a village in his latest project. "Gigs like this are hard to come by. Everyone thinks they can go to the thrift store to pick up what they need. They've lost sight of the importance of detail."

I stifled the urge to share my own experiences with making fake jewelry. Maybe some other time.

Sloan's plan had been to take advantage of the late afternoon glow, but the sound man got stuck in traffic. I spent my downtime reading through the revisions in the script, while Bettina, the Brit who did triple-duty as wardrobe mistress, make-up artist, and hairdresser, sprayed mousse on my burnt orange wig and tortured it with a curling iron. Bettina was the first person from the north of England I'd met and I was crazy for her accent.

"I've done all I can to show you off as the epitome of bad taste," she cracked.

"Is that your specialty?"

"Don't be cheeky with me, Sandie, unless you fancy some streaks in your mascara."

We had time to kid around like this because Sloan was busy straightening out a misunderstanding with the police about the shooting permit. By the time we were ready to begin, the sun was a dull flashlight in the sky and the LD had to send for another key light and some reflectors. Sloan huddled in the director's chair with his head in his hands, while the crew wrestled with the tripods.

Meanwhile, passers-by were gathering around the barricades, mainly tourists since native New Yorkers make a point of not gawking. There were so many distractions that when the time came to shoot my scene, I barely noticed the camera lens tracking my every movement.

Until now, I had tried to "inhabit" Janine, to imagine her thoughts and feelings as my own. But when Sloan called, "Action!" it was Janine who took control of me, moving my arms and legs in sync with how *she* felt, changing my tone of voice from strident to resonant when *she* spoke, using my eyes to see Theo and to react, not to his words but to his undertones of insecurity and innocence. I was surprised at how much compassion ran through Janine's tough nature like veins of gold crisscrossing a bed of granite. *I guess you can afford it, being financially secure and all*, I thought, then laughed at myself for feeling the need to justify myself to a fictitious character.

Sloan was satisfied with the first take. I wouldn't have minded if he'd taken eleven, because Janine was thoroughly in possession of me, as if this had always been so and she would never leave. Then Sloan cried, "Cut and print!" and there was nothing I could do to prevent my second self from wrenching free. A feeling of loss, of loneliness came over me. Did other actors feel this way when they disconnected from a role? *That's what happens when your life is one long string of abandonments.* I banished the self-pity before it could take hold. At the Ranch and later, when I'd worked scams with Russell, I'd mastered the art of switching my feelings on and off. I'd have to apply this skill to acting if I didn't want to end up a total basket case.

***

On the last day of shooting, I played opposite Estevan in a short pick-up scene. His character, Mario, mercilessly chided me about my obsession with Victor. "It's not easy finding a fresh spin on the gay-best-friend-know-it-all bit," he commented, and then proceeded to do just that by improvising his lines. Instead of "girlfriend, you should know better," he came up with "Darling, even a bitch in heat slinks away when it's over." I was too busy listening for the written line to react in the moment and lost focus completely. It took three more takes for me to relax into the new feel of the scene and although Sloan said little, I was sure my inexperience and lack of training was costing him money.

I'd never been to a wrap party and tried on three different dresses at the neighborhood thrift store on Amsterdam before choosing a simple black number to wear on Friday night.

On East 119th, Estevan opened the street door to a dilapidated, four-story building to let me in. The noise from the party upstairs drifted out from behind him like a soundtrack in search of a story. His short curly hair wrapped around his skull like a Persian lambskin and although the gray leather elbow patches on his sports jacket gave him a professorial look, the velvet collar hinted otherwise. He was quick to pick up on my reaction to the rundown condition of the building.

"The tenants are trying to raise money to buy this place before some Harlem developer snaps it up and throws us all out." He gestured disparagingly at some fresh patches of white plaster slathered on the peeling green walls. "In the meantime, we do the best we can."

The celebratory atmosphere in the apartment on the second floor defied the shabbiness of the hallway. The party was in full swing, the techno-pop I hated thankfully drowned out by the hubbub of yelled conversation. Chris and Nicki were the only other cast members from *Careless Love* to show up. They waved at me like "friends at a distance," signaling that our close connection would end when the film wrapped. A cold practice I assumed was no different between actors in LA. Nothing personal.

I needn't have worried about being overdressed. Estevan and Neal's friends, whether business types slumming in jeans, upwardly mobile artists in three-piece suits, or theater people in satin and leather, all showed a keen sense of style. They also shared an aura of specialness that Estevan expanded to include me by saying, "This is Sandie, she stole an entire scene in Sloan's new film."

As I drifted between clusters, every conversation I overheard was either about landing an acting gig or meeting someone who could help you find work. I doubted any of these people were full-time actors. Most of them looked like nine-to-fivers like me, waiting for their big break. Russell's voice started up in my head. *All of them work like dogs at jobs they despise and spend their weekends pretending to be somebody else. You and me, we're free to take off anywhere, anytime, with anyone we please. I ask you — who has it better?*

Not you, Russell.

I decided I was enjoying the company of this deluded but talented crowd. So much so, that I risked being swept away by their air of shared purpose. This wanting to belong, to be a bona fide member of the tribe, was a thousand times more frightening than the perils I'd faced on the shady side of the law. When criminals fail, they go to jail and no one notices. If an actor fails, you're condemned to obscurity by a large audience that witnesses your being thrown out of the club.

"That G&T looks like it could use more gin." He was more than a foot taller than me, his shoulder-length russet hair streaked with enough grey to soften the sharply honed features of his heart-shaped face. His blue eyes were warm as the Caribbean. They stayed on my glass while he poured, then pivoted up at meet mine, as if he'd decided something.

"I'm Ben Kaplan, better known here as Leslie Ann's husband." He shrugged in recognition of this inadequate introduction. "Leslie doesn't usually include me in this sort of thing but she's out of town and asked me to sub for her."

"I'm Sandie Doyle. Nice to meet you."

"Sloan speaks highly of you, said you've got authenticity up the ying-yang." He lifted my chin with his fingertips, examining my face as if to check the director's accuracy. "Did anyone ever tell you that you look like a solemn elf?"

His childlike directness caught me off guard and I turned away so he wouldn't think I was a soft touch.

He tapped my elbow, not ready to let me go. "I hear you did a great job. Too bad the project is so far over budget. Leslie Ann told me she's had a bad hit in the market and can't cover the overages. Sloan will probably have to lay off the crew and suspend shooting."

This casual announcement of doom rerouted my upward trajectory into a nosedive. I poured myself some white wine, too dispirited to care about the ill effects of mixing it with gin. "Salud," I toasted. "The lady vanishes."

"A great film title," Ben said, "but not what I'd care to see happen in this case. Do you have any work lined up, a play or a film?"

"Something always comes along when you lead a charmed life like I do."

Ben looked at me curiously, having caught the sarcasm and not sure what to do with it. His expression was so befuddled, it threw me for a loop.

"I like you," I said.

My forwardness surprised us both and for a few seconds the baritone notes of Ben's laughter harmonized with my chuckle. I felt his open palm plant itself on my partially bare back, the warm touch sending a message up my spine.

"It looks like we could both use a little comfort tonight," he suggested.

In a more sober state, I might have asked him why he too felt in need of consolation. I might also have reasoned that sleeping with the producer's husband was a sure way to sabotage whatever chances I had of being cast in Leslie Ann's next film. Tonight, however, there was no contest— body ten, reason zero— pure chemistry.

As Ben and I said goodnight to Estevan, I ignored our host's obvious disapproval of my choice of companion and concentrated on descending the stairs without breaking my neck.

I gave the taxi driver Tiff's address in the Heights and we rode uptown, Ben's hot hand glued to my thigh.

He earned some points by not jumping me in the elevator, although he did reach over and play with the ends of my hair. "You're a lot younger than I thought," he said.

"I'm an old soul," I said, fumbling for the key to the apartment.

I got him seated on the couch and then headed for the bathroom to wash my face. I hated having sex with make-up clogging my pores.

"Tell me about yourself," he said, after I came and sat down beside him.

At first I thought Ben's interest was a pose, something he thought was expected of him, like carefully opening an envelope to look at a birthday card when what you really want to do is rip it open. He waited expectantly for me to answer, not prepared to let it slide, while I calculated how much I could safely tell him.

"I'm from Yonkers but I've been out west. I stayed with my relatives and took acting classes at Santa Monica College. Now I'm working as a cosmetologist to pay my New York rent until I can find something that pays better."

"I know all about struggling to meet the rent. If it weren't for online sales, I'd have closed my store a long time ago. Fortunately, old movies are in demand. You'd be surprised how many people have kept their old VCRs."

By this time Ben had spun me around on the couch so he could massage my shoulders. He knew what he was doing and I responded by standing up and pulling him toward the bedroom. He followed willingly enough, kicking off his shoes and using his other hand to unbuckle the bronze, western-style belt buckle that cinched his tight-fitting black jeans.

I let my silk dress drop to the floor in a black puddle and pulled the cherry blossom coverlet off the futon. The only other furnishings in the room were a teak nightstand and an ugly goose-necked lamp. *I've got to fix this place up,* I thought, watching Ben struggle with the long-sleeved shirt he was trying to pull over his head. I heard the top button pop and then his head burst through. "I can't do this."

"It's not a problem. I've got a sewing kit somewhere around here," I said, not realizing my mistake until I saw him put the shirt back on and look around for his shoes.

Back in the living room, Ben sipped the re-heated coffee I gave him.

"What's the matter?"

"Leslie Ann's not on vacation. She has cancer. She's at the Mayo Clinic in Florida. I'd be there with her but she doesn't want me. I'm terrible at hiding my feelings and I think when she looks at me she imagines her death, visualizes me going on without her and she can't stand it."

"I'm so sorry."

101

Ben leaned over and put his head in his hands, talking to the floor. "I'm going to lose her. Leslie Ann needs my support and all I can see is the abyss. That's why she wouldn't let me go with her to Miami."

He poured out his fears that he was not strong enough to provide his wife with the love and support she needed during her illness. I held his hand but I was not in the room. Kidnapped by memory, I watched Brenda's coffin being lowered into the ground. If I hadn't been so young, maybe Mom would have talked to me about her fears.

I pulled myself together and kissed Ben on the cheek. "It's alright. I completely understand. I lost my mom to emphysema."

"How terrible for you. When was that?"

"I was thirteen. It's a long story."

Fortunately, he didn't ask to hear more and we sat in silence, listening to the hum of the city, thoughts of death thick as a wall of smoke between us.

"Do you believe?" he asked.

"In what?"

"Anything, I guess."

"I don't think about it. The here and now takes up most of my time, although tonight..."

"What?"

"Nothing."

"You seem so — self-sufficient, Sandie."

He may have meant this as a compliment, but for the second time since we'd met at the party, tears loomed.

"Don't listen to my drunken babbling," I said.

"Why not? You listened to mine." He caressed my cheek as he said this and I felt the negative and positive poles of my being collide with a thud, as if my heart had been resuscitated by a machine. Sensing my distress, Ben moved away. I started to pull him back, despite my fear that touching him would transmit a current too strong for either of us to bear. And then I remembered something one of my male friends had said in a rare moment of candor. "When I

102

was married, I could have all the women I wanted. They knew I'd been tamed by one of their sisters and I was safe to pet."

I went to get us beers from the fridge and by the time I returned, the danger had passed. We talked of more inconsequential things, like Ben's trip to the Burning Man festival last year, when he broke his leg on a rock climb. Since my own adventures were a lot more hard-edged than I felt he could handle, I substituted gossip about my colorful friends from my days in the theatre program in California, describing them as easygoing eccentrics, non-judgmental if a bit superficial. *What a crock. He's gonna think you're a bimbo.* But the gratitude in Ben's eyes was unmistakable.

"You're a sweetheart for putting up with me and I'm glad we connected. What a soulful woman you are, Sandie. Someone I'd like to know better. It may sound trite but I mean it."

He watched me carefully to make sure his words had sunk in and then pulled me into a lingering goodnight kiss.

11. Saucy Salsa

Two months had passed since Estevan's party and I hadn't heard from Ben. I'd almost given up hope when he got in touch to invite me to dinner.

"I'm sorry I didn't call sooner. I was too embarrassed by my behavior last time we saw each other. I promise I won't cry on your shoulder this time."

I was surprised at the rush of pleasure I felt at the sound of his voice.

"How's Leslie Ann?"

"She's still in Florida and everything's up in the air. We've agreed on a trial separation."

I had no idea how that worked but the fact that he'd called me overrode my doubts.

I spent the afternoon demonstrating Naturel's new line of moisturizing creams. Unable to remember the last time I'd been on a "real" date, I showed up at the Moroccan restaurant in my second-hand best, black Aquazzura pumps, dark green silk slacks, and an indigo, V-necked blouse.

Ben wore a dark blue shirt with a maroon tie. With his shaggy chestnut-gray hair and cherubic face, he looked like an Irish writer. We chatted over Pastilla and Kefta and he told me that Leslie Ann and Sloan had raised enough money to finish *Careless Love*.

"In a few weeks you and I can go to the opening at the little theatre at NYU. You're gonna' be a star."

"I sincerely doubt that," I said, secretly thrilled.

When Ben got around to asking about my family, I told him that after Mom died, my father was killed in a car crash and I'd been raised by an aunt in Queens (at least that part was true). I didn't like lying to him but if I started down the path to full disclosure I was sure I'd end up freaking him out. Maybe after we knew each other better...

"How about you? You're not from the city, are you?"

"Very observant, Sandie. You know a hick when you see one. I grew up in Pennsylvania, in a small city most people in New York have never heard of. My parents were extremely strict."

"What were they, Amish or something?" I pictured him as a boy, peeking out from under a broad-rimmed black hat fallen down around his ears.

"Not quite. My father was raised as a conservative Mennonite. No TV or radio in the house when we were growing up. Maybe that's why I love film so much. He and my grandparents were dismayed when I was accepted at NYU. They wanted me to work in the pretzel business.

"You're kidding me, aren't you?"

I realized my mistake when his face fell. "Sorry, it's such an incongruous picture, you sprinkling salt on coiled up dough."

Ben laughed in the middle of taking a sip of tea and some of the brown beverage sloshed onto his nice white shirt.

"Now look what you've made me do. And no, they don't make the pretzels by hand. There are machines that do all that."

"I get why you'd want to get away from Pennsylvania. Is NYU where you met Leslie Ann?"

106

"She was my film history instructor. We started dating after I graduated."

I'd figured Ben and Leslie Ann didn't make much money off the indie films they produced with Sloan. Tonight I learned that Ben made a small fortune in the early years of the video rental business by selling his store to Blockbuster before everything went digital.

"I rented a smaller location and made the switch to selling hard to find DVDs. I also carry vinyl records 'cause people still love the warmth of analog sound—along with its memorabilia. We've got movie scripts and photos of the writers and directors. People drive in from New England just to grab up collectibles, since I don't sell online. I'd love to show the store to you sometime."

He was a proud father bragging about his kid. I wondered what I'd ever created that I could be so proud of, putting aside the fake jewelry, which was—in Russell's repetitive vocabulary—a "dubious accomplishment."

Ben dabbed at the stain on his shirt with a napkin he'd dipped in water. "For someone without much experience, you're a good actor, Sandie. I'm glad we get to finish that film just so I can watch you on the big screen."

I was flabbergasted at how he'd read my mind and filled in the blanks with my dream come true.

After the baklava, Ben paid the check and said, "Don't get too comfortable. I've got a little surprise for you. We're going to see *New York at Sea*."

"You're kidding!"

He was talking about a musical extravaganza staged on a barge that floated around the city. It was almost impossible to get tickets.

"Hope you don't mind, I got us the cheap seats, on the top deck. If the troupe runs out of extras, we'll have to walk the gangplank and swim for it." He had me there for a moment.

***

107

Our drive to Long Island was an adventure in itself. Ben revved up the Bentley as fast as any Porsche, with me ecstatically pinned by the g-force to the passenger seat. With Russell, I'd felt a different kind of excitement, like a caged animal about to be set free, emboldened to run wild but also craving the approval of its liberator. Hanging out with Ben felt different, entirely, as if my real identity were a mystery we were both trying to solve. Maybe someday I'd tell him everything. Ben had patience, unlike Russell, who hated it when I "went all quiet" on him. As if the act of thinking was some kind of threat.

At the concert, Ben and I were crammed in next to hundreds of hearty souls seated on hard wooden benches on the hillside. My feet were beginning to freeze. "Wait 'til you see this, Sandie. From everything I've heard, this is one terrific show," Ben enthused.

We stared out over the water at the star-filled blackness, listening to the murmur of the audience, a hum of voices accompanied by the irregular drumbeats of surf slapping the shore. The show started and three spotlights switched on, piercing the sky to illuminate a gigantic barge cleverly disguised as an old fashioned, triple-masted schooner. I was impressed by the bombastic voices of the off-shore actors, by the sparks of light radiating from the sequins on their wet suits as they high-dived into the bay. Still, the water acrobatics and swirling colored lights were no match for the thrill I felt when Ben slid his arm around my shoulders and pulled me close.

For days afterward, little things he said had a habit of popping into my mind, like bursts of flavor from within a hard candy. *I love how the actors use the water as a stage. It's like watching sea otters at play.* And later, on the way back to the car, when he took my hand. *Your eyes are like seaweed that's baked in the sun.* I wondered where he got this stuff and why I liked it so much.

We went out every weekend after that but we kept it platonic. I respected his caution about jumping from one relationship to another. It was refreshing to be with a man who held me in high regard and was affectionate with no strings attached. Even if he teased me for being "raised in the backyard of the Bronx," as he called Yonkers, and jokingly accused me of "putting on a second face when the first one is ugly enough," when he thought I was wearing too much make-up.

Ben spent most of his time hanging out at the *Video Trove*. He didn't need to work, not with the investments he and Leslie had made, but he prided himself on keeping current with hard-to-find releases. His DVD library would have made Sloan drool—everything from cult horror films, like *The Atomic Brain* to the latest South Korean tribute to the moodiness of life. Viewing a movie with him at the loft was like experiencing a football game with someone who knew all the plays in advance and didn't hesitate to hit the rewind button whenever he thought you'd missed something. He had this idea that everyone had seen *Rear Window* at least three times—so what did it matter if he shouted out a spoiler and ruined the suspense?

He liked cooking dinners for us at his place and I did the same at Tiff's, where I was beginning to feel more at home. Our kisses grew longer every time we parted and he called me every night before I went to bed. I liked to think it was because he wanted to make sure I was alone. It also reassured me that he was flying solo too.

We were snuggled on Tiff's couch, watching a Romanian cult film, when he turned the sound down. "Can we make this a regular thing?"

"Are there really so many Romanian films?"

He tickled my ribs until I cried for mercy, something no one had ever done to me.

"You know exactly what I mean, Sandie Doyle."

"What about your wife, Ben Kaplan?"

"Leslie Ann's back from Florida. She got her test results and she's in remission. I can hardly believe it."

"That's great. And...?"

"We're getting a divorce. I think having such a close call motivated her to change her life. Out with the old—that's me. I'm leaving the loft as soon as I can find a hotel where I can stay while I look for an apartment."

He didn't sound especially heartbroken and this lifted my spirits. When he announced we were going dancing, I ran into the bedroom to exchange my heels for some flats. I don't know how Lady Gaga manages those moves in her stilettos.

**

Club 86 was packed—a cauldron overflowing with fiercely bubbling energy and music that pulsed at an ear-bursting volume. The frenetic lighting was perfectly synced with the clave keeping time on the soundtrack, exaggerating the speed and grace of the Salsa-dancers gliding over the polished wooden floor.

It took two Tanqueray and Tonics before Ben could coax me out there. *Three steps forward, three steps back*, not so hard after all. He was patient and endearingly funny and there was something else, the way he kept eye contact when we danced— grabbing me around the waist—as if to say, "I've got you now."

I was wanting him in a no-hurry sort of way, like we were already lovers and playing hard to get. Every time we moved apart to take our solo steps, Ben peered at me over his shoulder, as if he couldn't bear the separation. And each time we reunited, he pulled me to him so quickly I had to grab his shoulders to keep from falling. This made me laugh so hard I lost time with the music and ended up stumbling and giggling while the more serious aficionados looked on with increasing alarm.

"We'd better get out of here before they eject us," Ben said.

"Are we going to the loft?"

"Nope."

"Where then?"

"You'll see."

In the car, I leaned back and closed my eyes, imagining us going to the country or the beach for the weekend. The drive was much too short for that. He parked in a loading zone in front of what looked like a bookstore. A neon sign in the window blinked *Video Trove* in bright pink letters.

Ben unlocked and disarmed the door. "You never know who might want to steal the last remaining DVD on earth," he said, ushering me inside. The shop was long and narrow, its display cases jam-packed with vintage videos. The overflow was stacked on the floor, making walking through the aisles difficult. Shelves against the wall overflowed with books about the cinema, not arranged in any obvious order and interspersed with spiral-bound movie scripts. The entire operation seemed more like a storehouse than a retail establishment. I looked around for Ben, who had disappeared and heard him call my name. Looking up, I saw him waving from an elevated space at the back of the store. "Do you want to see my etchings?" he called. As a matter of fact, I did.

The small loft was the Feng Shui opposite of the chaos below, neat and uncluttered, the top of a big oak desk covered with a sheet of glass that pinned down a map of a world. A coffee cup occupied London, a pencil holder sat atop Allahabad, a tissue box covered Milan. He'd been to so many places I'd never seen.

I flopped down on the couch, which was covered in coarse blue muslin. Ben pulled a couple of beers out of the mini-fridge and placed them on the coffee table before joining me.

He leaned in for a kiss, holding nothing back. I responded and he kept his mouth glued to mine as he

111

unbuttoned my blouse, reaching in to tweak my nipples while I unbuckled his pants. Although the *Trove* was locked up tight there was something extremely sexy about making out in such a public place. It turned me on to think of a salesclerk bringing up the mail the next day and sniffing our lingering scent.

By now we were both naked and Ben pulled me down on top of him, not moving, our shared body warmth generating a persistent flow of electricity. *We make a complete circuit.* The thought snuck up on me, pleasant and a little terrifying.

Below me, Ben started to move and from that point on it was all ardent lovemaking, each putting the moves on the other—him flipping me over and pinning my arms on either side of my head as he kissed my neck—me playing with his pubic hair, twirling it around my fingers.

We tried a little of everything, but in the end it was simple and breathtaking.

***

I woke in Ben's arms, couldn't remember ever having been held for so long without wanting to squirm free. He kissed me and got up to brew coffee in a little Italian espresso pot that hissed and gurgled on the hotplate. "Better get dressed—we open at ten," he said with a sly grin.

I pulled my dress on just in time to hear the beep of the alarm system announcing someone's arrival. "That's Denise. Don't worry, she's accustomed to seeing naked women up here."

"You'd better be kidding!" I took a swipe at Ben and he grabbed my hand before it could make contact, holding it up to his lips.

"I'll get you a cab."

Denise glanced at us as we left. Did she wink or was it a nervous tic—I couldn't tell.

After that I got in the habit of showing up at the *Trove* at eight o'clock with some Chinese take-out. We'd have dinner together and Ben would close the shop at ten, depositing the day's proceeds in a sidewalk vault a few blocks away. One time he handed me the canvas money bag to hold for him while he set the alarm, and then forgot to ask for it back. Walking down the street with his money in hand, I asked myself. *How would he react if he knew a similar satchel had been stolen at gunpoint by a desperate version of me?* I didn't want to find out.

12. Making Faces

My job at Naturel paid what housewives used to call "pocket money." I was now one of many New Yorkers who had to work multiple jobs to make ends meet. So, what would my third job be? Thinking it worth a try, I called Sloan and got Bettina's number.

"Hello?" Her bright English accent resounded half an octave higher on the phone than in the make-up trailer.

"Hi, it's Sandy Doyle. You did my face on Sloan's last shoot."

"Yes, of course. If Sloan needs my services, I've got a cupla' days free next week."

Bettina thought I was calling on the director's behalf to offer a gig.

"Actually, I'm thinking of training as a theatrical cosmetic artist and was wondering. Is there a demand?"

"Well, I'm not skint and I work more than most. From what I've seen, you've got a good eye for character lines when it comes to your own face. If you can heighten that skill, you might be able to get some film or theater work."

"Thanks. I did take a course in theatrical makeup at Santa Monica College but I mainly studied acting. Do you think it would hurt my chances if directors knew I was on call for both?"

"Not if you stick with indie productions," Bettina said. "The more jack-of-all-trades you are, the more they fancy you. That's why I'm able to switch between hair and costumes if they can't afford a real dresser. In Hollywood it's different, but you don't have to concern yourself about that, do you?"

"How about taking me on as an intern?"

"Well...maybe. I could use some help if you've got the right attitude. The way it works is I pay you pennies in return for exploiting the hell out of you as my assistant. If I ask you to go for coffee or mop the floor, you do a bang-up job without complaints. You spend most of your time observing and when I think you're ready I let you apply foundation and work your way up from there. After a while, if you prove yourself, I can give you enough recommendations to set you up on your own, as long as you don't nick my clients."

"When do I start?"

"How about tomorrow morning? I'll give you a list of what you need. Best place to go is Making Faces on Forty-Third Street. Tell them the order is from me and you'll get a discount."

Bettina wasn't kidding about the grunt work. In the beginning, she had me running around town in between my shifts at Macy's, buying supplies and food. Most of our work was what she called "basic maintenance"—creating a natural look that keeps the actors looking good but not overly-cosmeticized, as though they'd walked straight onto the movie set from the street. A little foundation, light mascara, eyebrow liner and you were good to go—nothing I hadn't mastered already. Every day I expected to learn something new and was disappointed.

A month into my apprenticeship, I showed up for a 6 a.m. call at a small sound stage in the Village that was popular with low-budget film producers. Bettina was already there, busy unloading supplies onto her makeup table. The crew had been working all night and had transformed the stage into a hospital emergency room, complete with beds and phony medical equipment.

Bettina breathed an obvious sigh of relief at the sight of me. "Sandie, we've got some work to do, a dozen burn victims and one victim of first-degree assault. We'll get to him first."

Watching my mentor carefully, I finally learned some trade secrets, like using collodion to create scar ridges and molding derma wax to fashion horrifically swollen and bloody bruises. And when I begged for some hands-on practice, Bettina let me try stippling maroon, blue and black cream liner around a "burn" to make it look like the real thing.

I proved myself on that job, working under pressure and improvising when necessary. After that Bettina started paying me. She even trusted me to sub for her when she was out of town. For years I used makeup to hide my true self, and here I was, painting peoples' faces to reveal, rather than conceal, what lay beneath. I realized I liked working behind the scenes as much as acting in front of the camera. And it was fun being part of a crew that got the job done like a well-oiled machine.

Bettina took in little theatre work, so I was surprised to get a call from her asking if I could sub for a production in Corona Park. My previous live stage gig had been *Othello* at the Outer Space in Park Slope and I winced when I recalled the tinge of green that had marred Desdemona's otherwise flawless complexion. The effect had been invisible backstage but was glaringly obvious under the yellow lights. After Act I, I had hurriedly fixed the problem, using a light beige cream.

I took the E Train to the Queens Theatre, an equity sized venue with at least two hundred seats. When I looked it up on the Internet I was surprised to find that the original curvy glass structure had been part of the 1964 World's Fair.

Today, the stage was covered with cockeyed wooden stands that tottered on spindly legs under the weight of brightly painted fruit, voluptuous baskets, and exotic silk flowers—a sprawling Middle Eastern bazaar.

The click of high heels was the only audible sound in the uncanny quiet, as someone crossed in front of the painted backdrop of narrow streets. From the way Leslie Ann smoothed her hair and straightened her bolero jacket at the sight of me, I guessed that she was as surprised to find me here as I was to see her.

"Sandie Doyle. Bettina said she was sending someone but I didn't know it was you." Her tone was brisk but friendly. "I'm co-producing a play based on the writings of Kahlil Gibran. Let's get you started."

I flipped through the book of Gibran's paintings that she gave me. The famous poet and writer was also a gifted artist. He had bestowed his women with classical features, but they were not the demure maidens one might expect, especially the voluptuous L'Autumne, with her thick red hair rising behind her like a cloud of fire.

"You'll need to get the eyes right. I want you to use colors and shapes to create nuances of mood."

"You mean "reflection pools," I said.

Leslie Ann nodded. "I see you know your stuff. I've got some paperwork for you to fill out."

After the formalities she invited me for coffee and we walked to the Spilled Beans. It was crowded inside, but not noisy, since most of the customers had only their laptops for company. After ordering at the counter, we sat down at a table near the window. Waiting for Leslie Ann to figure out what to say, I practiced the people-watching exercises that Darshon had assigned in class. A nun walked by and crossed herself. I wondered, *why now?*

"My husband is really smitten with you."

When I didn't respond, she fiddled with her scarf. "Ben likes to accept people at face value. I was the realist in our marriage. And I still care enough about his welfare to be

118

concerned when I see him get involved with someone so... sketchy."

The woman had good instincts. We'd barely exchanged hellos that one time at the loft. If I'd been in her shoes and met someone like me, I'd have had my doubts too. Her eyes never left my face as she waited for my response.

"Maybe I can put your mind at ease by telling you that Ben has absolutely nothing to fear from me. I genuinely like him and would never do anything to hurt him. Have you told him you disapprove?"

"What, are you crazy? He'd get pissed at me for interfering and dismiss my suspicions as the fabrications of a jealous mind."

"And are you jealous?"

The waiter brought our food and Leslie Ann paused, leaning her chair back from the table as he covered it with plates. "The truth is, I'd rather see Ben fall for a small time grifter who is truly fond of him than some cold bitch with money piled away in the Caymans."

"Why settle for either?"

"Because there's not enough time to find the perfect match and he's going to need someone to look after him when I'm gone."

When I'm gone. Leslie Ann was talking about the finish line, the big sleep, not some cruise to the Bahamas.

"I thought... I mean... Ben said you were in remission."

"That's not exactly true. After the next round of chemo, they'll re-evaluate. In the meantime I'd be a fool to take anything for granted. That's why I'm producing Gibran's *Path of the Heart*. To try to change my way of thinking about death."

Uncomfortable as I was with her sharing these intimate details, I admired Leslie Ann's willingness to search for meaning in the abyss. I thought about how my parents hid away Mom's disease like some shameful secret.

"What do you want?"

"What I want is your promise to become the person Ben thinks you are or get out of his life."

Mom had died without a word of advice about how I was expected to go on without her. She'd also left the planet without any last requests. Suddenly, a near stranger was asking me to make good on a promise that I had the power to keep. It was obvious she cared about Ben as much as I did. I put out my hand and we shook on it. It was hard, but we made some chitchat and finished our meal without the subject of Ben coming up again.

If Mom had half of Leslie Ann's chutzpah, she might have convinced Frank to transform himself into a responsible worker and parent after she was gone. *Yeah, and maybe Antarctica would stop melting.*

The play opened the following week. To add authenticity, the prop master placed essential oil diffusers throughout the theatre, inundating the place with orange, clove, cinnamon, and sandalwood. The actors in *The Path of the Heart* each played several parts, changing costumes and makeup frequently. Creating the 'reflection pools' that Leslie wanted for the eyes was challenging, in part because I thought this approach was corny and overly ornate for the simplicity of Gibran's writing. What a surprise when, sitting in the front row at the first dress rehearsal, I experienced first-hand the mesmerizing effect of the deep blue shadows and ornate curls I'd created, flowing out and upwards from Sophia's eyes.

Even as the stone of the fruit must break, that its heart may stand in the sun, so must you know pain.

"That's my favorite line," Leslie Ann had confided in me. Given her situation—and my own—it made sense. Frank had broken my peach-pit of a heart and Ben was all the sun I needed. I just hoped he wouldn't turn off the light switch when he learned the truth about me.

At the end of the month-long run, Leslie Ann paid the cast and crew a bonus. She then took me aside and said, "Promise me you won't tell Ben about our little talk."

"You can depend on me," I said. The woman had been through enough without having to worry that she'd told me too much.

13. Ex's and Whys

Ben's tiny room at the Charles Hotel on Third Avenue and East 16th had been designed a hundred years ago, when people were a lot smaller. The walls were elegantly paneled in mahogany with brass trim. There weren't many cozy places like this one left in Manhattan.

It was my first visit and Ben was showing off the amenities. "It's perfect, don't 'ya think? I've always wanted a crib like this, where I could order room service and watch movies in bed."

His words caused us both to gaze longingly at the king-sized mattress with its turned down blue coverlet and cream-colored sheets. Trying out the bed would have to wait if we were going to be on time for the advance showing of *Careless Love* at the Cantor Film Center at NYU. I kept my coat on, the one I bought new in November, when winter began to set in. Ben put on his anorak.

We trudged downtown, turning right on East Eighth, the sidewalks covered with a dusting of snow from earlier in the day. I was excited but also wary. Ben had told me Leslie Ann was back in town and would be at the opening. Although she'd supposedly given her stamp of approval, there was no telling how she'd react to seeing Ben and me together as a couple. So far I'd kept my promise to her and kept Ben in the dark about our conversation.

In the theatre lobby, I tried to focus on all the successful filmmakers and actors milling about, the players I'd been dying to meet. I had a big part in the movie they'd come to see. So why did I feel like a cat about to be caught out in enemy territory?

As if she'd heard my unspoken question, Leslie Ann came to stand right in front of me. In her black silk pants and angora sweater, she looked more like a 1950s movie heartthrob than the workaday producer who dressed in oversized flannel shirts and brewed coffee for actors and stagehands. Her dark eyes sparkled, holding less pain than I remembered. She smiled at me politely. "Nice to see you again, Sandie. How are you?"

Before I could answer she turned and asked Ben, "How do you like my wig?"

His face lit up like a laptop screen. "You look good. The color suits you."

I pictured Leslie Ann's bald scalp under the synthetic hair and felt an unwelcome rush of sympathy for my rival.

"It's great to see you, Ben," she said. "Really it is."

Ben tried to hide it but her sisterly tone had a devastating effect on him. I wondered how much he'd been missing her.

Leslie Ann wasn't done yet. "Did you see the revival of *Carousel*? It's a lot more believable than *Ghost*, especially with the restored color, and the romance…"

"They don't make them like they used to," Ben said.

It was the first cliché he'd uttered in my presence and I interpreted it as a sign of how helpless Ben was in Leslie Ann's presence. Maybe they thought they were exchanging movie trivia but their intimacy and Ben's protective aura were unmistakable. Cancer was trying to kill her but it also provided a weapon that made Leslie Ann invincible if she chose to lay siege to our little love nest.

124

Leslie Ann knew exactly where to hook her arm into Ben's, and he needed no persuading as she led him off to join a circle of their friends, stranding me like an understudy not wanted on the set. By this time, my empathy had evaporated and I felt justified in taking back my good wishes.

Ben returned to get me a few minutes later, but the damage was already done.

The film ran for more than an hour and I watched maybe fifteen minutes, breaking out of my daze only when Ben nudged me for a reaction to the scenes in which I played Janine. *She wants him back* was the only coherent thought in my head. *He doesn't know it yet, but she wants him back.*

We left right after the screening. "I understand why you're upset but you've got it wrong," Ben said. Clearly he could see through me a lot better than he was able to read his ex.

Slush was seeping into my boots. "Can we take a cab?"

On the short ride uptown, I decided there was nothing I could do except wait for the night when Ben failed to call, or even worse, began putting me off with flimsy excuses. "Never date a married man," was one of Aunt Stella's stock pieces of advice, one she followed religiously until the next time round.

In front of the Charles, Ben held the cab door open, watching my downturned face for a sign of whether I'd be joining him.

When I finally looked up, his eyes bored into mine, not taking no for an answer. "She's dating someone—a guy she met at a film festival in Europe. He wasn't there tonight."

"Is that meant to reassure me? The two of you toss around chitchat like Hepburn and Tracy in that film we saw last week—I forgot the title—what was it, Pat and somebody."

"*Pat and Mike.* And we weren't flirting. We know each other. It's a kind of shorthand."

"More like a secret code," I said bitterly, but now that things were out in the open, it looked like I might have overreacted. I slid over on the seat and took the hand he offered.

Ben sensed my attitude had softened and continued to press his point, all the way from the velvet tapestries in the lobby to the top of the carpeted stairs leading to his room. "Leslie Ann may know a lot more about movies and plays than you do, Sandie—she's a producer for crissake—but you're the one who's been around. You're the one who takes risks as an actor and in real life too."

Been around, if only he knew how much. Anyway, I was grateful to him for trying. Maybe he'd fallen for me because I was a younger, less controlling version of Leslie Ann. Someone who knew better than to push him away and then tantalize him. Someone he could count on. That last bit made me smile.

"What's so funny?"

"I'll let you know when I find out."

"Not necessary—it's one of the things I adore about you Sandie; you don't waste time analyzing everything."

Ben had my blouse unbuttoned before I took off my coat, pushing the advantage the compliment had given him. With Russell it had been pyrotechnics from start to finish, like a show with every moment perfectly timed in advance. Ben gave me a chance to come find him, in the same way he went after me if I wandered off. We were in this together. And he wasn't inhibited about where he applied his tongue, something I at first had to learn to enjoy and then couldn't do without.

I lay beside Ben after he'd fallen asleep, wakeful and filled with wonder that someone like him could love someone like me. He was my opposite and looked for the good in every situation. I wished I felt as comfortable in my own skin as he did in his. I hadn't even told him my real name. Maybe it was time to do something about that. The first step was to get some paper ID for the "real me." I'd show it to him as evidence of my redemption when I confessed my past misdeeds.

In the morning, Ben left for work and I had some time to myself before my shift at Macy's. I tried to recall any pleasant memories from my stay with Aunt Stella to counteract the sinking feeling caused by the thought of asking her for a favor. When nothing came, I forced myself to pick up the phone.

"Hi, it's Sandie. How are you, Aunt Stella?"

"I assume you're calling because you need something."

"I'm afraid you're right. I need my social security card and my birth certificate to apply for a driver's license."

There was a long pause on her end. "You still there?" I asked.

"It's about time you came for the documents you left behind. I wanted to burn them when you ran away but I'm not that kind of person."

I was relieved to hear she'd held on to my papers and encouraged when she said she had plans to come into the city the next day. No need to make the trek to Astoria and exhume all the old issues between us. We agreed on lunch at the Stage Deli on Seventh Avenue.

Five years had passed. Maybe enough time for us both to forgive and forget.

***

I understood how wrong I was as soon as I saw my aunt waiting outside the deli, a brown envelope tightly secured under her arm, head tucked against the wind but not enough to hide the scowl on her face. She looked older than I remembered, her dry skin dusted with a layer of hopelessness.

She also seemed a million miles away and I fidgeted as I waited for her to say something. "I'm sorry, Sandie. I thought I could do this but I can't." By "this" my aunt meant lunch. She gave me the envelope and walked away. I waited for a backward glance that never came. All these years I'd thought of myself as the receiver of hurts, large and small, many of them inflicted by my aunt. It had never occurred to me that the wounds were reciprocal.

"Wait!"

I ran after Stella, leaping over a sandwich board on the sidewalk in my haste. She turned around. "What?"

"I'm sorry."

"No, you're not."

I checked myself to see if this pronouncement was true. It wasn't. "I want to make amends."

Stella rolled her eyes. "I never thought I'd live to see the day. If you mean it, then come by the house for Gile's birthday. It's on October twelfth."

Ten months from now. Maybe Stella would be in a more forgiving mood by then. "Okay," I said, and we parted, a truce having been called with no swap of smiles or hugs.

On my way back to the subway, I opened the envelope, checking to make sure it contained the papers I needed. At the sight of my birth certificate and original social security card, my vision blurred. Sandie Donovan was coming back to life, although she wasn't there yet. I'd never had a driver's license with my real name on it. As soon as possible, I'd go to the DMV in Washington Heights and apply for one.

***

The following night Ben and I went to see a heist movie. Afterwards, walking down Lexington, he asked me, "What's on your mind Ms. Grumpy?" I hated when he called me that.

"You know what really ticked me off? It was that scene where they rob the bank and the girl sits outside in the car polishing her nails. That's not the way it would be at all. They'd be dark purple or black, her nails, not some dumb cherry red color. And it's much more likely they'd send *her* into the bank. I mean if a bank robber did have a girlfriend, and most of them are real loners, the only reason he'd keep her around is if he could talk her into doing jobs. I mean how else is she going to show him how much she loves him?"

"I kinda' liked the gadgets that technical guy came up with," Ben ventured."

I looked at him with total scorn. "Don't you wonder where they got the money to pay for that fancy equipment? Most likely they rolled some drunks or hustled a dope deal. I mean these people don't go to parties in tuxedos to rob rich widows. They smash windows and terrorize people."

"What makes you such an expert, Sandie?"

The conversation had moved to shaky ground but I was too far in to back off. "Most people are willing to step over half-dead winos and mentally ill mothers living in the street with their kids but they're oh so shocked when somebody grabs some money and evens things up a bit."

"Is that really you talking?"

"Who else would it be?"

Ben looked at me strangely. "Criminals waste so much time hatching plots and carrying them out—imagine what they could do with all that talent if they put it to good use. Happiness isn't tangible. It can't be stolen. It sleeps inside each of us waiting for a reason to awaken."

What a load of bull, I thought, inwardly sighing with relief that I'd resisted the temptation to come clean about my past with someone who understood so little about why people did what they did.

***

Two weeks before Christmas, Ben surprised me and Tiff with a miniature tree crafted of sterling silver and decorated with brightly painted wooden elves. When he asked about my own childhood holidays, I told him they'd been "quick and dirty," mainly because Frank made a tradition out of foraging for trees late on Christmas Eve, when prices were slashed and he could bring home a seven-footer for under five bucks.

"The tree went up, the presents came out—instant Christmas. It was kind of nice, not having the holiday season drag out for two months like it does now. Although my Aunt Stella said it was pathetic, having a cut-rate tree. My mom told her the only reason Frank let her buy a turkey at full price was because if you bought a bird at the last minute there was no time to defrost it. Typical of Stella that she didn't get the joke."

"I usually go home for Christmas," Ben said. "Do you want to come? You can meet my parents and my younger brother, Jerome."

"I'll think about it," I said, secretly thrilled that my lover wanted me to meet his family. I was also wary of facing an inquisition. I pictured Ben's mom tying me to a waterboard and covering my nose and mouth with a soaking wet rag. *Tell me who you really are!* the harridan in my fantasy demanded.

I kept my cool and waited a week to see if Ben would ask me again. When he failed to do this, I suspected he felt obliged to extend the invite but didn't really want me to come. There was only one way to be sure.

"Alright, I'll go," I informed him. "But only if you promise not to leave me alone in a room with your mother or let her rope me into baking cookies."

"Cool," Ben said, blissfully unaware his sincerity had been tested. Maybe my chances of being accepted by those I thought of as "normal people" were better than I thought.

14. Crossed Wires

Tiffany said she thought it was a big deal that Ben was going to introduce me to his family in Pennsylvania and that she was happy for me. As a result, I was unpleasantly surprised when she skipped a dinner we'd planned, came in at 2 am, and went off on me just for asking where she'd been and had she eaten.

"Last time I checked you weren't my mother."

"Ouch! Just being friendly. I have more good news. Sloan might be using me as an extra on a commercial shoot."

Tiffany laughed sourly. "*Use* is the operative word, isn't it?"

"You're wrong about him. And I got paid today. You can have it towards the rent and there's more coming."

An expression of manic righteousness commandeered Tiff's face. "People who depend on their friends for help shouldn't use up all the toilet paper and not replace it and if you were counting on me being too twisted not to miss the tampons you took or notice that you've been sneaking into my room and stealing everything that moves, you've got it wrong."

She ranted for a full five minutes, barely stopping to breathe while giving vent to her paranoid imaginings. I wanted to grab her and inspect her eyes to see if she was using crystal again. I'd learned a few things at the Ranch despite it being such a hellhole. But I was putting in heavy overtime at work, trying to save up some spending money so I wouldn't have to ask Ben for every little thing I needed during our trip.

Tiff and I barely spoke for the next ten days. The night before I left, she came into my room to apologize.

"Have a good time. You deserve it," she said. Her eyes were clear and she seemed back to normal. She even gave me a hug and wished me well.

"When you get back, let's go out to dinner at that Dominican place you love," she said.

"Great idea. Nobody makes *chuletas de cerdo* better than El Lina."

Tiff wrinkled her nose. "Ugh! Pork chops are not my thing. I'll have the fried plantains."

It was good to be back to arguing about our tastes in food instead of her taste for drugs. I hoped things would stay that way.

***

Listening to Ben talk so lovingly about his family on the train, I was carried back to the day before I ran away from Aunt Stella's, when she'd hugged me for the first time ever. *She knows what I'm up to and is relieved to see the back of me,* had been my thought at the time. Impossible as it was, I wished our last embrace had been more sincere on both sides.

We'd finished our sandwiches and were splitting a slice of chocolate cake in the dining car—generically decorated for the holidays with silver bells —when the conductor announced our arrival in the city of brotherly love. This talk of love made me nervous. Ben's folks must have been fond of Leslie Ann and there was no way of knowing how they'd react to a strange woman arriving in her place.

At the 30th Street station, under the stone angel memorializing the railroad workers who died in World War II, a middle-aged woman with features chiseled as finely as the statue overhead, threw her arms around Ben's neck. Despite the ankle-length black skirt and tailored white blouse with ruffles buttoned up to her neck, Claire was not the matronly type I'd expected. I liked the business-like cut of her short gray hair and her brief but firm handshake.

"Welcome. Ben has told me absolutely nothing about you."

"Then we're even," I said.

Claire responded with a clipped smile. She led us to a cobalt blue pick-up truck, with tricked out hub caps and a chrome grill, parked in the 10-minute waiting zone. "I had to borrow your brother's truck. Your dad took the Toyota to work."

Claire settled me next to her, in the passenger seat.

"Since when does Dad work on Christmas Eve?" Ben asked from the back.

"Up 'til three. It was Paul's idea to put in the overtime."

"Your son told me a little about the pretzel factory," was all I could think to say.

Claire chuckled. "When Ben was a kid my husband would bring him home a different flavor every night. His favorite was the cinnamon, then the cheese."

"In time I burned out on 'em," Ben said. "Haven't eaten a pretzel since 1998."

Though I'd known Ben was in his thirties, this revelation added more years to my guess at his actual age. Not that it mattered. Like Tiffany said, I was twenty-two going on forty.

The ancestral home was a red brick row house two blocks from the Schuylkill River, which Claire said was guaranteed to flood the neighborhood at least once a decade. "This place was an empty shell when we bought it in 1980

133

for fifteen thousand dollars. Paul is handy and I'm not bad with a paintbrush. Ben here probably doesn't remember the days when our only heat came from the fireplace. Now we've got a lovely gas furnace."

I'd never seen a house like this one, the kitchen bigger than the living room, a six-burner gas stove dead center, and the walls decorated with oak wainscoting and blue plaid wallpaper.

Claire refused to let me help with dinner. "You and Ben go and get settled."

I followed him upstairs, into his old room, where the bookcase sheltered copies of *Treasure Island* and the *Narnia* series. Movie posters for *Back to the Future* and *Witness* testified to his early obsession with film.

Leslie Ann saw all this first. I pushed the thought aside.

"Did you try to get a job as an extra when they were shooting *Witness*?"

Ben did a double take. "How could I? That was ten years before I was born. It's just as well. My mom would never have wanted me to be part of something that exploited the Amish."

He pulled me down beside him on the small bed and I ran my fingers over the wings of the biplane printed on the coverlet.

"I like the country in you, Ben. I mean, you don't chew straw or anything like that. It's more the way you tilt your head, as if you're listening to something far off in the hills."

"Right now it's you I'd like to hear from, Sandie. I'm sharing my roots with you. How about revealing some details about your own?"

Like I suspected, he hadn't fully bought my stories. Although I planned to level with him completely, today was not the day.

"All you need know is I'm a boat with no anchor, a kite broken loose from a string, an island castaway with no radio, a horse that's left the—"

"What I *do* know is one minute you're a classy ingénue berating me for being a country bumpkin too dumb to lock up his bike in the big city and the next you're asking if it's possible to pick up AIDS from a toilet seat."

Ben searched my eyes, checking to see if I could take my own medicine. He had no way of knowing how gentle his most caustic words were in comparison to Russell's. When I cracked a smile, he responded by wiggling his fingers above the spot he'd discovered on my rib cage where even the thought of being touched drove me into helpless giggles.

We sat down to dinner just as Jerome, who arrived late, brought a gust of cold air in from the front door. "Sorry, had to catch up on some work."

Ben introduced me as his "good friend from New York."

Jerome's buzz cut and weathered, muscular build called to mind a race car driver or maybe a crane operator. I was about to ask him what he did when Paul spoke up.

"Ben hasn't told me much about you, Sandie. How did you two meet?"

"Sandie acted in a film that Leslie Ann produced," Ben said.

Paul nodded with lukewarm approval.

Not so Jerome, who rolled his eyes. "What have we here, brother? A romance with a rising starlet?"

"Better than dating a has-been asteroid," I said, putting some stress on the first syllable of the last word.

Ben laughed a little too loudly. "Don't mind my brother. He thinks cops are exempt from the social graces."

Suddenly it all made sense—the wary eyes, the bulge under the jacket, the way Jerome had met my eyes for longer than necessary when we were introduced.

"Try the candied yams." Claire suggested. I assumed she was used to being the mediator.

The conversation moved back to what sounded like familiar territory, mainly the carousel that someone had the

135

bright idea of building in nearby Pottstown to revive downtown.

"Idiot!" Paul spewed. "It's like serving champagne when what people need is cash and food."

Claire told me she was glad to see a Hispanic be elected to the Reading city council. "It's about time. They make up almost half of the county's population."

"You mean it's about time they all went south," Paul sneered.

From the subtle way Ben winced at his father's pure bigotry, I thought he'd keep silent, bound by some unsaid family rule. Instead, he spoke up.

"Would any of us be here if they'd built a wall around Ellis Island?"

An uneasy silence filled the room.

"Where are you from, Sandie?" Claire asked, after a few beats had passed.

"Yonkers, originally."

"Her parents are no longer with us," Ben volunteered. I was touched by the way he'd saved me from the pain of sharing this myself.

"I'm glad you could come and spend time with *us*," Claire said softly, her tightness unwinding enough to permit a sad smile. I felt no guilt for arousing her compassion under false pretenses. One of my parents *was* dead and I wasn't sure about the other. So why not claim at least half the sympathy offered?

Throughout the meal, Jerome kept me under not-so-discreet observation. His chin was as pointed as Ben's was round. Only the tinge of red in his hair suggested a family resemblance. By my third glass of wine I was ready to take him on.

"How does a policeman go fishing?" I asked.

Ben sent a disapproving look my way, then changed his tune when he saw Jerome's eyes light up.

"How?" Jerome asked me.

136

"He catches one fish and beats it into telling him where the other one is."

Ben's younger brother snickered and came back with, "How many porn actresses does it take to change a light bulb?"

Don't get paranoid. No way in hell he knows about your brief, blue-movie career.

"It looks like it takes two, but there are really none. They're faking it," was my comeback.

Everyone laughed, especially Jerome, and the tension in the room broke.

I thought I'd disarmed the policeman and I was taken aback when he cornered me on the front porch, where I was sitting on the steps, taking a breather from the strain of trying to fit in.

"My sister-in-law called me last week and we had a little talk about you."

So this is what writers mean when they say, "her heart fell into her shoes."

Jerome closed in. "Leslie Ann seems to think you're not the person you say you are."

"Is anyone—really?" I said this as casually as I could, cursing Leslie Ann for posing as my friend and betraying me.

I backed up on the steps and then got onto the porch swing, stretching out my legs to keep Jerome at a distance as I swayed back and forth. *If he had anything solid we'd be down at the police station. Keep cool. It's all a misunderstanding that will go away.*

Jerome grabbed my ankle and I pulled it away, drawing my legs up under me.

He got in my face, nothing to stop him. "This is one sick game you play, isn't it? Barging in on families under false pretenses?"

I'd had enough. "Who do you think you are, the Rockefellers of Pretzel Land?"

"Can't leave you two alone for a minute, can I?" Ben slipped in beside me on the swing, now a squeaky loveseat. He put his arm around me, his fingers lightly gripping my left shoulder as he felt for a tense muscle to massage.

"I've got a live one here, bro."

"Just how live is the question," Jerome said and stalked off.

"I'm sorry I didn't forewarn you. He's always been protective of me. Must be a holdover from our younger days when I almost drowned in the Schuylkill River."

I made sure not to show Ben how shook up and blindsided I was. Of all my fears about meeting his family, his brother being a cop had never made the list.

***

Christmas morning we exchanged presents around the tree, small items guaranteed not to embarrass anyone with overgenerosity. Ben was pleased with my gifts—a subscription to *Film Comment* and a wool vest from J. Crew. In return he presented me with a small box pulled from his pocket. "Let's go upstairs before you unwrap this."

It was a silver ring, cleverly linked together like a chain. "Where's the ball?" The lame joke did nothing to prevent a few runaway tears from trickling down my face.

"I've been thinking," Ben said. "How would you like to take a trip to Europe with me this spring? There's so much I'd like to share with you."

I hugged him tightly, at first out of joy at the commitment the invitation implied and then out of panic, thinking how impossible it was for me to grant his request without obtaining a passport.

That night I snuck out of the guestroom Claire had made up for me and joined Ben in his childhood kingdom. I lay wide awake, scrunched beside him in the tiny bed, schemes swirling in my head. True, I'd gotten my papers from Aunt Stella. What better evidence of respectability could Jerome ask for than a recently issued passport? Except that my passport would be issued to Sandie Donovan and both brothers knew me as Sandie Doyle. As I'd gathered from watching Frank and from my own hard-knock experiences, a string of lies could easily become a tangled mess.

***

Midway through the train ride from Philly back to Manhattan, Ben answered a call through his glowing Bluetooth headset. "What time did it go off?" Then, "You did the right thing. The place is locked up tight. This was no false alarm."

Something unpleasant fluttered in my chest.

Ben sighed. "I should have known things were simply going too well."

"Did someone break into your store?"

"No, it's the loft. The dispatcher contacted NYPD. It sounds like a painting is missing. Do you mind if we stop by before I take you home?"

"No, of course not. What a hassle for you. So sorry this happened."

All my happiness at being with Ben was swept away in a wash of guilt that swiftly turned into anger. I knew exactly what painting had been stolen and who had taken it. Tiffany. What an idiot I'd been to spout off about my filmmaking friends' wealth in front of my unreliable roommate. I'd bought into Tiff's hard-working student act, ignoring the signs of relapse anyone else would have spotted right away. Obvious signs that I'd chosen to ignore before I left for Pennsylvania.

These unpleasant thoughts banged around in my head so loudly I feared Ben might hear them. We hurriedly walked through Penn Station to the Seventh Avenue exit.

On West 28th, a police cruiser was double-parked out front and upstairs, the door to the loft was propped open. At

139

the sight of Ben, a uniformed cop got up from the dining table, his notepad open at the ready.

"Your neighbor let us in." His world-weary voice complemented his tobacco-stained teeth. "I'm Officer Tomlin."

Ben stared fixedly at the yellow rectangle above the couch, several shades lighter than the mustard-colored wall. The empty space I had visualized the first time I saw *Flowers* was now an ugly reality.

"It looks like a painting's gone missing," Tomlin said.

"A Warhol valued at 200 grand. Can we get it back?"

The Officer, who was packing up his finger-printing kit, paused to whistle in appreciation of what a big score this was. "We'll do what we can but most of this stuff gets sold and shipped out of state before we've even filed a report. I trust you have the artwork insured?"

"I don't know," Ben said, with a sigh. "My wife and I are getting divorced. There's a lot of paperwork. I'm not sure what might have fallen through the cracks."

I didn't know what upset me most—that Ben's troubles had become my own or knowing that I was responsible for them in the first place. That I didn't set him up on purpose was no excuse. This was my fault. I should have known that Tiffany would want to pull off something like this. I'd underestimated her from the beginning. I wondered who she'd paired up with to pull off the robbery. She certainly didn't have the guts or the ability to do it herself.

"I'm so sorry, Ben."

"Why? It's not your fault." He squeezed my fingers and smiled wanly. "This is what comes with big city life."

"Any idea how the thieves knew there was valuable artwork on the premises?" the cop asked.

"Not really. Although my wife has got in the habit of adopting actors and giving them the run of the place." Ben said this without a trace of suspicion aimed my way, which more than doubled my remorse.

140

He inspected the loft thoroughly and said he was fairly sure nothing else had been taken. We'd spent a lot of time there lately, and a few times I'd caught him on the verge of asking me to move in. There was no question of that happening now. When he heard about the burglary, Jerome would be looking over my shoulder. Even if I proved my innocence, he'd fit me up for guilt by association.

After Officer Tomlin left, Ben poured us two whiskies and joined me at the library table in the room where Sloan had first auditioned me. I was much less nervous then than now.

"The thief was clever enough to cut the phone line coming out of the control box but not smart enough to spot the wireless backup system with a silent alarm we installed last year. The Brinks security people called the police. Too bad they got here too late."

"It's a real shame, Ben. I'm so sorry this happened."

I was dying to leave, to go home and confront Tiff, but I stayed with Ben. There was no reason to think he suspected me of being involved in the theft and I wanted to keep it that way. We shared a second drink and I listened to him vent. He was mainly angry with himself for having kept the painting in plain view in the loft, where so many people came and went.

After he'd calmed down, I said, "I wish I could spend the night but I've got an early appointment." *An appointment with a two-faced bitch who'd taken advantage of me being out of town to rob my boyfriend.*

Ben was too upset at having his home invaded to pick up anything odd in my behavior. He called an Uber and insisted on paying for it.

15. Ready or Not

I was aiming my key at the lock when the sound of two voices, one male and one female, reached me through Tiff's door. I stood there like a fool, my brain unwilling to register what my ears were sure they'd heard. *If you lose your cool it will make matters worse.* A slow minute went by as I collected myself to make my entrance.

"Sandie! I thought you wouldn't be home 'til tomorrow." Tiffany's voice was unusually bright, like she'd been caught with her hand in more than a cookie jar.

"It's okay Tiff, no harm done." Russell had his back bent over the glass coffee table, fingers paused in the middle of filling a hollow cigar with weed. He put down the blunt and looked over at me, anger radiating from his bloodshot eyes.

He's done all this to get back at me. If he was counting on a knee-jerk reaction, he wasn't getting one.

"Nice work, you two," I said. "Very clean. Although I wish you'd prepared me in advance. I hope you haven't damaged the painting."

Russell's confounded look inspired me to adopt a British accent like Bettina's for the remainder of my little speech. "No matter. It's all among friends. And since the tip came from yours truly, she expects no less than an equal share." I was Emma Thompson at her bitchy best in *Late Night*.

Tiffany's jaw dropped and Sandie the actress applauded from the wings. Neither of my co-called friends bothered to deny what they'd done.

"Sandstorm, you've grown up. Welcome to the club."

"Don't look so surprised, Rusty. Surviving you was the price of admission."

"Touché." There was grudging admiration in his voice. We hadn't seen each other in eight months. It felt like much longer.

"Where is it?" I asked.

"Russell's fence has got it," Tiffany said, unable to contain herself. "She lives downtown but he hasn't told me who she is and—"

"Tiff, shut up!"

"Don't talk to me that way! You promised we wouldn't cut Sandie out, so what's the big deal about her knowing our plans?" Opposing forces were warring on Tiff's face—*he's got the power to shut me out of the deal* vs. *I'm gonna kill the asshole anyway.*

Russell smoothed the surface of the cigar blunt in preparation for lighting up. "I'll talk to you any way I want crankhead, if you insist on acting like a moron who can't keep her mouth shut."

Speechless, Tiff just stood there and I seized my chance. "Look. I already know too much, so you'd better cut me in, unless you're planning to kill me."

"Don't give me any ideas," Russell muttered, taking a deep toke.

"Let me finish. The only way Tiff and I can be sure you won't double-cross us is for you tell us who your fence is."

Still holding the blunt between his fingers, Russell rose from the couch. Unlike the last time I'd seen him, he'd come up in the world and was dressed for success, down to the bleached cuffs of his stonewashed jeans and the polished tips of his expensive-looking shoes. "You'll have to trust me on this one. My contact would cut me off like a gangrenous toe if I gave away her identity."

Tiffany looked at the ceiling and I didn't buy his BS either. "If you handle all the business by yourself," I asked, "what's to keep you from taking off and leaving us in the lurch?"

"In the lurch? Are we in a play? Will I also be uncouth and forsake you?" Russell mocked.

I laughed involuntarily. The Russell with a knack for turning drama into comedy was still alive and kicking. I had to admire him for that. But he'd made a mistake when he confirmed that his fence was a woman. If this was who I suspected it was...

Watching Russell check his smug face in the mirror near the front door, I kept my thoughts to myself.

"I'll be in touch when it's time to share the proceeds," he said, orchestrating his departure by slinging his leather jacket, probably Armani, over his shoulder.

***

Tiff opened her mouth to say something and the sight of her pleading expression set me off like a bottle rocket. "I trusted you and you ruined everything!"

Her face crumpled and she fled into the kitchen.

I followed her. My throat squeezed tight with regret for what I'd said. I wanted to strangle Tiff for falling under Russell's spell yet how could I blame her when I'd done the same thing? She never thought things through, like an out-of-control three-year-old running into the street. True, she also didn't think it through when she impulsively whispered, "Give me a sec," and found a way for me to sneak into the back of the van. If it weren't for Tiff I would have been caught and punished for attacking a counselor at Recovery Ranch and injuring a resident. I could still hear her voice wishing me good luck. I owed Tiff my life.

I put up the kettle and placed two cups on the table. "I'm sorry, Tiff. I should listen to your side of the story. It's almost four a.m. and we'll never get to sleep anyway. Do you have any decent coffee?"

Tiff pulled an insulated bag out of the freezer and got the French press going. We'd shared this ritual so many times before that it almost made the scene feel natural. Maybe Russell was right and we *were* in a play.

"Look, when Russ called and asked me how you were, Sandie, he sounded sincere. It just slipped out, the part about the painting and your wealthy friends. I was sharing my admiration for the way you landed on your feet. The next thing I know, he shows up here. You were away in Pennsylvania with Ben and the rest, well, sort of happened. We're talking big money here, Sandie. And he promised we'd split it with you. We still can."

It was no use. He'd brainwashed her. Since deprogramming would take too much time, all I had left was shock treatment. "Tell me, Tiff. Are you going to split the guilt for betraying someone I love who's asked me to go to Europe with him and hinted at marriage? Are you going to share my prison sentence when Ben banishes me from his life?"

She avoided my eyes, leaving her coffee untouched. "Like I told you, it was all Russell's idea."

"And if he told you to stab me with a carving knife you'd just do it?"

Tiff gasped as if I'd hit her in the gut. "I'd do anything to make things right with you if I could."

"Sure you would, like a dog can take back shitting on the carpet," I snapped. Losing all patience, I stormed out of the kitchen and locked myself in my room.

Tiff's words were as empty as her brain. There was nothing she could do to change the situation. On the other hand, maybe *I* was the one who could set things straight.

What Russell didn't know was that when we visited his friend Andrea during our "cross-country tour," she'd pulled me aside. "It must be a big disappointment to see your man reduced to petty theft. Russell's a master craftsman and I miss selling his pieces. I once moved an Art Deco statuette of his for ten grand and I'm sure no one will ever detect it's a copy."

If Andrea was Russell's fence I knew where I could find her.

The next day, I finished my shift at Macy's at 8 p.m. and after taking the South Ferry train to Christopher Street, walked over to Sheridan Square. I was pretty sure Andrea lived on Barrow Street, in a two-story building next door to a shop with some kind of awning. It wasn't much to go on, until I remembered a hand-lettered placard I'd seen in the window below street level, advertising dance lessons. "I'll bet they knocked out a few walls to make some room," Russell had remarked. "Either that or they only teach close dancing."

Barrow Street was a bust. I kept at it, winding my way through the charming tree-lined lanes that once inspired people to call this neighborhood the Village. The streets may have been narrow but the rents were colossal and I wondered how Andrea came up with her monthly nut.

The drizzled mist on my shoulders had turned into freezing raindrops by the time I spotted a wine store with a red awning on Jones Street. Two doors down, a neon sign flickered in the second story window of a red brick townhouse. *Dance Studio*. It looked like they'd made a go of it.

By now I was soaking wet and shivering. I pressed the bell button next to *Andrea Dawson* and spoke into the intercom. "It's Sandie. Russell's friend."

The speaker crackled. "Russell said not to talk to you."

"At least let me in to take a break from the rain. It's miserable out here."

To my surprise, Andrea buzzed me in.

Her apartment had changed since my last visit. The smell of paint lingered and there was no trace of the hippie-

147

style beanbag chairs or the garish disco ball hanging from a light fixture in the foyer. Andrea Dawson was likewise transformed. She'd added metallic copper streaks to her black hair and replaced the silver-headed cane with a pair of sturdy Eskimo boots. Only the clove cigarette had survived.

Seeing my bedraggled state, my reluctant host shocked me again by popping into the bathroom and bringing me a towel. "Russell told me you might stop by and try to sabotage our operation."

She gently wrapped the terrycloth around my shoulders and I repressed a shudder before asking, "Did Russell also say he stole the Warhol because he wanted to ruin what's left of my life?" The teardrops welling in my eyes were not difficult to summon when I thought of Mom's painful death and all the chaos that followed. If Andrea's goal was to make a helpless waif out of me, maybe I could get somewhere by playing the part.

She came closer, like a magnet attracted to negativity. "The buyer picked up the painting this afternoon." Her voice was icicle sharp. "If you make trouble, you'll forfeit a generous finder's fee."

"What if I could promise you other, more valuable finds?"

I'd never seen a whole face twist into a smirk. "Look, Sandie. Even if I wanted to make some kind of ridiculous trade, it's too late. The buyer will wait for the Warhol to cool off and then move it out of his shop faster than the fake Rauschenberg he sold for me last month. *Flowers* is the real deal and he knows it. He's already given me a nice down payment and Russell has your share."

"If that's so, I'll never see a dime. He's long gone by now." The plaintive note I added to my voice came easily.

"You should have thought of that before you counted yourself out. Now if that's all you've got to say, I have things to do."

"It's a long subway ride uptown. May I use your bathroom?" The "may I" stuck in my throat but my meekness had to be convincing.

Andrea's cell phone vibrated. She nodded an irritated "yes," and took the call.

The bathroom was directly opposite an alcove at the back of the apartment, a cozy setting for an office. I scanned the top of the desk and, on a hunch, rifled through the business cards stacked in a small, metal holder. Her hairdresser, an eastside boutique, and a doctor were at the front. I skipped to the last card. *Louis Sperling, Old World Gallery* and pocketed it, along with another one for *Fishburg Fine Art.*

Russell's pal was still on the phone when I left. She didn't bother looking up. I'd pulled off my performance and she'd discounted me as an adversary. I doubted she'd miss the two business cards I'd pocketed, at least not before it was too late to squash my plans.

***

It was past 10 p.m. and I was lucky to find a Dominican take-out place open on Vermilyea Avenue. While I waited for my empanadas, I listened to the music blaring from a speaker outside the dance club next door. People were lined up, waiting to get in. It was the kind of place Ben would have liked. If ever I got this mess straightened out, I'd invite him.

As soon as I got home and dropped my container of *Arroz con Pollo* on the kitchen table, I knew that Tiffany and Russell were gone. I stood in front of Tiff's empty closet with her favorite Springsteen song, *Take the Money and Run,* echoing inside my head.

She'd left an envelope on the bedside table with my name on it. The note was clipped to a check written out in a childish hand for the exact amount of next month's rent. *Russell and I are leaving for Mexico. You can have the apartment. Here's a start on paying for it on your own. I*

149

owe you that much. Believe it or not, I remain your friend, Tiff. I was grateful for the money but talk about delusions. Helping someone in the past doesn't give you carte blanche to betray them at random in the future.

I slept badly and called in sick the next day. My supervisor wasn't happy. From the irritated way Marla responded you'd think I did this often. I was tempted to tell her I was feeling fine and needed the time off to plan a crime.

My second call was to the *Fishburg Gallery.* "I understand you sold a Rauschenberg last month and I'm interested in purchasing one."

"Sorry," said the woman who answered the phone. "I'm afraid we've never been so fortunate as to sell one of Mr. Rauschenberg's paintings. However—"

"Thanks for your time." I hung up on her and googled *Old World Gallery, Madison Avenue* on my phone. Clicking around, I learned the gallery specialized in antiquities and sold fine art 'on consignment.' I stared at a picture of the gallery's interior and imagined the Warhol stored somewhere in the basement.

For more than an hour I explored the online catalog of Sperling's treasures. The man was a modern-day horse trader with a taste for the exotic that from the look of things seemed inexhaustible. There were Greek vases inlaid with centaurs and pan pipe players, a bronze bear from Rome, and an early Victorian 'snake engagement ring' like the one given by Prince Albert to the Queen. According to Russell, men with obsessions were the most easily conned. I combed through Sperling's offerings, looking for an item that stirred my imagination, an item I was sure he wouldn't want to lose.

It would be dangerous. Anyone who dealt with stolen art in a big way was bound to be both ruthless and clever. One false move and he'd wipe me off his sleeve like a pesky insect. I went through a mental list of what I would need. I'd be playing for keeps. No re-do's allowed. And I'd need some help.

***

"Hi, Jeff. It's Sandie Doyle. I played Janine in *Careless Love*."

"Sure, I remember you from the set on Prince Street. What's up?"

"I've got some jewelry I need recast as a replica of an antique ring. It's got to look real enough to fool a professional if you know what I mean."

"I hear you. What makes you think I'd be willing to do something like that?"

"Do you like money?"

"As much as the next person. I'm at the Muse Theatre downtown, mounting a new play. Come by and I'll take a break so we can talk." I heard snippets of conversation and laughter in the background.

"If you don't mind, I'd rather meet somewhere else. Do you have a workshop at home?"

"No problem. I'm in Ozone Park. Make it after four."

I was pleased with his attitude and willingness to help. Although I'd learned a few things working on replicas with Russell, this was one project I couldn't handle on my own.

***

A sliver of sunlight ran along the sidewalk on Liberty Avenue in defiance of the permanent shade cast by the elevated tracks. I passed the Xing Bin Laundromat and turned left. Two blocks down a pair of gargoyles grinned down at me from above the entrance to what Jeff had called his 'pre-war' building. I wondered which war he'd meant.

The intercom was busted so the prop master came down to let me in. His apartment was about as dust free as one can get in New York City, light and airy, with high ceilings that made me imagine I was in Europe. Maybe if Ben and I survived as a couple, we'd take that trip. It was the second time I'd pictured us together since Tiff and Russ

151

destroyed my new world. I pushed past that foolish idea to the business at hand.

"I see you're up and running."

Jeff had his sculpting tools and jeweler's wax laid out on his worktable. He picked up a pair of metal tongs and opened the door to a small, circular kiln from which he extracted a tiny, half-moon cutout that sizzled when he dunked it in cold water. The enamel pin was expertly painted with miniature sand dunes and palm trees.

"You do nice work."

"Thanks. Did you bring the ring you want copied?"

"I emailed you some pictures."

He opened his iPad and clicked through the photos. "When you said antique I didn't realize you meant ancient."

I pointed out the ring engraved with the image of a winged horse.

"That's the one."

"It's a seal ring," Jeff explained. "The caption says it's Etruscan Bronze age, which means it's from Crete and at least 3,000 years old. Couldn't you find something more difficult for me to replicate?" He studied the picture under a magnifying glass for several minutes, while I contained my impatience.

"Can you do it?"

"Maybe."

I opened the pouch I'd carried around for so many years and plucked out Mom's wedding ring. "Is this enough for you to work with?"

Jeff tossed the orb in the air, letting it land on his open palm, feeling the heft of it. "I can melt it down and add enough impurities to give it the appearance of alluvial gold. This will fool the naked eye but it won't stand up to XRF."

"What's that?" I'd heard Russell mention this test but forgotten the details.

"X-ray fluorescence testing. The X-rays excite the atoms and when you count the number of photons emitted, they identify the trace elements in the gold. Modern, refined

152

gold is very pure. Ancient gold shows elevated levels of impurities. If you — "

"Don't worry about XRF testing — it won't come to that." I met his doubtful eyes confidently. "How long will it take?"

"This is a complex job. The wax carving has to be good, but not too perfect. And I need to learn more about the aging process. There's a formula I've heard about that simulates the pinkish/reddish patina of archaic pieces." He paused, thinking it over. "You know, if you try to pass this off as genuine, you could end up in jail."

I laughed. "Maybe worse. But don't worry. The person I have in mind would never go to the cops. And I promise to keep you out of it. I can always say I bought the ring at a flea market."

"Give me a week."

"I'm sorry I don't have the cash for a down payment."

"If you pull this off you'll rake in a fortune. Shouldn't I get a percentage?"

We haggled for a while and then I left, feeling both satisfied and bereft. Mom's wedding and engagement rings were all that had remained of her legacy. I'd hung on to them, even gone hungry, rather than sell her treasures. I still had the engagement ring and took some comfort in knowing the wedding band would be used to put something right. She would have liked that.

***

That evening Ben called while I was at Macy's applying lipstick to a mouth that wouldn't keep still. I went into the bathroom to listen to his message asking if I wanted to join him for dinner and a show. It seemed Jerome had kept his promise to stay quiet about what a misfit he thought I was.

Afraid I'd be incapable of lying to Ben on the phone in real time, I texted him. "Thanks for the invite and I'd love to get together. I'm a bit under the weather. Nothing serious, just need some rest. I'll call you when I'm feeling better." I felt like a complete fraud when I tapped the Send button.

Immediately my cell vibrated with a call from a number I knew only too well. "It's me, Russell. Before you hang up, I'm telling you to lay off any ideas you've got about taking on Andrea and her high-class dealer. They'll eat you for breakfast. Sperling runs a legit operation and acts like a big shot in the art world. But don't let him fool you. His real profits come from the underbelly. If he sees you as a threat, he'll burn you. There was a rumor going around that some artist tried to reclaim a stolen sculpture and ended up dead. Nothing anyone could prove. He's too smart for that."

"I don't know what you're talking about," I said, fulfilling Russell's prophecy by cutting him off. His faux gangster talk was no surprise but I'd underestimated Andrea's paranoia. Of course she would be sure I'd taken something during my visit with her. I pictured her office in chaos as she rifled through the filing cabinet and ransacked her desk after I left. Horrified to discover the missing item was Sterling's business card, I could hear her calling Russell to complain.

I did take a few moments to consider Russell's warning, since my plan depended on Andrea keeping her mouth shut when it came to Sperling. But the way I read this woman, she would never admit to making a mistake involving a rich client. Her accidentally giving me access to her rolodex had been a doozy. That's exactly how Russell would have put it. Funny how one short conversation could put his crazy words back in my head.

16. Here I Come

Monday was my next scheduled day off from Macy's. Phase one of Operation Bait and Switch was the only event scheduled. I rose early and took the subway to 81st Street, where I switched to the crosstown bus and rode through Central Park. It was a windy day and my carefully permed red wig rapidly turned into a rat's nest on the walk down Madison, fraying my already jittery nerves. I ducked into a coffee shop a block from Sperling's gallery to buy a quick cup of soup and use the Ladies.

I primped in front of the mirror and waited for my confidence to return. My coat collar was trimmed in real mink, nails polished with respectable burgundy. I was hoping my cashmere sweater set and wool skirt, purchased from the *Make Ends Meet* thrift shop, gave me a mature look that suggested toned-down old money. The Egyptian-style pieces I'd borrowed from Jeff Vega's stock of costume jewelry were meant to suggest a "wealthy woman in her early thirties who wants to make an artsy impression." Sloan would have been proud of me.

Through the window of the *Old World Gallery*, I recognized Louis Sperling, sporting the same goatee and carefully messed up wavy gray hair that graced the photo on his website. He was deep into animated conversation with a female customer. Her luxury designer bag dangled from her arm, tantalizing Sperling, who stared at it with unabashed relish. He was short and slight, his pinstriped blazer and a blue silk scarf suggesting a troll who cultivated an air of elegance.

The dealer approached me as soon as I set foot in the gallery, his *well-heeled customer* antennae fully extended, along with his right hand. "Louis Sperling at your service. May I help you?"

I relaxed my hand in his as we shook, looking around with the awe expected of someone worshipping at the altar of good taste. "I'm looking for a nice painting to surprise my sister's husband on his birthday. It's in January."

"You've given yourself plenty of time to find the perfect piece," he gushed. "Any style or period in particular?"

"I'll know it when I see it."

He flashed a toothy smile and showed me a few paintings by some early 19th century artists I'd never heard of.

"Don't you have something more modern, maybe from the 60's? The 1960's that is."

Sperling eyed me closely. "Is there something specific you're looking for, Ms.—?

"Braughn, Melanie Braughn. No preference, but my brother-in-law should recognize the painter's name."

Sperling adjusted his blue paisley ascot and took a respectful step back, a would-be king transformed into a courtier. He'd obviously heard of the Braughns. My late-night research into rich art collectors in New York had paid off.

"Perhaps you know my sister, Dorothy?" I asked, praying that he didn't.

Sperling smiled. "I've never had the pleasure. How delightful that you've chosen my humble establishment to find a piece worthy of the Braughn collection."

Earnest and Dorothy had made the list of top ten art collectors published by *The Insider's Guide to Art*. Dorothy's sister, Melanie, however, was a character born in my imagination.

"So you *do* have something in mind," I said, with a wink.

It was fun to watch the confusion on the crook's face as he flittered from greed to caution and back again, trying to find a way to play it safe.

"Actually, yes. There is something special coming on the market soon. The seller lives in Connecticut and is trying to make up his mind. I could call him and say you're interested. That is, if you're willing to go higher than one-fifty."

I smiled and nodded, as if one-hundred-and-fifty grand was peanuts. "Who's the artist?'"

Sperling took on a regretful air. "As I'm sure you know, collectors are a security-minded bunch, especially before a sale. What I *can* tell you is that this is an important work by a famous pop-artist."

It had to be the Warhol.

"If you'll give me first dibs, I'll be grateful," I crooned and gave him the card I'd mocked up at the Copy Spot on my lunch break the previous day. *Melanie Braughn* was printed in elegant script above an equally impressive address on York Avenue. The address was real. The mobile number was a throwaway.

"I'll be staying in New York with my sister prior to our leaving for Europe in the spring."

"That sounds perfect. Perhaps we can have lunch the next time you stop in. I'm a regular at *Frank's Deli*. You'll find me there at noon almost every day."

What a hoot that his favorite haunt was named after someone as two-faced as he was.

I left the gallery satisfied that Andrea was right. Sperling had been holding on to the Warhol, waiting for it to cool off. He'd have it on hand when I came to get it.

***

157

Jeff made his delivery on Friday, meeting me in Herald Square Park, a few blocks from Macy's. Next to the fake antique ring in the box, Vega had placed a card on which he'd neatly inscribed, *Winged Horse (Pegasus), Seal Ring, Crete, approx. 1400 BC*. In the sunlight, the gold showed creased pockets of red, like an old woman with rouge ground into her wrinkles.

"It looks prehistoric."

"That's because I consulted with an expert. He showed me how to coat the crevices with a mixture of red ochre, titanium oxide, and some carpenter's woodworking glue as a binder. That lovely reddish/pinkish color you see mimics the aging process."

Jeff started in on how he had added impurities to the gold to make it convincingly alluvial, but I was listening with half an ear, my nerves jangling. I'd been so caught up in preparing for the job that I'd avoided thinking about the risks. If Sperling suspected he was being had, he'd come after me. Calling the cops would not be an option.

Once again, I cruised through the *Make Ends Meet* thrift store in the Bronx, doing my best to avoid the aisles packed with tasteless pantsuits and polyether jackets. I needed a new outfit for my new part. Like Russell once said, "the only difference between a thief and a conman is that one takes the loot and runs, while the other rewrites the story so all the money is delivered to him, or in your case, her." A model that, unlike him, I planned to live up to.

It amazed me, what some women threw away. Take this rayon vest with silken tassels, I thought. It's the height of fashion... somewhere. The fawn-colored, ruffled chiffon dress I chose to try on in the dressing room made me look like an upside-down lampshade. Outlandish as it was, it provided the long sleeves required for the job. Into the cart it went.

I looked through the junk jewelry section, most of the pieces too cheap to bother putting in a case behind glass. More than ever I wished I hadn't sold Mom's cameo brooch to Navid when I first got to town. At least the substitute I settled for had the same kind of Victorian tube clasp.

***

When Monday came around again, I was in place and ready. At noon on the dot, Sperling left the gallery as he'd described. This gave me an hour at most. I paused at the entrance to the *Old World Gallery* and inhaled deeply before pulling the elliptical, bronze handle to open the glass door. I was wearing the chiffon dress and praying Sperling's assistant wouldn't get a close enough view of the brooch pinned to my dress to place it as a fake.

"Good afternoon. I'm Richard. May I help you?"

He wore an expensive, pin-striped suit, that needed only an ascot to make him his boss's twin. Like Sperling, he approached me immediately, a credit to his training. *Take control of the customer as soon as she walks in.*

"Are you looking for something in particular, madam?"

It was the first time anyone had addressed me by that title. The upside-down-lampshade look had worked better than expected.

"I hear you have some antique gold jewelry that *is* actually older than the hills."

Richard smiled coyly. "We have a few pieces from the Late Bronze age that definitely meet your criteria."

I followed him toward the back of the gallery, stealing glances along the way at statuettes of Egyptian cats and sphinxes, fragments of stone reliefs of gods at play, and wide, gilded frames that seemed worth more than the faded images they surrounded. My ignorance felt like a weight pressing down on me in the face of these art treasures.

Russell's voice sounded in my head. *You've entered Aladdin's Cave of Wonders and unless you awaken the clever genie within, you may be trapped by the sorcerer.* How typical of that hypocrite to tell me to gather my wits in a situation that was entirely his own fault.

Richard offered me a seat at the display table and disappeared for a few moments, coming back with a tray. Two gold bracelets nestled in folds of red velvet. I hid my disappointment and picked up the more ornate piece. "Lovely."

"It's an armband from Denmark, also called an oath ring because the Vikings swore vows on them before they went to war."

"For real?" I asked, packing my voice with awe.

"Well, that's the story." He showed me a hollow compartment at the end of the golden circle forming the bracelet. "Who knows what was hidden inside? It's the mystery that makes this piece so valuable. It's appraised at close to a million."

"It's beautiful but doesn't speak to my heart," I said. "Do you have any rings?"

Richard scooped up the bracelets and said he'd be right back. I hoped so. Sperling's lunch hour was ticking away.

When Richard returned, he deposited two rings on the cloth with a slight flourish. One was the *Winged Horse*. I let out a gasp of appreciation and reached for the ring, placing it with appropriate reverence in my palm.

"You have good taste," he said. "This one is 3200 years old. Exceedingly rare." Maintaining his friendly smile, he kept his sharp eyes trained on the object in my hand. It was now or never.

"I thought all Greek antiquities were government property," I said. He looked away briefly to hide his embarrassment. My remark had hit home.

"Luckily, we're not in Greece, are we?" I added, watching him return his gaze to the ring. It was too late. I'd already made the switch. I dropped Jeff's forgery gently on the cloth and waited for Sperling's assistant to return both rings to the case and walk me to the door. I was long gone before Sperling, who would never have fallen for such a simple trick, returned.

160

The second part of my plan required a helper and although I'd succeeded in recruiting Jeff, I regretted not being able to give Tiffany a second chance, not now and possibly not ever. Yesterday I'd gone into her bathroom to look for a fresh bar of soap. On the top shelf of the medicine cabinet, I found something I'd hoped I wouldn't.

What a huge mistake I'd made, taking Tiff's word that she was clean. She hadn't bothered to hide the syringe, or the baggie lined with a thin coating of white powder not worth taking with her.

It was obvious why Tiffany had signed on to Russell's scheme. That monkey on your back is a habit you've got to pay for while it feeds on you. If I looked at the schoolwork on Tiff's desk, I suspected I'd find a neglected mess, more evidence I'd failed to notice. Not that she had been paying me much mind either. Two survivors standing back-to-back don't have time to take stock of each other. And now, there was only one.

On the phone, I laid out my plan to Jeff, full disclosure, including my small but undeniable role in Ben's loss of his art treasure. I could have lied but I was sick of all that.

"Sandie, have you thought about what happens if this Sperling person doesn't like being blackmailed and calls the police?"

"It's simple. He won't want the Art and Antiquities investigators poking around his stock of stolen pieces."

When I offered to sweeten the deal because he'd be taking a risk, Jeff responded by asking, "What if he shoots us? You said yourself that he's got a reputation for violence when he's crossed."

This question encouraged me. He was already seeing himself in the situation. The first step to saying yes.

"Sperling's not the violent one, Jeff. It's his minions. If I pick a spot that's out in the open, we'll be safe."

161

"This is not my thing, Sandie. You know that. I'm happy making things in my workshop, not playing cops and robbers."

Just when I thought I'd had him. Discouraged, I stayed on the line and waited for him to cut me loose.

"You're doing this because you love Ben, aren't you?"

"Yes. That's true."

"I wish I had someone like that."

"Does that mean you're in?"

"For the right price."

"I'll add another thousand. Not half bad."

"Half-witted is more like it."

I had him.

***

The following Monday morning, Jeff parked his Ford Escort wagon in the loading zone in front of Sperling's gallery, with the motor running. I was the first customer inside. I stayed close to the front window, letting Louis Sperling come to me.

"Good day madam. How can I help you?" He had replaced the blue paisley ascot with its rose-colored twin and it took him a few moments to recognize me and launch into his act.

"Ms. Braughn. What a pleasure. I didn't expect you to come back so soon. I have the painting here, ready for viewing if you'd like to follow me downstairs."

"What I would like to do,'" I said, "is propose a friendly bargain. I'll return the real Pegasus ring in exchange for the stolen Warhol and twenty thousand in cash."

Awareness that I wasn't who he'd thought I was flashed in his eyes and then colored his cheeks bright pink. "I'm not sure I understand."

He understood perfectly. He was buying time.

"Ask Richard," I said. "He made the mistake of showing me the ring yesterday."

162

Without a word, the dealer turned and disappeared into the depths of the gallery. Saliva turned metallic in my mouth and I sweated it out for a full ten minutes before the art dealer returned. He was unarmed as far as I could tell.

"Give me the ring and we'll talk," he said. Behind him stood a bulky menace with a caved-in face to go with his muscular body. I backed up toward the window looking out on the crowded street. "Lots of people out there who can see us," I reminded them.

"Jordy keeps the peace, that's all." Sperling's man looked like he'd been typecast as a tough and had no intention of trying out for another part. And the art dealer's high-handed manner reminded me I was dealing with someone who held his own in a violent world. I remembered Russell's warning about the sculptor who ended up dead.

Working hard to keep my hand steady, I placed a folded paper on the table between us. "Here are your directions to the exchange site here. Bring the Warhol. If it looks good, I'll hand over the ring."

Sperling glared but his shoulders seemed oddly relaxed for someone being given this kind of ultimatum. "All right. You're calling the shots. I'll bring my x-ray tester."

"I'm sure you will," I said.

***

As I approached the Escort, the passenger door flew open. "You took so long. I was afraid you weren't coming back," Jeff complained.

"No worries," I said, with such a casual air that he looked at me like I'd lost my mind. The relief of having completed stage two of the plan was coursing through my veins, leaving no room for misgivings about stage three.

"Sperling took his time looking at the replica. I could see he was trying to think his way out of the exchange. After you drop me off at the park, drive over to Lex and find a good spot where you won't get boxed in. I won't be long, twenty minutes max."

For the change of hands I had chosen a curved, overhead walkway that crossed the bridle path near the reservoir. We'd be in full view of the horseback riders and joggers without our business being totally public. A bit of insurance.

Sperling was already there, waiting in the middle of the bridge. An observer might have taken us for father and daughter, the mutual glare of hatred in our eyes caused by some family squabble. I passed him the ring box and he put it in his pocket, licking his lips which were chapped with cold.

"You should be working for me. I'd teach you not to play games you don't fully understand," he said. The dealer stood unnaturally still, like his wounded pride had left him paralyzed and incapable of fulfilling his end of the bargain. I grabbed the handle of the portfolio case from one of his hands and took the envelope filled with cash from the other. He offered no resistance, letting me take what was due, and turned on his heel.

From opposite ends of the bridge span, we examined our prizes. Using the scanner Jeff had given me, I located the tiny microchip embedded in the Warhol's gilded frame, while Sperling analyzed the gold in the ring with a portable XRF tester. I looked up to see the crooked broker waving goodbye, an unpleasant smile on his face. Whatever that smirk was about, it filled me with foreboding.

Clutching the portfolio, I fast-walked out of the park and down eighty-second toward Lexington, dodging and diving in between pedestrians who threatened to slow me down. It felt like the longest six blocks my feet had pounded since I ran from the police in Kansas City and my neck grew stiff from twisting around to see if I was being followed.

I jumped into the Escort with barely enough time for my butt to hit the seat before we were speeding through Central Park on the 79th Street transverse. Jeff was tailgating the school bus ahead of us so closely I shut my eyes, not a good thing if your job is to monitor the side view mirror. I pried my lids open and the first thing I saw in the curved glass was a black Suburban, tight behind us, Jordy at the wheel.

Jeff took evasive action, winding through side streets, but our pursuer stuck to us like a recurring nightmare, appearing and disappearing, running red lights to stay with us. On the Henry Hudson Parkway, he merged into the fast lane and tried to shake the Suburban but the underpowered Escort didn't have the juice.

The roadway darkened as we raced under the George Washington Bridge and that's where Jordy made his move. He veered over, angling dangerously close to my side of the car. Jeff struggled to avoid crashing into the median and yelled, "He's trying to kill us! Let's pull off and give him the goddamn painting!"

I punched 911 on my cell. "There's a reckless driver in a Suburban, on the Henry Hudson Highway just north of the George Washington Bridge."

The response time was quick and sirens split the air a quarter mile or so behind us. Jordy reacted by zipping over two lanes and taking the Fort Tyron exit. We stayed on until Dyckman Street, and then headed south, Jeff driving slowly, giving both of us time to calm down. In a few minutes he pulled up in front of the u-shaped apartment building on West 171st Street.

"Thanks Jeff. Come on up and I'll pay you," I said. "And if you're as shaken up as I am, there's some weed my roommate left behind we can chill on."

17. Setback

After Jeff took his cash, kissed me on the cheek, and saw himself out, I carefully removed *Flowers* from the portfolio and propped it on the mantle of the fake fireplace. I finished off Tiff's stock of cannabis while allowing myself the luxury of imagining Ben's happy face when I returned the painting. Maybe it was the weed. I felt on top of my world, in control of my destiny. No one was going to dictate my actions, not anymore. For years I'd focused on what I needed to do to survive, much of it not pretty. What I needed now was a touch of whatever caused Andy Warhol to trade in his soup cans for painting flowers.

I decided to call Ben before the high wore off and I lost courage.

"Hi, it's me. Can we get together?"

"Right now?"

"If that's okay. There's something important I need to tell you."

"Sure. I'm at the store. Take a cab, Sandie. Call me when you get here and I'll pay the fare. Can't wait to see you!"

He sounded so matter of fact, no questions asked, like it was no big deal I hadn't answered his calls and it hit me hard how much I wanted to be with him.

I took a long, hot shower and scarfed down two poached eggs on toast before packing up *Flowers* and calling the taxi service.

Outside, the sun was a weak version of itself, maybe a sign of better things to come. The taxi arrived in record time and I was thinking *I'm on a roll* when someone grabbed me by the wrist and spun me around.

"Hey! Let her go before I call the cops!" yelled the cab driver.

"That would be me!" Jerome shouted over his shoulder. "Get lost before I arrest you for obstructing justice."

The cab took off and Ben's brother wrested the portfolio out of my hand. I watched helplessly as he unzipped the case and extracted the painting.

"What have we here? Turns out Leslie Ann knows a thief when she sees one."

Jerome wore his cop face so convincingly I had trouble remembering what he'd looked like when we met in Pennsylvania.

"I know you've heard this phrase a thousand times, but I'm telling you it's not what you think," I said. "Please. Just hear me out."

"Not a chance. You think you'll get me talking and then you'll get me going. Too bad for you, I'm not Ben — that's why Leslie Ann called me.

"Look, I can explain—"

"Explain what? That you're a thief and con artist with a flair for acting that makes people think you're cool?"

"You've got it so wrong, Jerome. Yes, I did steal the painting, but not from Ben. I stole it from a fence who runs an art gallery, and at great personal risk. And I did it for your brother. I'm on my way to return the painting to him now."

Jerome looked at me disdainfully. His light blue eyes had only a vague hint of Ben's, an ice storm compared to a summer shower.

"You're nothing but a petty criminal and you're not a particularly good one. The social security number for Sandie

Doyle that you used on your W-9 forms for both Leslie Ann and Sloan was a total dud, and when I ran your fingerprints — yes, I got them when you stayed with us in Pennsylvania— someone named Sandra Storm came up in the national database as wanted for armed robbery in Kansas. She's probably not a real person either. Who the hell are you?"

I'd be damned if I'd tell him my real name. "There were circumstances, nothing you'd understand. How long have you been following me?"

"Long enough. It's pathetic how you telegraphed your little operation. Every time you walked out of this building you'd done a makeover and I knew you were up to something. You saw those men out in the open in Central Park, making it easy for me to ID them. I'm not sure how you convinced Sperling to give you the painting — probably a falling out among thieves — and I don't care."

It was obvious there was nothing I could say to change his mind. "What happens now?"

"You've got one chance to stay out of prison. Keep away from Ben and disappear under the rock from whence you crawled. I'm giving you twelve hours to leave New York before I tell my friends in the department where to find you. I'd arrest you right now if my brother wasn't so blinded by love. He's such a ..."

Lost for words to describe Ben's naivete, Jerome slid *Flowers* back into its case. "I'll tell him I recovered this through my connections at NYPD. Now get out of my sight."

***

A strange calm descended on me as I rode the elevator back up to the apartment. Some people lose everything in a hurricane and there's no one they can blame. Not me.

I climbed into bed and stayed there, trapped in a depression so deep it took a Herculean effort to get up and walk to the bathroom. Like the faulty airlock of a doomed spacecraft, my room sucked in cruel memories of happier times Ben and I had shared in this very space. As night fell, along with it came a deeper hopelessness than I'd ever experienced. There was no way to tell if Jerome was bluffing about turning me in and nothing to stop him from making good on his promise. The only way to tell would be to wait for the police to knock at my door, a risky proposition. I couldn't afford to move to a hotel room and wait them out, having given Jeff the last of my cash 'til payday. And there was no sense in going back to work since Naturel would fire me as soon as they sent Sandie Doyle's tax info to the IRS and it bounced back. Russell may have done great work counterfeiting jewelry, but he'd done a lousy job forging my back-up identity.

I thought about calling Sloan or Bettina, whom I'd begun to think of as friends. It didn't seem right, dragging them into my mess after they'd been so generous. If I stayed in New York, Jerome would track me down eventually and he seemed the type to exact retribution from anyone who helped me.

I flashed back to furtive evenings at the Ranch, sipping paper cups of homemade saguaro wine and listening to Tiffany's stories about living in the Park & Ride outside of Phoenix, where she'd occupied a different vehicle every night. What the hell, it was that or sleep on a park bench or in a subway car, waiting for the cops to roust me. It was a short-term solution and once I'd raised some funds one way or another, I'd leave New York for good.

I dragged myself out of bed, dressed in the warmest garments I could find, and then packed a suitcase—throwing whatever food was left in the fridge on top of the clothes. Standing in the doorway, I took one last look at the apartment that I'd begun to think of as home.

At a newsstand near the subway station, I bought some candy bars before catching the train to Whitehall Street. I walked to the ferry terminal, where I picked up a Staten Island Railroad map that I studied carefully. Next to the

Dongan Hills station was a *P* with a circle around it. As good a destination as any.

***

It took me an hour to find the right vehicle, a beat-up Toyota wagon. It was a real junker, unworthy of an alarm, although the stick through the steering wheel was proof of the owner's paranoia. I pushed down the reclining passenger seat as far as it would go, repressing useless thoughts of the comfortable bed I'd left behind. I tried to fend off an attack of déjà vu that went far beyond the terrible night I'd spent under the viaduct in Kansas City. Images from all the desperate situations I'd experienced fused into a suffocating montage. I felt like a rabbit condemned to live in a warren where all the tunnels led to the same sad place. How foolish to think it could ever be otherwise.

I set the buzzer on my wristwatch for 5 a.m., in case the car's owner was an early bird. Sleep teased but did not deliver, receding every time a car engine revved or a headlight penetrated the interior of the car, sweeping over me like a searchlight mounted on a prison tower.

At 3 a.m., I got out of the car. Under a charcoal black sky streaked with grey clouds, I crept over to an unlit traffic island to pee on the grass. I was pulling up my layers of sweatpants when a gravelly voice made me jump. "Got some smokes sister?"

"No, sorry. How about a candy bar?" Damned stupid of me to have left the pepper spray in my backpack in the car. I reached into my pocket, keeping my eyes on his, pressing the fear deep down and out of sight.

He smiled, brown teeth only a shade lighter than the grime covering his face. I held out the Mars bar, willing him to take it and go, working on keeping my expression neutral as I waited for him to make up his mind. *He's probably thinking about some other treats he might take by force.* It was taking too long. I was calculating a karate kick to his

171

head, when to my immense relief, he took the peace offering and faded into the darkness.

Two hours later, the sun came up—so beautiful, so unaware of my troubles. No matter where I started, the route took me full circle to nowhere. It was high time for a change — but how?

Despite the cold, it was stuffy in the car. I rolled down the window an inch, heard the strains of pop music as a minivan took possession of the space opposite mine. Out popped a little girl in a pink satin gown, a tiara tilted on her pretty head. The mother followed quickly, grabbing the princess's arm before she could dart in front of an oncoming car.

For a moment I wished that I too lived in a spotless, suburban home, where the worst thing that could happen was running out of milk and cookies and you didn't have to risk everything, every day, just to stay on the planet. A nice fantasy but not for me. Even the "respectable" work I did was fraught with danger. The emotional risks of being an actress tied my stomach in knots so tight I might as well have been robbing a bank. And unless you were a star...

My mind churned with ideas going nowhere. The one thing I was sure of was the pointlessness of drifting through life with no other plan than survival. *Think small and you'll be small.*

As the mother and daughter walked past the Toyota, the girl's eyes sought mine and she waved hello with her sparkling wand. *Fake diamonds made real by a genuine smile.* Now that was a familiar concept.

Plagued by a stiff neck and a chill that wouldn't quit, I vacated the car and walked back to the train station, pondering my next move. I'd kept my cell turned off. If I replied to the texts from Ben that were sure to have piled up, Jerome would make good on his threats. I could say to hell with the consequences and tell Ben everything, but even a big-hearted guy like him was going to have a hard time dealing with the truth of who I was.

172

Once I had played out my self-pity, something else came to replace it, the bald fact that I couldn't blame Jerome for believing he had to protect his family from the likes of me. I'd given him no reason to trust me, just the opposite. Why hadn't I called him as soon as I learned what Russell and Tiffany had done? It would have been embarrassing, yes, to admit my loose tongue was partially responsible for what happened. It would also have been smart. I owed Ben's family an explanation. That, at least, was still in my power to give.

An incoming call showed Leslie Ann's ID. I couldn't help but laugh. *Be careful what you wish for, Sandie.*

"Is Ben with you?" At first I didn't recognize the weak, tired voice as hers.

"No, he's not, Leslie Ann. What's wrong?"

"I just got back from Spain. Ben was supposed to meet me at the airport, but he never showed and isn't picking up his phone. That's so not like him. I took a taxi home and called Doreen at the *Video Trove*. He hasn't been to work for two days and missed an important meeting with a customer. She went over to the Charles Hotel and no one there has seen him. I'm worried, Sandie."

Her anxiety transmitted itself directly into my chest. Gulping air, I sat down on a bench overlooking the tracks.

"Tell me, Sandie. Did you piss off one of your partners in crime when you hijacked the painting for yourself?"

So that was the story Jerome was selling.

"Tell me. Is Ben caught in the middle of something ugly?" Her voice verged on hysteria.

Sharing my side of things with Leslie Ann would be a waste of time but we did have a common interest in Ben's safety. I'd stick with that.

"Don't worry, I promise I'll find him," I said, determined to keep the premonition that gripped my throat from choking off my voice. "Try to get some rest. Soon as I know anything I'll be in touch."

173

She grunted her agreement—I'd say more out of exhaustion than any confidence in me.

The train came and left as I checked my messages. There were so many missed calls from Ben that now I wished I'd taken. None were more recent than two days ago and, mixed in with these was a day-old message from an unidentified caller.

The voice had a mechanical quality, clipped, over-enunciated British verbs produced by text-to-speech technology. "Sandie, you know who this is. Did you think you could win the set without a return match? I now possess something — or to be precise, someone — who belongs to you. If you want to see him again in one piece, you need to follow the encrypted instructions I have sent via SMS. However, before you can decode that text, you'll have to download the Blackout software. And you can start convincing me of your good faith by deleting this voicemail upon receipt."

Sperling — I was sure it was him—wasn't bluffing. As Melanie Braughn I'd given him the number of a burner. He had no way of getting my real number without access to Ben and his phone. I wasn't ready to face what this implied. Instead, I tried to calculate how many of the twelve hours had passed since the message was sent. My mind felt sluggish, unwilling to fully grasp what had happened.

How could I not have foreseen how easy it would be for Sperling to take revenge? I should have taken steps to protect Ben. I'd put the safety of my own skin first. And I was totally unprepared when I needed to be at the top of my game.

Get a grip, Sandie. There's too much at stake. Guzzling a cup of coffee, I got to work. After writing down the name of the encryption software, I deleted the voice message as per Sperling's instructions. A new text message arrived within seconds. It looked blank, except for an ominous black bubble displayed above the message window.

Eleven hours' worth of Sperling's deadline had elapsed, leaving me exactly one hour to download the Blackout app to my phone, create a password, and decode the message. As I thumbed the keys and navigated to the Blackout site, I felt my lungs hyperventilate and tried to slow down my breathing. *Got to concentrate. Got to get this done.* By the time I'd installed the app, I'd used up precious minutes.

I created and entered a password as directed before tapping the black bubble. The message opened. I read slowly and carefully, taking notes, praying the words were not coded to self-destruct before I finished.

> *Next week, art collector Priscilla Donnelly will send five pieces from her collection to the Philadelphia Museum of Art, to be included in a three-month exhibition. One of the works is a recently discovered Jacob Lawrence painting from his Builders series.*
>
> *Donnelly's agreement with the museum stipulates they will send someone to help her pack the artwork properly for shipping.*
>
> *On Wednesday, a packing expert will arrive by air at Martha's Vineyard and proceed to the collector's residence.*
>
> *You will find a way to take his or her place and deliver Builders #5 to me at a time and place of my choosing.*
>
> *I will provide you with the airline and flight number after I confirm this message has been deleted.*
>
> *Remember, Ben Kaplan's life depends on your following these instructions perfectly.*

I tapped Reply and typed: **What flight?** Then I deleted the original message and waited.

A few endless minutes passed before the answer came:
Flight 9K 301

I felt like a kid who'd passed a surprise math test despite being shamefully prepared.

I entered the flight number and Google spit out only one, scheduled for early Wednesday, tomorrow, Cape Air from Boston to Martha's Vineyard. Then I searched for 'fine arts packer' and found:

Develops methods and procedures for packing art objects, according to weight and characteristics of shipment. Selects protective or preservative materials to protect shipment against vibration, moisture, impact, or other hazards. Designs special crates, modules, brackets, and traveling frames to meet insurance and museum shipping specifications.

Now I knew what kind of person to look for on the plane, without any idea what they looked *like*.

***

I had to go back to the apartment and pick up some things. I didn't care if Jerome caught me out and sent an entire regiment. On the way, I made a quick trip to the hardware store to purchase a pair of coveralls. I needed to look the part and if Ben's life was in danger, I vowed to use everything I knew about stealing and every ounce of my acting ability to save him.

18. The Game

On Wednesday morning, the Cessna light aircraft buzzed like an angry insect and took off into the thick layer of clouds blanketing Boston Harbor.

It was a windy day and seated close to the tail yet only ten feet from the instruments in the cockpit, I alternated between surrendering to the roller coaster ride and feeling trapped inside a cocktail shaker.

Of the eight passengers aboard, one had to be the fine arts packer. My top candidate wore a baseball cap and wire-rim spectacles. His long thin fingers seemed made for delicate work. My second choice was a young woman who fiddled with her imitation alligator handbag and stared intently at the dark blue metal walls of our cocoon, as if wishing the fog away.

Thirty-five minutes later, my eardrums popped and the Cessna dropped out of the clouds onto the runway. We took turns on the steps of the tiny exit ladder and clustered around the plane as the pilot lifted our bags out of the wings.

One of the smaller suitcases was plastered with a bright sticker: *Masterpiece F.A. Packers.* My first break and I planned to make the most of it. I was pleased when my favorite actor for the part (except that this was no movie), showed up to claim the carry-all and wheel it out behind him. Slipping on my backpack, I followed him at a distance into the terminal, which was the size of a large barn yet surprisingly modern. To my great relief, he walked past the car rental booth and through the exit to the line of waiting taxis. He hopped aboard one of the vans and it was the most natural thing in the world for me to climb in and sit beside him.

"Where to?" asked the driver, whose straw hat and dark sunglasses gave him a friendly air.

"Oak Bluffs," my seatmate said. "The Waterfront Inn."

I consulted my mental map of the island, landmarks memorized on the plane from New York. "You can drop him off first. I'm staying close by."

"That's nice of you but I'm in no hurry," the art packer said.

I took the opening. "Bumpy flight. I'm Teresa Stanley."

"Dave Tinsley," I'm glad I skipped breakfast. Is this your first visit to the Vineyard?"

"Yes."

"Surprised you'd choose to visit in winter. Even the locals take a break and go south."

"I don't blame them." I looked out at the bare trees lining the road, their naked branches a stark reminder of my own situation. If I didn't sprout some good ideas soon and pull off this job, Ben's fate would be sealed.

"Are you here on business?" I asked Tinsley.

He nodded absently, and I didn't press him. Confidentiality was required in his line of work and there was no sense setting off alarm bells. Besides, I had the info I needed.

Entering Oak Bluffs, we drove along a street of quaint, 'gingerbread' houses, decorated with ornate scrollwork and gaily colored paint schemes.

Dave gave me a friendly, goodbye smile and I watched him carry the heavy tool-bag up the steps of a three-story hotel.

A few doors down I saw a guest house and told the driver, "This is me."

"Enjoy your stay," he said automatically to my back, as I left the van.

Under the cold blue of the recently cleared sky, I walked out on a jetty and parked myself on a bench overlooking Nantucket Bay. Dark choppy water sprayed the beach below and I wondered if the sea turned light turquoise in summer. Unlikely I'd ever find out.

I got out my cell and called the number listed for Masterpiece Fine Art Packers in New York. "May I speak to someone in Custom Packing?"

"This is Emily," said a brisk, cultured voice. May I help you?"

"I need to ship some art to a gallery in Chicago. Do you have anyone who works in the Boston area and could help me pack?"

A slight pause, then, "Yes, as a matter of fact one of our technicians is working with a client on Martha's Vineyard right now."

That would be Dave.

"Sounds perfect," I said. Can you give me his cell number? My schedule is flexible and I'd like to coordinate with him directly."

Another pause before she gave me the information. "Thank you," I said, and then—as if an afterthought, "By the way, will Mr. Tinsley bring the packing supplies with him or do I need to order some?"

"We order the packing materials and have them delivered in advance, along with all of his tools. Just give Dave the specs for the job and he'll call us to make the arrangements."

"Thanks very much. I'll get in touch with him shortly."

That was no exaggeration. In less than a minute I had Tinsley on the phone. "This is Sarah, Ms. Donnelly's assistant. I'm glad I caught you before you came over to the

179

house. She's a bit under the weather. Would you mind staying over and coming to us first thing tomorrow?"

"I wish I'd known earlier but if that's the way it has to be, no problem. I'll see you then." Dave sounded a little put out but he had no choice.

I walked over to Oak Bluffs Car Rental and rented a nondescript Honda. The stage was set and all I needed was the right costume. Over at the beach, I used the public bathhouse to change into my recently purchased coveralls and pulled my hair back into a sensible ponytail. Mumbling softly to myself, I memorized a few lines from my "script" while walking over to Priscilla Donnelley's house.

Every inch of the rambling, gothic style residence—with its elaborate porches, balconies, and window frames— looked like it had been crafted by a master woodworker. Inside, the oak and mahogany tones added warmth to spaces that would otherwise have felt cavernous. Two New York apartments could have fit inside the main room.

Ms. Donnelley herself was a surprise. Not the grasping, "I've got more of everything than you do" sort of person I associated with the word "collector."

"Funny," she said. "I expected them to send a burly man to do the packing and I expect *you* thought I'd be a delicate White woman."

I had to laugh. Damned if I didn't like this stoutly built, forthright person from whom I was about to steal a treasured artwork.

"Did they deliver my tool-bag?"

Priscilla pointed to a leather satchel parked near the door and I checked through it, finding a T-square, tape gun, tape measure, box cutter, sharpie, box-sizer, and a shipping scale.

I followed the trusting art collector into a large parlor that had been converted into a professionally lit art gallery. The windows were heavily draped to keep out damaging UV rays. The paintings were spaced closely together, using up every inch of wall space in the room. Most of the work was realistic and there was no particular theme, although there were many Black faces represented in both rural and urban settings. "You should have been here last year for the Harlem Fine Arts Show. It was a seven-day extravaganza — artists came from as far away as the Caribbean and we threw in a golf tournament."

"Now I understand why the Obama family vacations here."

Priscilla smiled and pointed to five paintings lined up against the wall at floor level. "Just make sure you take good care of these. The Jacob Lawrence is worth a fortune — no one knew there was a *Builders #5*, not even the foundation that maintains a searchable archive of his work. The museum wants to buy it from me but I can't bear to let it go."

At first glance it was a simple painting of four carpenters at work. Until the pulsating colors drew me into the overlapping, three-dimensional shapes that looked like you could peel them right off the canvas.

Priscilla put a hand on my shoulder. "Mesmerizing, isn't it? He called his style dynamic cubism."

Afraid we were starting to bond and I'd make a wrong move, I told her I had to unpack the tools. "I'd better get started if I'm going to make the afternoon ferry. I'll get everything packed for you and the truck will come tomorrow."

Priscilla frowned, looking a little confused. Maybe she'd thought that all art packers were art lovers and would want to discuss more than the physical dimensions of the paintings. She showed me the box containing the insulation material and left.

The paintings had been pre-measured, making it easy to follow the online instructions saved on my phone. I wrapped Lawrence's painting in plastic palette wrap, then laid it out in the middle of a stiff piece of cardboard, folding and taping the overlap to seal the cardboard into a neat package. It was a lot of trouble but I was glad of it when

Priscilla came in briefly to check my work and nod her approval.

I assembled five more cardboard, bubble-wrapped packages, for a total of six. They all contained paintings except for the one I padded with a few of Priscilla's books to give it the same heft as the others.

The last step was to slide the five packages into their outer boxes and stuff the air pockets with bubble wrap before taping the containers shut. I tucked the sixth box, the one containing *Builders #5*, into Dave's empty tool bag. With a little jiggling, it was a snug fit.

***

I drove the Honda onto the hi-speed Woods Hole Ferry satisfied I'd done a good enough job packing up the paintings to pass surface inspection. When Dave came by the Donnelley place next day he'd find his tool bag missing and a job mysteriously completed. He might unpack the five cartons before taking them off-island or he might not. Either way, I'd be long gone by the time he discovered the theft.

19. Racing the Clock

Blackness so deep that all hope for light was lost. No movement being possible, the signals from his brain received zero response from his body, although his breathing went on of its own accord, taking in the moldy, stale air of his tiny prison. Ben fixed his mind on the rise and fall of his chest, thinking of Nestor, the Persian cat who lived with his family on and off for years and had been accidentally locked in the attic when they went on vacation to Atlantic City. A week later they'd found Nestor, curled up quietly in acceptance of his fate, dehydration the only sign of his ordeal. The boy had been puzzled by this feline capacity for fatalism. Now the man tried to mimic the cat as best he could.

***

I let the white noise of the ferry's diesel engine calm my mind enough to think, not that it did much good. As matters stood, Sperling could go back on his end of the bargain and kill Ben with no trail leading back to him, no incriminating evidence. The wily art dealer had encrypted his messages and forced me to delete all of them after the fact.

As if cued by my discouragement, a blacked-out text bubble popped up on my phone. I signed into Blackout and read:

Deliver in 6 hours or all bets are off. Acknowledge receipt of package.

It was 2 pm. I replied *package obtained* and erased Sperling's message as per the drill.

When I scanned the latest voicemails, all of them were from Leslie Ann, except one. I switched from Vibrate Only to Low Volume and the ringtone played immediately. The caller ID displayed *Jerome Kaplan*. I should have known Leslie Ann would call in the cavalry. I would have done it myself if I'd thought Jerome would believe my complicated story and even if he did, get here in time to be of any use. Against my better judgment, I picked up.

"Sandie, have you located Ben?"

"No. There was something I had to do first."

"What could possibly be more important?" Jerome was treating me like a low-level rookie in his squad room.

I took a deep breath of salt air to keep from blowing my top. "We don't have time for this, Jerome."

"You'll be doing time yourself if you withhold information. If you want to help Ben, you can't lock me out."

He was right. He might be a pushy cop who saw me as a threat to his family, but we had to work together. It was the only choice.

I began by explaining how I'd tricked Sperling into trading Ben's painting for an even more valuable ring and the dealer had retaliated by kidnapping Ben and forcing me to steal a Jacob Lawrence from a collector on Martha's Vineyard. "I'm waiting for instructions on where to drop off the painting."

"This doesn't make sense. Are you putting one over on me? Why didn't Sperling simply demand you return *Flowers*?"

"Do you think I'd lie to you with Ben's life at stake? All I can think of is that Sperling's strongman Jordy was watching me and saw a cop confiscate the painting. Sperling must have gone ballistic knowing that he'd never get it back."

I waited for my words to sink in. For Jerome to comprehend just how much he had screwed things up.

"Can you think of where they'd take Ben?" he asked, now all business. We could trade accusations later.

"If I had any idea, I'd be on my way there right now."

"Where do you want to meet, Sandie? I can be in New York in three hours."

"That's cutting it close. He's given me another six hours. We'll need to move quickly once Sperling tells us where the drop-off point is."

"Shit. That could be anywhere."

"Don't I know it."

***

Five hours later, I dropped the Honda at the Enterprise lot in Yonkers and took the subway to my meeting with Jerome at a bistro on the Upper West Side. In his hooded sweatshirt and jeans, Ben's brother blended in so well with the crowd I wasn't sure it was him until he sat down at my table.

"You have to tell me everything. Even the smallest detail could have relevance."

I told him about Sperling's text-to-speech voice messages and the encrypted texts that followed each one.

"What makes you so sure it's him?"

"The voice sounds like an automaton, but it says things only Sperling would know."

"Did you save the messages?"

"No. I was instructed to delete each message upon receipt. He uses some kind of gadget to monitor what I do."

Jerome's lopsided smile reminded me of Charlie Brown. "Nothing's ever totally deleted. You just have to know where to look."

For the first time since Ben's abduction, I felt a glimmer of hope. I sipped my cappuccino and considered that maybe, by calling in Jerome, Leslie Ann had done the right thing.

***

Sperling had chosen a tiny and infrequently visited pocket of green on the corner of Amsterdam and 111th Street. At 6 p.m. I was waiting on a bench in the park, the shipping box cradled in my lap, looking around expectantly, and checking my watch every second. In the dim light reflected from the street, I had a view of a bird bath and two tree trunks curving upwards, bowing to each other, their top branches meeting in a kiss. This is what Ben and I might have had if my life wasn't so fucked up.

I didn't recognize Jordy at first, in his New York City Parks Department t-shirt, carrying a trash pick-up stick, and wheeling a grey plastic can in front of him. He took the package from me and placed it carefully in the can. Then he motioned for me to come with him.

This was not part of the plan, but neither was it unexpected. Sperling had me at his mercy as long as Ben was his pawn. Before we left the park, Jordy patted me down none too gently. He took my cell phone and threw it in the bushes with an evil grin. So much for Jerome keeping track of me.

***

What do you think about when you're about to die? Had his life held any meaning? Did making films matter when climate change was burning up the earth? Was Sandie the person his kidnapper meant when he taunted him, saying "Your life is in the hands of a con woman who might decide you're not worth the effort of saving." Had he entirely misjudged her? The litany of uncertainties went on for a while and then gradually crawled to a stop. Lack of oxygen

186

had made him terribly tired. The temptation to slip into the void was interrupted by two angry voices that invaded his tomb. In his drugged state he could barely make out the words, which sounded like they were spoken through a guitarist's wah-wah effects box.

"I gave you the Warhol in good faith," the female voice said. It's not my fault you were tricked out of it. You promised me a fifty-fifty split on the Lawrence when Sandie delivered, a full partnership. Do you think you can buy me off with a lousy two grand?"

"You're too ignorant to be a partner. Greed is not knowledge." The male's voice was filled with contempt.

"You pompous twit!"

A loud pop! Then silence.

As the minutes—or was it hours?—passed, the memory faded. What did it matter if he'd imagined the whole thing? Soon he would be beyond caring.

***

Eyes front. Don't let Jordy catch you looking for Jerome in the side view mirror. With no way to track my cell phone, the Pennsylvania cop would be forced to surveil us in real time, not easy in heavy traffic. If he *was* tailing Jordy as promised. My fate was in the hands of someone I barely knew. *He's a professional. Yeah, but don't forget this is New York City and the guy is more used to cruising around corn fields.* I pushed Jerome from my mind and forced my shoulders to relax. I would need my wits about me when the time came.

Jordy drove us south on the Henry Hudson Parkway and then took U.S. 1 to Jersey City. Within a half hour of leaving Manhattan, we were parked in front of a square monolith that looked like it had once been a war-time factory. The sign out front read Climate Controlled Storage.

Carrying the heavily wrapped Lawrence, Sperling's hired muscle pushed me in front of him as we walked toward

187

a formidable, steel-plated door. He pressed his thumb on a display screen to gain entry and we walked down a long hallway, past lockers on both sides, their corrugated steel entrances rolled up, all of them empty.

"The place is brand new. No tenants yet. My boss owns it." Jordy was telling me there'd be no witnesses to whatever it was they had in mind for me and Ben.

One locker door was closed. I felt a stab of anxiety at the sight of the climate control lights blinking green on the panel in front, the LED showing 88.8 F. This was hotter than the recommended temperature and not a good sign.

The door opened from the inside and the first thing I saw was a pair of legs in herringbone patterned pants, one stretched out, the other bent at a weird angle on the concrete floor. The feet were clad in expensive Italian boots I had a feeling would never touch pavement again.

Ben always wore tennis shoes — even with a suit. It wasn't him.

At the sight of the body on the floor, Jordy reached for his gun. Too late. The shot that killed him was fired from close range. Andrea grabbed the package from his arm as he fell, then swiveled and pointed the gun at me with her free hand. "You learn quick but you'll never catch up."

"Where's Ben?" I frantically scanned Sperling's treasures, my eyes coming to rest on an Egyptian sarcophagus three feet off the ground, resting on a metal table. It looked like the real thing and knowing Sperling, I had no doubt it was.

The sarcophagus was sealed shut, with a straw sticking out of the face mask. Although my mind raced forward to a dreadful conclusion, I forced myself to hope against hope. Not easy, given the two dead bodies on the bloody concrete floor.

"Name your price," I said. "I'm the one who should pay — not Ben."

"There's no reason you both shouldn't pay," Andrea said, keeping the gun steady and aimed at my heart. "The little trick you played on Sperling ruined my reputation and has cost me thousands of dollars. You don't deserve to walk away and neither will your boyfriend. End of story."

"Ben has access to lots of money. Think about it, Andrea. Isn't doing well the best revenge?" *Where the fuck are you Jerome?! I won't be able to stall her much longer.*

"You've got the Lawrence now and there are a lot more where this one came from."

Andrea made no answer. Either she was thinking about my offer or trying to figure out the best escape route to take after she killed me.

The sound of Sandie's voice sent a rush of adrenaline through Ben's frame. His dead arms and legs came to life and he rocked back and forth, this being the only motion he could manage. He felt something beneath him give way and then a falling sensation. He braced himself for the impact.

***

In the corner of my vision, the sarcophagus swayed infinitesimally back and forth. I braced myself. This might be my one and only chance. When the crash came, Andrea whirled around and her gun-arm followed. I grabbed the statue of Hermes and with the superhuman strength of desperation, swung the bronze statue in an arc aimed at the back of her head. The statue was a lot heavier than the plank that nearly killed Tash. So heavy that gravity interfered and the bronze collided with the back of Andrea's knees instead. She screamed in pain and fell forward, knocking her forehead on a stone tablet inscribed with some words in an unknown tongue. Face down, she lay limp and possibly lifeless on the floor.

I rushed to where Ben was trying to extract himself from the fragments of the sarcophagus. When I cradled his head in my arms a miraculous smile animated his pale lips.

189

"You came for me," he said, and slipped into unconsciousness.

Jerome chose that moment to burst into the building with what I later learned was a battering ram, accompanied by a half dozen NYPD swat team members. He took in the scene impassively, as if his training had kicked in and the three bodies on the floor of the storage unit were no more than dummies in a practice exercise.

"This place is like a fortress." His eyes swiveled in many directions at once, making it difficult to tell if he was talking to me or someone out in the hall. He checked on Ben to make sure he was alive and came over and squeezed my arm in a brief gesture of solidarity. "I couldn't get in without summoning help," he added. There's an ambulance waiting."

Three medics rushed in. "It's too late for these two," Jerome told them, pointing at Jordy's body and then Sterling's.

One of the medics, a woman, gently disengaged Ben from my arms while the other took his vitals and got an oxygen feed started before they moved him onto a stretcher.

Jerome hovered over them. "How's he doing?"

"His pulse is steady and the oxygen's bringing him round," one of the men responded as they wheeled Ben out. A third medic examined Andrea, whose moans indicated she had some life in her.

A uniformed officer introduced himself as Detective Laau.

"Did you kill the deceased men?" he asked me.

"No. I wish I had."

"Really? Your wish came true without any help from you?"

"She's with me," Jerome said, flashing his ID.

"So you're both cops from Pennsylvania?"

Jerome had a lot of explaining to do and Detective Laau wasn't satisfied until he'd done a powder test on my hands and obtained a written statement.

He asked me why one of the victims had driven me to the storage facility and I kept my answer simple. "I heard from Jordy that my friend Ben was being held here against his will and I asked Detective Kaplan for assistance."

I showed Laau my brand new, New York State Driver's license in the name of Sandie Donovan. At least I had Naturel as an employment reference. Even Jerome seemed impressed by that. He said not a word to contradict me and I was sure this was the only reason Laau didn't haul me into the precinct for more questioning.

When at last we were permitted to leave the scene, I picked up the package containing *Builders #5*.

"Give it here," Jerome demanded.

I mustered my outrage. "What? If you don't trust me to return this painting to its rightful owner in Martha's Vineyard I'd say it's your problem, not mine."

"I'd say you were a complete idiot, if so many parts weren't missing. Stop pushing your luck," he retorted.

I surrendered the painting and went to climb into the back of the mobile intensive care unit.

"Where do you think you're going?" Jerome shoved me away from the ambulance. "Yes, I covered for you. But that was a one-time deal. I'm Ben's family; you're not."

His steely tone matched his unflinching eyes. "I've had my brother's best interests at heart my whole life. You barely know him. You do one selfless thing and you think you've earned redemption. It's not how things work in my world. I'm retaining my right to turn you in for the Kansas City robbery anytime. However, if you stay away from Ben I don't see why you can't continue to live in New York City. I saw the driver's license you showed Detective Laau, and now I know your real name, right? Sandie Donovan. Displeased to meet you."

Jerome scrambled into the vehicle and took his place across from Ben, who was wrapped head to toe in a blanket, an oxygen mask covering most of his face. The wail of the siren shattered my heart as the red and white sped away.

20. Lucky at Cards

In my dreams Ben wore a red silk sheet wrapped around his waist. I'd take one end and pull, turning him over and over, trying to draw him closer. But the more I yanked the longer the sheet grew. There was no end to it.

I'd wake up wanting to call him. But the new cell phone I'd bought—after fruitlessly searching the bushes where Jordy had thrown the old one—stayed in my purse, a testimony to Jerome's power over me.

I wondered where Ben had recuperated after being released from the hospital. Probably at the loft with his ex-wife-best-friend. It hurt to think he believed I'd deserted him at the time of his greatest need, when I had done the exact opposite and saved his life. But I'd given him no reason to doubt his brother's version of events. And maybe the obnoxious cop was right. How could a few good deeds on one side of the scale outweigh years of misdeeds piled on the other? Jerome had me cornered and the more I thought about it, the more I was sure the cop was unlikely to keep his end of the bargain. He owed me nothing. Once Ben had "gotten over" me, his self-righteous brother would do as he pleased. If that happened, I'd better be prepared to leave the country. I would have to apply for a passport, a risky proposition since it meant appearing in person.

***

I walked by the entrance to the Radio City Post Office on West Fifty-Second several times, thinking how easy it had been for Jerome to find Sandra Storm's prints in a national database after they were lifted off the license I'd lost in Kansas City. It was impossible to know if anyone had matched these prints with the ones on file for Sandie Donovan at Recovery Ranch. Once I passed through those official looking doors, I would find out.

If they measure my blood pressure, I'll be arrested. I joined the long line in front of the aptly named Acceptance Facility to have my picture taken. By the time I'd filled out all the convoluted forms and was called to the window, I was ready to cut my losses and run.

As it turned out, the civil servant barely glanced at my face to compare it with the passport-sized photo on my application. He took the postal money order I'd brought with me, along with my birth certificate and social security card, and tapped away on his keyboard. He seemed the kind who would tape his glasses together and then forget to go have them fixed. I could have hugged him. That's how thankful I was for his obliviousness.

"You should receive your passport in four to six weeks."

I left feeling like I'd stolen something. I was a block away before I recognized that something as me. If Ben ever got back in touch, I'd tell him the truth. Let Jerome do his worst. It was simple. If I became someone who lived her life free of lies and in the open, then that vindictive cop would have no power over me.

I went home and submitted three cosmetic consultant applications as Sandie Donovan. Thanks to Tiffany's "generosity" my rent was paid for the month. Small comfort, since my absences from my job at Macy's had cost me my day job. My best bet was to call Bettina and pray that Jerome had kept his promise not to trash my name. Reputation

194

means everything in show business, especially when cosmetics are involved.

"Sandie, I was just thinking of you."

"What's up," I asked when I got control of my voice. Bettina's friendly tone had thrown me.

"You've got a steady hand, Sandie. How'd you like to accumulate enough hours to join Local 798?"

"You're kidding me. How many hours do I need?"

"At least one hundred and eighty."

"That's six months' worth. I don't have anywhere near that amount."

"You might, if you get hired by my friend's opera company to do the makeup for *Rigoletto*. You already have some film and stage experience and this could put you in the running with the union."

After all the crap that had happened I could barely believe my luck was changing. "Wow, Bettina. This is a plum. Can I ask why you're not taking it for yourself?"

"Looking a gift horse in the mouth are we? Suffice it to say I would never pass this on to you if I wasn't double-booked. The ink's already dry on my contract with the DiCapo Opera Theatre, and since I'm responsible for finding a replacement, this is your lucky day. Or more accurately, tomorrow, which is when you start. I'd anticipate a two-month run, enough to get you going in the right direction."

Bettina dictated all the info I needed and in a happy daze I scribbled it down.

In the morning, I stopped by the library on St. Nicholas Avenue to check out a book on operatic make-up that I read on the subway. I picked up some necessities at Abracadabra, a store in Chelsea that stocks Mehron makeup and splurged on a cab to get to the theatre on East Seventy-Sixth. When I walked in the door, my total net worth was below ten dollars.

The stage manager at the DiCapo, a young guy named Steve who'd mastered that popular grizzled look, told me to start with Gilda, the singer playing Rigoletto's daughter. Within two hours I'd made up the entire cast for the

195

matinee. I was hired on the spot. The pay was generous, at least by my standards.

***

I chilled at home on my night off, heartbroken that I couldn't share my newfound success with Ben. Happiness with him hadn't exactly slipped through my fingers—how could you say that about something you never got a firm grip on in the first place—but that didn't make losing him any easier.

When the intercom buzzed, I pressed the speaker button with caution. Friends usually called first.

"I'm here, in the lobby." There was only one person I knew with a voice this young. It was Griffin, my little savior from the International Hostel who'd helped me out on my first night back in New York City almost a year ago. The kid I'd felt sorry for and then totally forgotten in the midst of my own troubles.

"Come on up."

I watched for him through the peephole and opened the door as he walked toward me down the hallway. I'd last seen Griffin in Brooklyn, getting into a gold Lexus driven by a chicken hawk. He'd grown at least an inch and filled out nicely. Minus the freckles, the brown curls cascading to his shoulders would have made him a teen heartthrob.

I used two fingers to raise his chin. A colorful bruise had puffed up under his left eye and his lower lip was split and raw.

"It was an accident. He was aiming for my body and my face got in the way. He threw me out. Said I'm shelf ware to him until this heals."

"Sit on the couch," I ordered. "I've got plenty of ice."

I improvised a cold pack with ice and a washcloth and gave it to him to hold over his eye. "Who did this to you? Was it the man in the Lexus? The one who picked you up at Daisy Studios?"

196

Griffin shook his head slightly. More movement would have caused more pain.

"No. It was Monty, the guy who owns Daisy Studios. He lets me crash at his place when we're working. I thought he was okay. He pays good cheddar, says I'm uber-different from the others, that he respects me. So how can I say no when he sets me up with Stuart Danner, this hotshot film distributor with a hard on to take me to his place and shoot some video.

"When I get there, Stu asks me to do some nasty things way out of my orbit. That's not what I signed up for, and when I tell him that he goes ballistic—at me, but mostly at Monty—and I hear him yelling on the phone: 'You should've broken the kid in first! He's not what you promised. Why do you think I keep you around? Your films are crap and so are you.'

"So Monty comes to get me. He takes me home and tells me I'm his bitch and if I fuck him over I have to pay. Then he messes up my face and locks me in the basement overnight."

I took the cold pack off Griffin's eye and he followed me into the kitchen. My hands shook as I grabbed a fresh tray of ice from the freezer and banged it on the counter. Seeing how he folded his arms and watched my every move, as if the rage in my hands would get loose and target him, made my heart collapse.

I remembered how when I was down my Mom, who was miles ahead of Frank when it came to basic humanity, used to say, "If you can't help yourself help somebody else." Then she'd assign me a chore to make me feel useful. I'd seen right through her while I washed the dishes but the trick always worked and I did feel better. I might not be Mother Teresa, but I would do my best.

"You can stay here for a while."

"Really? It's a palace you've got here." He paced around the apartment, peering into cupboards and closets as if he were a cat sniffing out its lair.

"Tell me, Griffin. How come you never called even though I offered you a place to stay?"

"I didn't know anything about you. What you wanted in return. There's always a price."

On the street, certain things were never discussed, especially bad things everyone took for granted. Like trading sex for basic necessities. The less said about it the better. It was bad enough as it was.

"You remind me a lot of myself and I want to help you."

"How do you know I won't kill you in your sleep?"

"Yeah, that's it. I have a death wish."

"Poison or kitchen knife?"

It was coming back, why I liked him in the first place.

I got some food into him and we stayed up late talking. We both hated sharing personal information, so it was awkward at first. Luckily, books and movies were safe. When he wasn't cracking jokes, Griffin was a deep thinker, much better read than me. His favorite writer was Hunter Thompson and he was shocked that all I knew about his hero was that he'd committed suicide.

"People don't get him. He believed life was meant to be a wild ride instead of a safe trip to the grave. If that means we get hurt sometimes for being who we are, that's how it goes."

If someone without a recent black eye had said this, I might have laughed. Instead, I said "You sound like my high school English teacher. Now I know what Mrs. Golden meant when she said that character is destiny," and left it at that.

**

The next afternoon I took my houseguest to the thrift store to get some clothes. He was firm about paying with his own money and that was fine with me.

"You know you can stay at the apartment as long as you like," I said.

198

"It ain't that simple. Monty knows my parents live in Sioux Falls. He's gonna' send them some videos of me if I don't go back to Stu's house and apologize."

"Did you tell him you won't go?"

When he didn't answer, I took the plunge and asked, "Should I call the police?"

"Hell no! They'll put me in Juvie or a foster home and even if they bag Monty, he'll skip bail. He's done it before. He picks up and moves to another state. He'll get even by outing me to my parents — they don't know I'm gay. That's why I cut out. It'll kill my mom. She's a devout Mormon."

"It will kill your mom even more if you continue what you're doing now," I said. "Don't you think it's time to change direction?"

I told Griffin about how I'd broken free from Russell in Kansas City. "I did a lot of things I'm not proud of after that but at least I had only myself to blame."

I'm not sure that sharing my story with him is what convinced him not to go back to Monty's. I only know that Griffin looked at me differently after that and before I left for the theatre, he said "You're right. I've got to start sticking up for myself."

It felt strange leaving Griffin alone in the apartment. It wasn't that I expected him to clean me out. It was the anguish I'd heard breaking through his cynical laugh when we clowned around; his fragility made me uneasy about other things he might do.

I got home from work at 1 a.m., worn out from the quick changes and make-overs at the theatre. On the ride home, I'd had a think.

"If you're gonna' stay here, Griffin, you'll need to go to school."

"Whatever you say, Mom."

I didn't know whether to slap or hug him.

21. Reunion

Bettina was wrong about one thing. *Rigoletto's* run. It was the longest the DiCapo had ever had and at six months we were still counting. Griffin, who had just turned sixteen, got his GED through the Jump Start program and enrolled in a coding class downtown to learn how to create apps. We settled into a routine much like any family. Maybe that's why I decided to accept Aunt Stella's invite to Gile's birthday, issued so many months ago.

On a cold day in October, I found myself walking through the crowded streets of Astoria toward the big blue whale of a building that housed my aunt's condo. I hoped that Giles had grown up as much as I had since the last time we breathed the same air. My passport had come in the mail a few months ago, and if I ever carried out my plan to leave the country, maybe for England or Australia, it was likely I'd never see him or Stella again.

Her apartment looked just as I remembered it, spacious and airy, with the addition of a modular, red couch that faced a giant plasma TV. Two men were watching the NFL game, the backs of their heads visible over the low-backed couch. I recognized Gile's thick, close-cropped hair, the same style he'd always worn. The unkempt salt-and-pepper tangle also seemed familiar and its owner, feeling my presence, turned his head. It was Frank, his face the same thin shell I remembered from Arizona.

He stood up and slowly made his way around the couch, as if having trouble finding his balance. The noise from the TV made it difficult for me to decipher the hoarse phrases tumbling from his mouth in hesitant clusters. "You look great... gave up hope... after what happened..." Frank stopped in his tracks when he saw me back away.

"Why didn't you tell me he'd be here?" I asked Stella, not caring if Frank heard me over the blare of the TV. "You could at least have given me a heads-up."

"We were afraid you wouldn't come." She went into the kitchen, followed by Giles, to give me and Dad time and space to talk.

Frank propped himself up, using the back of a blue velveteen easy chair for support. "Can you forgive me?" He looked up and away from me when he said this, as if awaiting an answer from a higher source. When none came, he awkwardly navigated around the chair and took a seat.

I grudgingly sat down opposite him. "How long have you been living with Aunt Stella?"

A tremor rippled through his hand. "Since I got sick."

I waited for some details on his situation; no way was I going to ask.

"It's no excuse," he croaked, "but you should know that Stella refused to take you back when I called her from Tucson. That's why I took you to the Ranch. It wasn't a good choice, the place ended up being shut down, but at the time I had no idea that it was such a ..."

"Snake pit? What did you think? That the hot box and the barbed wire were for stress reduction?"

He looked away.

Sick of his evasiveness, I was about to get up when he answered. "I've got one, maybe two months to live. It's throat cancer. Stella's taking me to a hospice in the Bronx tomorrow. It would mean a lot to me if you came to visit, while I'm, you know, still there."

202

"I'm sorry, Dad." I left my chair and came and sat beside him, taking his hand, trying to turn off the inner voice that said how unfair it was, him asking me to play dutiful daughter after he'd fed me to the wolves. I wasn't sure I could forgive him. On the other hand, I remembered how painful it was to have Ben and his family sit in judgment of me—and I was no angel myself.

"If your mom had lived we'd all be together," Frank said wistfully.

If she'd lived Brenda would have divorced you and found someone willing to carry their own weight, was what I wanted to say. "Yeah, well you did the best you could," was the lie I settled for, as Stella's voice called us to dinner.

Over roast chicken, string beans, and mashed potatoes, Giles tried to keep the conversation going. "Tell us what's new, Sandie."

"I'm working as a make-up artist," I told them, skipping the part about being a small-time actress as potentially embarrassing. "And I'm getting married next year. In the Bahamas." God. Why had these words fallen out of my mouth like a skydiver with no parachute?

After singing the birthday song and sharing some cake, I wished Giles the best and prepared to leave the gathering before anyone could question me further. Stella and I exchanged a hug that had been a long time coming and on the way out I aimed a quick, "I'll be seeing you," at Frank. I planned to visit him at the hospice but couldn't bring myself to tell him outright.

***

Over breakfast, Griffin asked me how the reunion went.

"Being with my dad made me feel like a cross between Cordelia and her evil sister, Goneril."

"You've got a bad case of Shakespeare."

"DiCapo is producing *Lear* next season and they gave me the libretto."

203

Griffin left for class and a few minutes after, I heard a knock on the door. I thought he'd forgotten something and was too lazy to use his key. Through the fisheye lens of the peephole, I made out a guy in a suit and a pink shirt who looked harmless enough. It was 9 a.m. Not prime time for home invasions. "Who is it?"

"Delivery," he said.

I opened the door a crack.

"Sandie Donovan?"

"Yes."

A single sheet of paper glided through the opening. The return address said District Attorney of New York.

"You've been served."

It was a subpoena issued by the Supreme Court of New York County, Criminal Branch, commanding one Sandie Donovan "to appear at the time, date, and place set out below to testify in a criminal case." I skipped past the boilerplate and read, *the following matters, or those set out in an attachment: THE PEOPLE OF THE STATE OF NEW YORK against ANDREA DAWSON.*

So this is what I got for trying to become an upright citizen. I shut the door and leaned on it. Maybe my body weight could stave off what lay beyond. I had been planning to go to the gym at the Y for some exercise. Instead, I cursed my bad luck and poured myself a whiskey.

At noon, I heard Griffin bounce through the door, fresh from biology class. He found the subpoena lying on the floor where I'd thrown it and brought it to my room. "What's this?"

"The end of my life as I know it."

"What's that mean?"

"I have to go to court and testify about something unpleasant a friend of mine did."

"What'd she do that was so terrible? Were you there? It's risky, being an eyewitness."

I had to hand it to Griffin, he had an instinct for the complete picture. "I'm the one who's supposed to take care of you, not the other way round," was my best comeback.

He hounded me incessantly all afternoon, even after I cooked up a late lunch using my special eggplant recipe made with Ricotta and Asiago cheese and handed down by my mother. Griffin was sharp and even if I could get away with it, I didn't want to lie to him. He'd been deceived and used too much in his young life for that. Over forkfuls of tomato-covered eggplant, I ended up telling him more about myself than even Tiff knew. It was strange how someone as young as him could be so worldly, unless you counted scars as years.

I told Griffin about discovering Ben inside the sarcophagus, how terrifying it had been not knowing if he was alive or dead. When I got to the part where Jerome banned me from the ambulance, Griffin let out a groan of disgust. "All some people can see are the backs of their eyeballs."

"Jerome thinks he's protecting his brother from me and my ilk."

"What about Andrea? Isn't she the one who whacked two people in cold blood? Ben's brother is a real ass-wipe."

"He's a cop, Griffin. Can't help himself. When you're covered in other people's muck all day that's what you come to expect."

"Maybe if you testify at the trial, he'll call it quits."

"I wish things were that simple."

"You'll never know unless you try."

"They're not giving me a choice. But I don't have to like it," I said.

"I wouldn't want people digging around in my life in public court either." Griffin carried our lunch dishes to the sink. "Text me the date. I want to be there."

"What about school?"

"You wouldn't deny me a lesson in civics, would you?"

205

The conversation would have continued in circles if I hadn't been saved by a text alert from the theatre, asking me to come to work early for a cast and crew meeting.

***

As the date for my deposition neared, my anxiety grew. I tried to hide my fear from Griffin, pushing down my panic by discussing his homework, where he might get hired after completing his courses at *Codesmith*, or his current favorite video game. He was a good cook, although like me he repeated the same recipes and was prone to burning things in the oven when experimenting.

They had me scheduled to testify as an eyewitness for the prosecution against Andrea and there was no doubt the defense would dig up everything they could to discredit me. I tried not to worry, telling myself that all the physical evidence found at the scene by Detective Laau pointed to Andrea — otherwise, they would have detained *me*. I tried not to dwell on being the sole witness and what that could mean. Andrea had unsavory friends. And what if Griffin got in the way?

I had my passport and there was nothing to prevent me from leaving the country. Except that if I ran away from the court I would also be running away from Griffin. I could not imagine leaving him, becoming just another person in his world who had done him wrong. I wasn't gonna' become my dad.

***

On the first day of Andrea's trial, I gathered my courage and Griffin and I took the subway downtown to 100 Centre Street. We were fifteen minutes early and spent the time in Foley Square, watching a large group of people performing T'ai Chi exercises in the center island. Their strong, calm movements were rooted in a different universe than mine.

Griffin opened one of the doors leading into the New York State Supreme Court and bowed deeply. "I'm not allowed to provide you with moral support, having such low morals myself," he said. "I do, however, know some lawyer jokes I'll tell you if you come inside."

That was enough to prevent me from fleeing on the spot.

We rode up to the 5th floor in an elevator packed with apprehensive people and found the courtroom listed on the summons.

In the courtroom, Griffin and I slid our butts to the middle of a smooth wooden bench close to the back wall. I sat ramrod straight, my invisible force field in place. Turning my head slightly to the left gave me a view of the defense table and the back of Andrea's head, her black hair cut short and businesslike above a white collared blouse. The attorney sitting next to her was busy writing on a yellow pad. To the right of them, the jury sat in two rows, seven women and five men.

"All rise for the Honorable Judge Nyberg," a disembodied voice proclaimed.

Never having attended a trial before, I hoped to be the first witness called after the opening statement by David Jacobsen, the prosecutor — who would lay out how the state intended to substantiate the double-murder charge against Andrea Dawson—followed by the proclamation of innocence by the defense attorney, as often shown on TV.

Instead, I sat for hours, enduring an endless parade of motions made by the defense and denied by the judge, as well as the detailed testimony of several police officers about what they had observed upon arriving at the storage locker. Andrea's defense attorney, Purcell Jones — short of stature and loud of voice — went at his job like a Pitbull. Jones added bite to the most innocuous of questions, such as "Did you read the defendant her Miranda rights?" and his cross-examinations were peppered with implied accusations.

If Jerome Kaplan was somewhere in the crowded courtroom, I didn't spot him. Maybe he was back on his beat in Pennsylvania and would drive into the city at some point during the trial. I imagined him telling the court about following me to the storage locker, where I was supposed to deliver a stolen painting as ransom for his brother Ben. Would that discredit my testimony as a witness? What had Jerome already told the prosecutor?

Amidst these fearful speculations, I heard my name called. Griffin squeezed my hand. "I'm proud of you," he mouthed silently. I hurried down the aisle to take a seat in the witness box, wishing more than ever that I could avoid testifying.

The court clerk swore me in and Jacobsen began his questioning. The prosecutor spoke rapidly, even for a New Yorker, his words zipping by like a blurry movie. I nicknamed him *Speedy*.

Speedy started out with easy questions, like what was my name and what did I do for a living. "I'm an actress and a cosmetologist," I said. *You're a thief and an imposter* resounded in my head.

He began to work his way through what happened on that terrible day. I presumed he'd read my statement to the police and was basing his questions on that.

"Why were you at the storage locker?"

"To deliver a painting to Mr. Sperling."

"Did you arrive alone?"

"No, I was with his assistant, Jordy."

"What did you see when you entered the locker?"

"Mr. Sperling's legs. He was lying on the floor. I could tell he was dead."

"And then what happened?"

I was about to describe how, at the sight of Sperling's body, Jordy pulled out his gun and Andrea shot him when a scream from the direction of the defense table froze the words in my mouth. "You bitch! You liar! You killed him yourself and framed me!"

Andrea sprang to her feet, kicking over her chair. She scrambled around the table and had covered most of the space between us before one of the Court Officers managed to grab and restrain her. Judge Nyberg ordered Andrea evicted from the courtroom and told Purcell Jones that his client would not be permitted to return until the court was assured there would be no further outbursts.

"We are now adjourned. Hopefully by tomorrow Mr. Jones will have control of his client. If not, we will proceed without her."

I was relieved. If Purcell Jones was going to support his client's accusations and try to make me look like a murderer, I was not looking forward to his eventual cross-examination.

***

The next morning it rained heavily. When Griffin saw what a foul mood I was in, he offered to skip class and accompany me to the courtroom. I turned him down and made my way to the subway, hugging the brick facades of the buildings to avoid the icy puddle-spray produced by each passing car. I stopped before crossing Amsterdam to adjust my hood against the slanting downpour and felt a jab of pain in my arm. Looking down I saw a hand jerking a hypodermic out of the spandex fabric of my coat. A stranger's face leered down at me — emotionless eyes, a cruel mouth.

I willed my legs to run. Nothing happened. I pitched forward and he caught me on the fly, my head so close to the sidewalk that my skull would have been smashed a second later.

Whatever was in that hypo worked fast. Barely conscious, I was aware of being laid out on the backseat of a car, plastic ties digging into my wrists as he tightened them, my hands placed in an upside down prayer position over my chest.

Minutes passed or it might have been hours before the car stopped and I revived slightly. My captor pulled me out and pushed me into an upright position, guiding me along a narrow walkway leading onto the bridge. I could walk a little better now but my vision was fuzzy. When I looked up, the storm clouds merged with patches of dark blue to form a deep, threatening purple.

I stumbled on ahead, a heavy hand on my shoulder reminding me who was boss. The metal planks beneath us hummed with the energy of the traffic on the other side of the divider. Tumbling green water raged below, the river's voice amplified by the vibrations from the bridge into a terrifying roar.

"Just a little farther and you'll be fine." His harsh tone mixed with the whoosh of the wind.

I sensed the hitman's eyes trained on my staggering footsteps, waiting for me to trip so he could give me a push over the railing. So many suicides chose the Washington Bridge. One more would hardly be noticed.

The dense fog was rent by the scream of a large bird, or so I thought. I stopped and turned in time to see a body tumbling head over heels into nowhere. *That was supposed to be me.* Confused, I turned to walk back but instead the wind spun me in a circle to face the railing overlooking the water. I was balanced impossibly on one leg, my muddied senses struggling to warn me like a group of mountaineers shouting from a far-off peak. My one grounded limb lost its footing, my neck stretching forward like a swan's, and I teetered and began to fall, arms stretched out like wings, flopping helplessly. The river waited.

Two hands came from nowhere, seizing my waist in a vice-like grip strong enough to counteract my downward motion. My body twisted and shuddered in defiance of gravity as I dangled above the water.

"I'm not letting you go," Griffin said between clenched teeth. His feet firmly planted, his slim torso pinned against the railing, he stubbornly pulled my dead weight upward until I tumbled backward over the railing to safety. We held each other so tightly that our overworked heartbeats palpitated as one.

By this time, all traffic on the bridge had stopped and a policeman walked toward us on the deck, carrying a blanket with a comic mixture of relief and horror on his face. "I stayed back when I saw the kid running to your rescue. The first time I've seen a jumper caught in mid-air."

22. Saving Brandy

After my near-death experience, I had this idea I would get back to normal, whatever that was. It helped when Andrea copped a plea—after some people she'd ripped off testified about the nature of her business—and my involvement in her case ended. When they fished Mr. Doomsday out of the river, I half expected some brilliant cop to unearth the thug's connection with Sperling and make an arrest. There was a better chance of my mom coming back from the dead.

The police did come after Griffin and he spent a night in jail before I could bail him out. It was a good thing his encounter with the thug on the bridge was witnessed by the same cop who brought me the blanket. We heard from the public defender assigned to Griffin's case that the officer was interviewed by the DA and said he saw Griffin push my attacker aside as he was running to my rescue. Accidents happen. No charges were filed.

I expected Griffin to be glad I was alive and proud of his role in making that happen. Which was why his ongoing grumpiness was so confusing. When I tried to make conversation or asked him how he was doing, he'd get up and leave the room.

At least he was getting on with his education, leaving every morning at nine and usually back by three. I wanted to ask if any high-tech recruiters had approached him, like the school promised they would, but I didn't want to sound like his mom. He'd already told me how she bugged the hell out of him, poking around in his life.

"She wanted proof I was a hetero to show to her narrow-minded friends. She wanted me to deny who I was when I didn't even know myself."

That was the closest Griffin got to fully confiding in me. Until one night during dinner I dropped a remark about what a kick I got out of doing operatic make-up, even though film-acting was my first love.

"People should go with their best choice," Griffin insisted. "That's what I'm doing. Getting it together to design video games."

"You'll succeed," I said. "I can feel it."

At first, from the way his eyes misted up, I thought he was going to thank me. So it came as a shock when he mumbled, to himself more than me, "It makes no difference. I'm still a wimp."

"How can you say that? You're a hero, Griffin. I'll never forget what you did."

"Or what I didn't do," he grunted, averting his eyes and getting up from the table.

I wanted to pull the kid back into his chair and ask what was going on. Whatever it was I could tell it ran deep. Not having Russell's talent for "cracking people's shells," I let it go.

Nevertheless, Griffin's remark about sticking with your first choice replayed in my mind next morning, when Sloan called to ask me to work as an extra on a high-end commercial. My "yes" slipped out faster than mascara runs in the shower.

***

The shoot was in Madison Square Park, just south of West 26th and Broadway. The crew had set up near the Shake

214

Shack, a hamburger joint on the south side of the park, with an outdoor patio attracting long lines of customers on sunny days like this one. Sloan looked directorial in a safari jacket and baseball cap. "It's good to see you, Sandie. Glad you could make it."

He placed me on a bench with two bored-looking actors and gave me a copy of the *NY Times*. "When you're not reading the paper, look straight ahead, as if you're a typical New Yorker, blasé in the face of all that happens, no matter how bizarre."

The afternoon was devoted to capturing one dolly shot: a model in an evening gown running barefoot through the grass, high heels in hand, ethereally graceful until she trips over a fallen branch and into the arms of a sleazy, gigolo-type decked out in a tuxedo. A perfume ad, I bet. Sloan confirmed this and explained that special effects would later turn the background into a futuristic city, complete with flying electric cars.

Once Sloan and the creative director of the ad agency were satisfied that they'd shot sufficient variations of the model's running style, route, and encounter with her fantasy man, I picked up my fifty from the production assistant. While they were breaking down, Sloan came over to chat.

"You've been out of the loop for a while."

"I'm working as a make-up artist for an opera company."

"Nice work if you can get it."

"You're right but I prefer acting."

"You should. It's something you're good at, Sandie. I suppose you've heard Ben and Leslie Ann are in Europe. She's trying another experimental treatment."

"Sorry to hear that. I thought she was better. Tough times for them."

"Extremely tough," Sloan agreed. "As Ben told me, divorce or no divorce, Leslie Ann needs him. Seems their friendship outlived their marriage. They're staying in Spain for a while, until they get some test results after the treatments are over."

I hadn't seen Ben in... how many months was it? My losing count meant something.

***

That night, as usual, I kept my cell phone switched off during my stint at the Di Capo. This meant that I didn't see Griffin's text, sent at 9 p.m., until well after eleven. *Sandie, I thought I could deal with this but it went wrong. He's gonna kill me.*

Whatever was bothering Griffin had finally pushed him into action. Too bad he hadn't consulted me before doing something stupid.

I messaged him, *where are you? How can I help?*

He sent me an address in Bushwick. *Trapped in basement.*

Set your phone to vibrate. Will ping you when I get there, I texted back and left the theatre to hail a cab. The driver was a fast one and needed no urging. In the back seat I thought about Griffin's troubled past and how much it resembled my own. I knew what it was like to stuff your uneasiness down into the depths of you, until it came alive, in my case as an angry animal clawing its way out to deal with Frank's desertion after Mom died, the cruelty at Recovery Ranch, the way I'd let myself be exploited by Russell. Like Griffin's, my misfortunes had piled on like a squad of football players. We were still throwing them off our backs but at least we had each other.

***

Monty's lair was a nondescript row house, with a flat roof and colorless shingles curled up at the edges. A high, chain link fence lit by dim streetlights surrounded the barren front yard. The gate was locked and the darkened windows

216

heavily barred, even the ones on the second floor. It looked like a setup designed to hold kids in and keep trespassers out.

I told the cabbie to park in the rear alley. "We might need to leave in a hurry."

"Whatever," he said; pocketing the extra twenty I gave him.

At the back of the house, I found the weak spot I was looking for and texted Griffin — *Basement door. Now!*

A minute later, the knob jiggled from the inside but didn't open. Taking a closer look, I noticed an iron bolt attached to the bottom of the door, engineered to slide into the ground and lock securely. I pulled up on the handhold with all my strength. No result. I tried twisting the handle and the bar slid upwards. Griffin pushed from the other side. The door held fast. We were making noise and running out of time. I examined the top of the door and released the second bolt. The door swung free.

Griffin grabbed my arm, pulling me into a dark, dank room.

"What are you doing?! Let's get out of here!" I cried in a hoarse whisper.

"Not yet. There's someone else who needs an assist."

Dim moonlight filtered through the iron-meshed windows, sketching eerie lines on the concrete floor as I followed the teenager and tiptoed across the basement. I watched Griffin reach behind a shelf attached to a workbench and, with a click, pull the bench away from the wall. The space behind was in total darkness. A frightened gasp came from inside.

"It's me," Griffin said. "Don't be afraid."

The girl came out and threw herself into Griffin's arms, sobbing with relief. "I thought you'd forgotten me."

"This is Brandy," Griffin said. With her blonde hair in a ponytail, she'd have looked no more than eleven if it weren't for the tight-fitting sweater and garish eye makeup.

217

With a jolt, the basement flooded with light, fluorescent and glaring, revealing every corner. I heard the abrasive sound of metal on metal, like bolts moving, and Monty burst through the doorway to observe the invaders from the top of the steps. Short and balding, his sallow face had more than enough rage to compensate for his feeble body. A gun dangled from his right hand.

"You're trespassing. Give me one reason not to shoot you."

With lightning speed, Griffin returned Brandy to the crawl space and shoved the workbench back in place to protect her. I stepped forward to make sure Monty knew he had a witness to deal with. The pornographer responded by raising the gun, aiming it first at Griffin, then at me, his arm shaking as he brandished the pistol back and forth. Any second I expected it to go off.

Something slammed into Monty's head, and when it bounced off, I saw it was a baseball. Monty fell and the gun clattered down the steps as Griffin ran up. I grabbed the pistol off the floor and by the time I looked up, Griffin was standing over Monty, the baseball bat raised over his head like a lethal weapon.

Blood dripped down over Monty's left eye and ear. He tried to scramble to his feet and Griffin brought down the bat, narrowly missing his tormentor, who returned to the floor and lay still. Aware his life depended on it, Monty put his hands together in prayer. Griffin laughed.

I grabbed a rag and a roll of duct tape off a shelf and climbed the stairs. I threw the dirty cloth at Monty to wrap around his head wound and then I placed the muzzle of the gun under his undamaged ear. "You're gonna' show me your operation. Griffin and Brandy will wait in the taxi."

At gunpoint, I forced Monty to stand up and then used the bat to prod him forward and through the doorway that led to his office in the house. I imagined him calmly working up here while listening to the cries coming from the latest victim he'd imprisoned in the lower depths.

On his desk, a late-model laptop was hooked up to an external hard drive and a large monitor.

"Disconnect the drive and give it to me."

"You planning to sell it to the highest bidder?"

"I'm taking it home to erase it, you fuckhead."

"I've seen you somewhere before, haven't I?"

In a moment he'd remember me as Yellow Rose.

I used the knob on the handle of the bat to flip the laptop onto the floor. Nothing like a little random violence to distract him from any memories he had of me lying on the bed at Daisy Studios. Running out on that gig was the best decision I'd ever made.

"Monty, this is your lucky night. Griffin doesn't want the police involved so let's pretend I'm here in their stead. I want you to connect to every one of the servers where you store your filth and permanently delete the files. That includes disabling the backup. I'll be watching and if I think you're cheating, I'll kill you."

I waved the gun at him for emphasis and Monty, who had no way of knowing what kind of person he was dealing with, sat down at his desk and did as he was told. Afterwards, I tied him up with the duct tape and smashed the electronics.

I exited through the basement and joined Griffin and Brandy in the backseat of the cab. Griffin hugged me tight. "I thought we'd lost you!" Next to him, Brandy had curled herself into a ball.

The nervous cabbie gunned the accelerator and we drove back to civilization.

***

As soon as we got home, I tucked Brandie into my bed and stayed with her until she fell asleep. I knew she couldn't stay with us but there would be time in the morning to figure things out. I tiptoed out of my room to use the bathroom and saw that Griffin was still up.

219

"Have you got a clean towel?"

"Sure." I pulled the plushest bath towel we had out of the linen closet and was handing it over when something in his face, a tightening around the jaw, stopped me.

"What happened that you're not telling me?"

Griffin swayed and I caught him before he fell to the floor. I walked him over to a chair and knelt beside him. "You can tell me. You know you can."

He struggled to speak the words. "It hurts where he did me."

"Who? Monty?"

"No. It was Stu. I went over there to free Brandy from Monty's basement. I didn't know Stu would be there. They dragged me upstairs to one of the bedrooms. Monty said I had it coming. After they left I untied myself and called you."

I felt a burning sensation in my chest, like hot lava and fought to control the urge to vomit.

"I should take you to the hospital so they can do a rape kit. We'll get Stu's DNA and send him to jail."

Griffin shook his head violently. "No! They'll put me in a home. I told you before. No cops."

"All right, I understand."

When he came out of the bathroom, his hair still wet from the shower, I saw that he'd been crying. I wanted to hold him but was afraid my touch might bring on a flashback and make things worse. We sat on the couch together and he reached over to touch the top of my head, as if *I* were the one who needed comforting. I'm sure he had no idea how much this tore me apart.

"Thanks for coming to get me," he said.

After Griffin turned in for the night in what was now known as Tiff's old room, I thought about getting rid of the gun. I didn't like having it in the apartment with a young man who had every reason to kill his tormentors if given the chance.

On the Web I found a buy-back event sponsored by a church on Staten Island. *No questions asked* it read. I'd

220

heard that was the protocol. It was also the right thing to do. On top of that they were offering a two-hundred-dollar gift card. I'd make the trip as soon as possible. In the meantime, I stowed the weapon in a box and hid it under the bed before climbing in next to Brandy. I fell asleep to the sound of her gentle breathing and in the morning, woke to the touch of little fingers running through my hair.

I fed the kids breakfast and since Brandie didn't seem ready to talk, I put her in front of the TV while I called Children Services. I told the receptionist that I'd found a little girl wandering around the street looking confused and taken her home with me. "She says her name is Brandy but she doesn't have any ID."

They sent over a young social worker named Lydia, decked out in a pink angora sweater and clutching a clipboard for security. Griffin stayed hidden in the bedroom while Lydia interviewed Brandy.

"What's your last name and how can we get in touch with your parents?" she asked. No time for "how brave you've been" or "I'm here to make sure you are safe."

Brandy pursed her lips.

"Your parents," Lydia insisted, "how can I reach them?"

"Don't know." Brandy, who had kept her tears at bay after being rescued from a cellar in the middle of the night, trembled in the face of this question.

The social worker sighed. "Do you have some clothes with you?"

"She's lucky to have what she's wearing."

Brandy was not eager to leave the apartment with this robot-like stranger. To convince her it was okay, I accompanied them downstairs, holding the little girl's hand as we walked to Lydia's car.

"These are good people who will figure out what you need and help you. They're much better at this kind of thing than I am. Trust me, things will work out." I hated myself for saying these words with no way of knowing if they were true.

23. Getting Danner

Griffin slowly recovered from his ordeal and I was relieved to see him dive back into his schoolwork. "There's a recruiter from Microsoft coming next month," he told me. "I'm gonna put together a killer portfolio. It's cool. I might get a job before I finish the program."

His optimism had to be genetic since life had treated him much too harshly to justify his positive outlook. If only I could follow his example. I couldn't get away from the awful images of those men brutalizing him. I'd promised no cops. That didn't mean I couldn't find another way.

The first thing I did was call Sloan and ask if he knew Stuart Danner.

"Not personally. He runs a home-entertainment company. If we're lucky, he'll be adding *Careless Love* to his Blu-Ray catalog. Why do you ask?"

"I've heard some unsavory things about him. He offered a friend of mine a job and she's nervous and asked me to check him out."

"I don't know what to say, Sandie. Stuart's one of the biggest distributors of Indie films in New York."

I'd seen Danner pick up Griffin in his Lexus and was astounded that someone with such a high profile would take the risks that he did. Maybe this was what people meant when they talked about privilege.

Sloan coughed nervously into the phone. "I wouldn't want him to drop my film because I was spreading rumors about him. We're just starting to get some interest from festivals."

He had a clear conflict of interest here and I was about to let him off the hook when he said, "You might want to talk to Estevan. He's got his reasons for keeping track of certain people and if there's an issue with Stu…"

"Thanks, I'll do that. And keep me posted on *Careless Love.* It would be great to see it on TV. Maybe you could do a series—they're streaming like crazy now."

No kidding. How dope would that be, Sandie? Good to talk with you. Take care."

***

I hadn't seen Estevan since the showing of *Careless Love* at NYU and was surprised at how cordial he was on the phone. I told him I had a problem I hoped he could help me with. With no hesitation, he asked me out for brunch at a café in Harlem.

When I got there, Estevan apologized for insisting that we eat outside. "The food here is great but I can't stand small spaces. It's a long story," he said.

Weak sunlight washed across the table, stealing enough chill from the air to make it bearable. I wasn't hungry, so I watched my friend eat while I told him what had happened to Griffin. Maybe I should have saved the grisly details for after the meal. Estevan pushed his plate aside in disgust.

"I can tell you from experience that Griffin won't breathe easy until he's sure Stuart Danner won't ever touch him again. This is personal for me, Sandie. I'm gay, I'm Puerto Rican and I was victimized as a kid. My family took a long time to accept my true nature and to this day it bowls me over that they eventually did. Otherwise, I'd have been

224

cut off at the knees like Griffin. They blackmailed him with his fear of being judged by the people who raised him... and then they used him like a piece of meat."

The breeze picked up and the red and blue plastic flags on the awning overhead flapped so loudly I had to lean in to hear what Estevan said next.

"We need to get this guy, to stomp him and scrape the crap off our shoes."

I had sensed this side of Estevan. During rehearsal he was the one who gave everything he had while the others carefully saved their energy for "when it mattered." It made sense that he would be as uncompromising about righting a wrong as he was fanatical about perfecting a part.

"When's your next night off?" he asked.

"Monday. What do you have in mind?"

"A lot depends on how young you can make yourself look, Sandie. It's a good cause — worth our while — but we might end up breaking some laws. I should tell you that up front."

He wanted to pull off a con and feared I might shy off. How ironic. "I can try for fifteen. But why bother when Danner prefers little boys?"

"You've got a younger brother. And if he's half as delicious as you are..."

"Are you sure we can get to this guy? I did some research and Danner's film distribution company is in a high-security building."

"There are places where chicken hawks hang out, places where they meet and feel safe. I know someone who can get us in."

"How?"

"He'll vouch for me. That's all it takes in Danner's world."

"Your friend isn't an undercover cop is he? I don't want Griffin caught up in the legal system again — he's been through enough. And you should know right now that I'm not somebody who testifies in court. Not anymore."

"Don't worry. Spencer's not a cop — he's an ex-junkie. Two years ago, he'd have sold his mother for a fix. He's worked for some unsavory people in the sex trade and he knows that scene inside out. Plus he owes me a favor."

The last of my doubts slipped away. "What's next?"

"I'll call Spencer and set things up for Monday night. It's a two-part operation so keep the day free as well. Remember to put together a killer, baby-doll outfit. And don't forget to bandage your breasts."

"I'm a good actor. You don't have to worry about me."

Darshon reached across the table and shook my hand. "For Griffin."

I repeated the words, feeling the bond between us strengthen and hold.

***

On Sunday, after the matinee at the DaCapo, I hit *Cinderella's Closet*, the new consignment store on St. Nicholas Avenue. Within minutes I found the exact item I was looking for, and it was in my size. The cashier, still on the cheerful side of eighty, was amused at my enthusiasm. "This is my kind of place," I said, putting all my change in their Children's Hospital collection jar.

Come Monday, I put on my recently acquired costume and arrived in Red Hook around noon. There were plenty of bars and well-labeled small businesses along Van Brunt Street. In contrast, anyone who went a few blocks west—like I did—would walk past the white-washed building that was once a shoe factory without guessing it housed the Magpie League.

Estevan met me out front. Thanks to his connected friend, we were welcomed into a heavily curtained room on the ground floor, where obsequious waiters in starched uniforms scurried between plump leather chairs set apart at discreet distances on a plush red rug. The chandeliers and old-fashioned light fixtures on the walls were there to give the room an air of respectability, all the usual trappings of a British gentleman's club. Until you noticed the gaudily framed pictures of young children in provocative poses mounted on the wall facing the bar. Estevan's informant had said there was a hidden screening room upstairs, complete with couches used for far more nefarious purposes than film-viewing.

It was Thursday and, as predicted, Stuart Danner sat near the window, against a backdrop of soft velvet drapes the color of blood.

"Spencer said I'd find you here," Estevan said. He nudged me forward and I stood there, the picture of shyness in my tight-fitting pinafore with ruffles at the hem, blonde hair in ringlets, eyes round with seductive innocence above peach-like cheeks with just a hint of naughty rouge.

Stu Danner put down his newspaper and took off his reading glasses. No hint of recognition flickered in his eyes and I swallowed my relief at his not having recognized me from our brief encounter when he was parked outside Daisy Studios.

Danner finished looking me over and shook his head. "Not my type. Wrong age and wrong sex."

Estevan's face collapsed in disappointment. "I'm sorry. I was misinformed." He paused for a beat or two and then his expression brightened as if welcoming an unexpected idea. "It seems you're in luck. Her brother looks just like her and is three years younger."

"Then bring him to the club." Danner's deep voice had turned breathy and querulous.

"That's the thing," Estevan explained. "The boy and his sister are staying at a shelter for runaways. Only family members can visit or take the kids out for meals. But I can get you access."

Danner looked skeptical. "Far too risky. I'll pass." He put on his reading glasses and picked up his newspaper.

"There might be another way... but it will cost you," Estevan said, touching Danner's sleeve to create complicity. It was a nice touch.

We both waited for the degenerate's response. A cardinal rule — make the mark come to you.

"How much and what do you have in mind?"

"Five grand buys you home delivery."

It was a calculated risk. The outcome depended on lust beating out paranoia and the high cost of untried goods. It seemed to take forever for the businessman to reach into his breast pocket for a pen and a business card to write on.

"Ten p.m. tonight. Just you and the boy. Don't be late."

We drove back to Manhattan in the dark blue Chevy Impala, a retrofitted police car that Estevan had recently purchased at the Brooklyn Navy Yard. "Can you pass for a boy?" he asked me.

I stared at him in disbelief. "Up to a point. But we're talking about a ten-year-old. It's impossible."

"A convincing profile, seen from a distance. That's all we need."

I visualized myself with short hair and a baseball cap. "Well, maybe — if the lighting is dim enough."

"It will be," he assured me. "We'll set the stage and he'll fall all over himself to make an entrance."

***

Back at my apartment, Estevan covered his straight, dark locks with a wig of curly auburn hair. "Can't be too careful about being recognized, not when you've been in as many unsuccessful films as me."

While he made a few phone calls, I worked on my own appearance in the bedroom until I was satisfied.

"Whaddya think?" I asked Estevan.

"Now I remember why Peter Pan's always played by a woman."

228

"Thanks. I'll put some cotton in my cheeks at the last minute to add some chipmunk."

We rehearsed a few of the trickier moves Estevan had scripted for himself and left at 9 p.m.

The trip to Long Island was quick, rush hour having ended three hours ago. We were both nervous and trying not to show it.

Stuart Danner lived in a new development in Roslyn. Estevan had used Google Street View to confirm that the sweeping, circular shape of the driveway made it difficult to see a car's occupants clearly, unless the vehicle sat directly out front. The other advantage was darkness.

As planned, we stopped about fifteen feet shy of the entrance and Estevan switched on the car's interior lights. He got out and walked the rest of the way, leaving me in the backseat as bait.

Ten minutes later, Estevan and Danner exited the massive front door that was more fitting for a fort than a private residence. As they walked toward us, Danner craned his neck for a better view of who was in the car and I turned my head to give him a glimpse of my profile and the brim of the baseball cap. He had been told that the boy, named Casey, was reluctant to enter the house because he'd been warned at the shelter about contact with strangers. Casey had supposedly agreed to ride in the car only after his sister told him that she and Estevan were friends.

Estevan opened the back door of the Impala and stuck his head in.

"It's alright, Casey," he said loudly enough for Danner to overhear. "There's someone here your sister wants you to meet. He's going to help the two of you find a nice place to live." For a few unpleasant seconds, the ominous implications of this sentence crawled along my skin.

As soon as Estevan stepped back from the door, Danner took his place, leaning in with one arm extended, as if to touch the "boy" reassuringly on the shoulder.

Estevan grabbed both of Danner's arms by the wrists and twisted them behind the pedophile's back, slamming them together and locking the handcuffs in place with a click. My arm still ached from letting the actor repeatedly practice this move on me earlier in the evening.

"Be quiet if you know what's good for you." Estevan shoved Stuart Danner into the back seat while I exited from the other side.

Danner hung his head in miserable compliance, not bothering to put up a fight. Types like him took out their anger on kids, not grownups. Thinking of what he'd done to Griffin made me want to punch him in the face, or worse.

Estevan drove the route we had mapped out to Bushwick. Our captive spoke only once. "I could make you rich."

"We're not here for you to make us rich. We're here to make you sorry." My words hung in the silence as Monty's house came into view and Estevan pulled round back. He shoved Danner through the basement door that Monty had obligingly left open in his hurried flight.

We had not discussed what we planned to do with Danner once we had him. Although violence wasn't Estevan's thing, I suspected unknown forces within him had been punched down. It wasn't about being persecuted for being gay or experiencing racism as a Puerto Rican. I could tell he'd come to terms with the world and found enough beauty within himself to match the ugliness outside. It was Estevan's sheer hatred of cruelty that stiffened his limbs and filled his core with rage on behalf of innocent children.

My own feelings were crammed inside, attached to a trigger waiting for the go-ahead.

No one was more aware of the emotions seeking release in that basement than Danner. His breathing accelerated and when he said "please" the word was broken in several places by his vibrato.

I retrieved the digital recorder from my purse.

Estevan made a fist and held it in front of his face like a scientist looking for a clue as to what he would do next. Banner braced himself for the punch, but it never came. Instead, the actor placed both hands on Danner's shoulders and shoved him down into the crawl space where Brandy had recently been imprisoned.

I tossed the recorder into the indigo blackness where Danner crouched in fear. "If you record your crimes in full, we'll think about letting you out."

I helped Estevan push the workbench into place and for a while we stood there, listening to the pounding and the sobs coming from behind the wall.

"Stop sniveling and start recording!" Estevan commanded.

We switched off the light and left.

***

"You do realize that busting Danner guarantees *Careless Love* won't be picked up for distribution?" I asked Estevan over the noise of the Impala's engine.

"Don't be so sure. Sloan has good connections and if the film succeeds at least we won't owe it to a monster."

"How long do you think we should keep him there?"

"At least two days," he said. "Long enough for the face of every child he's harmed to be carved indelibly on his soul. Then I'll call the police. It's not every day they find a criminal locked up alongside a recording of his confession."

***

A week later, I invited Estevan and Neal over for dinner. When they arrived, I took Estevan aside to prep him. "Griffin doesn't know we had anything to do with Danner's arrest. You should have seen the amazement on his face when I showed him the article in the Daily News. It was like he could hardly believe it. He said 'What's up with life? It's never played fair with me before.'"

Estevan grinned. "Neal suspects I'm hiding something. By the time I tell him, he'll be so relieved that I'm not seeing another guy he'll forget to be angry about the risks we took."

I watched Griffin devour the grilled swordfish and braised green beans, shoveling in forkfuls of rice in between. There was a healthy color in his cheeks and his eyes looked clearer than I'd ever seen them.

24. Of Babes and Arms

Disoriented, I scanned the crowd milling beneath the harsh lights around the Delta baggage carousel. Griffin had insisted on coming with me. A woman turned toward us and waved.

"Oh my God — you're an earth mother!" I was floored by the sight of Tiffany's denim jumper and embroidered white blouse.

Griffin, who had never met Tiff, had no memories of skimpy sundresses clinging to her pipe-cleaner legs. All he saw was a buxom beer maiden who made me look flat-chested in comparison.

He eyed the occupant of the baby stroller with equal awe. "He's so tiny."

"Tony's three weeks old. You can't get much younger than that." Tiff yanked at the handle of a pink duffel-bag on the conveyor belt and it fell to the floor. Griffin slung it onto the luggage cart and walked behind us on the way to the Air Train.

"Don't worry, Sandie. I promise I won't force you to listen to gushes of verbal diarrhea about my unique and wonderful child. And I apologize for using Griffin to get to you. He's a soft-boiled egg, that one."

"Yeah, well, Griffin saved my life and he wouldn't stop reminding me of how you did the same."

Griffin had also violated my privacy by taking my traitorous roommate's call on my cell while I was in the shower and conspiring with her to get me to take her back.

Tony let out a sharp cry and was immediately swept out of the stroller and into a Tiff's baby-carrier pouch. "I know, I know," she said. "I look like a mutant kangaroo."

The baby looked exactly like Russell, who predictably had promised his son the moon and delivered a patched-up beach ball leaking air as much as he did. I'd heard the whole story from Griffin. The only thing missing was a doting pair of grandparents to pick up the pieces. Fat chance. This honor had fallen to us.

The Russian driver, whose aged Coupe de Ville town car looked like it was used for stunts in a B movie, struggled to load the duffel bag and stroller into the trunk.

"I borrowed our neighbor's bassinette," Griffin said over his shoulder from the front seat. "She said not to bother returning it because she got her tubes tied. Talk about synchronicity."

Griffin and I had done what we could to baby-proof the apartment for Tony's arrival. We'd bought an apartment-sized washer and dryer on credit and he moved his stuff out of Tiff's old bedroom into the living room, where we set up a Sochi screen to hide his futon and the dresser. It was going to be a tight fit and I'd thought more than once about backing out of the arrangement. Each time, Brandy's brave little face as she was led away into the broken world of Children Services came back to haunt me. Sometimes life gave second chances when least expected.

As the taxi crossed the Whitestone Bridge, I cracked the window. Across the choppy water, the skyline spread flat against the gray-blue sky, impersonal and anonymous—two New York qualities I'd thought I loved and now seemed to have outgrown. Tiffany fumbled around in the monstrous pink bag and pulled out a black t-shirt she thrust at me with an embarrassed grin. *I DONE YOU WRONG AND I'M SORRY* was printed in red letters on the front.

"You expect me to wear this thing?"

"No, silly! *I'm* gonna wear it, every day until you forgive me."

***

On his first night with us, Tony wailed for hours. In desperation, I strapped him in his car seat and placed it atop the vibrating compact-size clothes dryer. When Tiff asked if this was standard motherly practice and wasn't I afraid the vibrations would shake up his internal organs, I grabbed the baby and walked him around the apartment until he finally fell asleep.

At 3 a.m. I was awakened by the booming bass of a passing car, probably someone driving home from an all-night party. The strident rap music was soon drowned out by the blare of approaching sirens. I pictured a fire engine and an ambulance speeding through the city's arteries—a red corpuscle followed by a white one. A reminder that somebody, somewhere, was a lot worse off than me.

Tiffany meant well but she needed a lot of help dealing with motherhood. Tony's round-the-clock demands were endless and it was impossible to tell if his frantic cries indicated hunger, a need for a changed diaper or something more urgent that I was at loss to imagine. I'd never guessed that something as natural as motherhood could be such a monumental challenge. We served at the beck and call of a month-old bundle of instincts who expressed them with colossal lungpower and who Tiffany said made her feel like a milk machine with a cleaning attachment.

Griffin helped us out but he was just a kid and needed to finish school. Although he'd set the stage for Tiff's return with the baby, once his fantasy family became a reality he acted like it was a huge inconvenience. As always, he wasn't easy to read and I didn't have time to use a pair of plyers to find out what was bugging him. It wasn't fear of Monty or Stu, of that I was sure. Since Monty's night of reckoning and

235

Danner's punishment, Griffin walked around with more confidence. Maybe babysitting didn't fit in with his new image of himself.

Tiffany started work again as a cocktail waitress and since I worked nights too, our childcare expenses went sky high. We took turns delivering Tony and his supplies of breast milk into the care of Arva, a warm yet businesslike Dominican woman who ran a popular daycare in her ground floor apartment across the street. Arva gave a cash discount and lots of advice, which was how Tiff learned how to enroll Tony in Child Health Plus, a state program that covered kids for less than ten dollars a month.

Tony shared a playpen with a three-month old girl, who looked enormous in comparison. I always hesitated in the doorway on my way out, but the expected wail of protest never came. Both Tiff and I felt guilty in spite of knowing our son was in good hands. It was hard to believe how quickly we'd begun to think of him as belonging to us both.

Because we knew almost nothing about baby development—what to expect and when to expect it—we took our cues from Tony's caregiver. "Today he lifted up his head," Arva would say. "The first time I've seen him do this."

A few weeks later, I was getting Tony into his pajamas, while heating up his night feeding, when he looked up at me, his legs curled like pink lobster tails above the changing table and smiled. It was as if he recognized a friend he hadn't seen for years. As I said to Tiffany, "It killed me, totally. I guess he decided it was time to let me see who was in there. Wait until I tell Arva."

After Tony started smiling and gurgling, everything Tiff and I had done up to that point—enduring the racket he made and taking turns comforting him when he had colic, getting up at 8 a.m. after a late night to feed Mr. Voracious, doing double duty when the other "mom" was sick—suddenly seemed worth it. The next time I dropped him off at Arva's, I couldn't help gloating.

"Last night he grabbed on to my finger and smiled. If you're lucky maybe he'll do the same for you."

I walked to the subway with a step lightened by the absence of motherly guilt.

Vacuum-packed in the downtown A train, I often came close to falling asleep on my feet on the way to the theatre. We were staging *Aida*, meaning make-up was front and center, requiring a lot of research to make it look authentic. To transform our mezzo soprano into *Amneris the Egyptian Princess*, I began with her smoky eyes, which took almost an hour. After applying foundation, I drew dark curving lines below her natural eyebrows, blending them together with a brush. Then I placed small pieces of tape angling down from the side of each eye, using them as guides for filling in the black, winged tails sweeping outward, adding drama. I stuck with the traditional, navy blue eye shadow but added my own touch around the edges, streaks of yellow painted between vivid strokes of ebony eyeliner.

Afterwards I rushed home to whatever chaos awaited me. The cast had long ago given up on inviting me to parties.

***

Tiff stopped breastfeeding when Tony was three months old, saying it was too much trouble using the pump and she'd given him a good head start on his nutrition. It didn't ring true and sure enough I found her stash hidden in the closet behind a bag of disposable diapers.

That night, as soon as she walked in the door after her shift at the diner, I confronted her. I had planned to start with sarcasm, giving her points for not wanting to poison our baby with her contaminated milk. That was before I became the object of the menace launched from her cranked up eyes.

I removed myself from striking distance while staying close enough for her to hear me. "If you don't deal with your problem, Tiffany, you'll lose custody of Tony."

I was prepared to defend myself but I shouldn't have worried. There was no fight left in her and when I shook the bottle of pills in her face, Tiff fell apart, wailing louder than the baby in the next room ever did.

"I swear, I didn't use while I was pregnant. Russell made sure of that. He watched me like a hawk, right up until I gave birth at Cedars-Sinai. I thought Russ would stay with us once he saw how beautiful Tony was. Unfortunately, he meant it when he said, 'I'll see this thing through, right until you drop the kid and not a day longer.' He's one cold-hearted son of a bitch."

"Maybe you should be grateful to Russell for forcing you to stay clean for that long."

The barb connected and Tiffany winced, her face muscles rippling as she fought to keep her cool. "Who do you think got me strung out in the first place?"

"When you were a teenager? You never told me Russell was behind you getting sent to the Ranch."

"Well now that you're enlightened, how does it feel? Shitty, right. Ignorance is bliss."

She was right. A lot of things were starting to make sense in a messed-up way. The only thing I was sure of was that the past didn't matter and Tony's welfare did. I put the question as strongly as I could. "Are you going to take care of things?"

She heard the ultimatum in my voice, because that evening, I witnessed a colorful whirlpool of multi-colored pills and white powder swirling down the toilet.

The next morning, Tiff and I went to her first Crystal Meth Anonymous meeting. I didn't stay until the bitter end and afterwards she came home to change into her waitress uniform. "I'm one day sober and counting. And I've got a sponsor. He'll be coming over to check on me sometime this week, unannounced, as they say."

She promised she'd look in on Tony, who was at Arva's, and pay our weekly childcare bill on the way to work. I had

238

an audition in the early afternoon or I would have been looking after the baby myself.

***

When the doorbell buzzed I assumed it was Tiff's over-eager sponsor. No such luck. It was Monty. Before I could react, he shoved me backwards, locking the door and flipping his jacket open to pull a knife from the sheath on his belt. "You'd better let me have my way or I'll cut off your face."

I knew he meant it and a jolt of fear shot through me. There was so much hatred in his eyes I pictured it overflowing into the street and traveling through a storm drain to poison the Hudson.

"I understand you're upset." I was having difficulty keeping my voice steady. "I've got some cash in my purse— you can have that right away and I'll arrange for more."

My hands shook as I fumbled around in my handbag for the Mace I always carried with me. Monty grabbed the bag and threw it across the room. "Money's not what I want."

Griffin's gun was hidden away in my room, waiting to be disposed of. I turned to run in that direction, hoping Monty wouldn't stab me in the back, and stumbled over the throw rug in the foyer, falling hard to the floor. Monty grabbed my arm and roughly pulled me to my feet.

"Strip," he ordered, pushing me into the middle of the room. Keeping a grip on the knife, he took a seat on the edge of an upholstered chair to watch the show.

With each piece of clothing I removed, I felt another part of myself detach, until my shivering body stood naked in front of him, my mind a million miles away.

"After you left, I remembered who you were. The cunt who came to my studio and then chickened out at the last minute. I'm one of those chumps who pay their taxes and I still had the form you filled out. The one with your name and address, Sandie Doyle."

"It's Sandie Donovan," I said. If I *was* going to die it wouldn't be under a false name.

Monty dropped his pants where he stood and waved the knife impatiently at the couch. "Lie down."

A second later I felt his full weight pinning me down. He gripped my shoulder with one hand, holding the knife over me with the other. I saw it in his eyes, the hope that I would fight back and give him an excuse to stab me. I forced myself to stay limp. All I could do was hope he'd get it over with and not kill me afterwards.

It took him forever but Monty finally got it up and pried my legs apart. For a moment, he let go of my shoulder so he could use his hand to guide his penis. He was halfway there when I made my move. I jammed my palm under his chin, making him jerk his head back and used all the strength in my other arm to heave him off. I heard the knife clatter on the wooden floor.

Scrambling across the living room floor on all fours, I reached my bedroom door and made it inside. There was no time to shut the door. I dove under the bed and felt around for the box I'd put there. Monty grabbed my legs and pulled me out, not seeing the gun in my hand until it was too late. I aimed in his direction and fired. My first shot ever taken outside of a pistol range found its mark. Monty toppled backwards, clutching his gut, and screaming in agony.

I called nine-one-one and the operator told me to pull the sheet off the bed and ball it up against the "victim's" stomach to stop the bleeding. In about ten seconds the sheet turned red and I knew he was going to die. He passed out when the EMTs came through the door.

Griffin told me later that Monty was DOA at the hospital. "It was you or him, Sandie. You did what you had to do."

25. Clearing the Air

Thanks to Officer Maria Sanchez from the Special Victims Unit—yes that's really a thing outside of TV land—the police drove me to the hospital instead of the precinct. Maria was one of those people who kept her ear to the ground and picked up on cases like mine. And since the gun was registered in Monty's name, I was never charged with a crime.

A reporter from the New York Post got wind of the story and for a time I was a celebrity, hailed on social media as a woman capable of defending herself. The main result of my short-lived notoriety was a shitload of threatening and sexually explicit emails sent to the address posted on the make-up artist website Griffin had designed for me. On the upside, I did get a few legitimate calls for freelance work to supplement my main gig at the DiCapo.

***

Tiff was up to twenty days sober and Tony had turned three months, when Ben texted me. I had presumed he would take Jerome's damning words at face value and delete me from his cell phone and his life, that he had dumped me at a distance, lacking the backbone to reject me in person.

I ignored the message and he called the next day.

"I heard what happened, how you fought off that bastard in your apartment. I would have contacted you sooner but I was out of town. I'm sorry. Can we get together?"

"I don't think it's a good idea. And your brother Jerome would agree."

Both my roommates strongly disagreed with this response. "If he wants to make it up to you," Tiff said, "you should let him. Otherwise, you'll never know what could have been."

In the end I messaged Ben saying I'd changed my mind.

***

Why did I let them talk me into this? I stood at the bar in a downtown restaurant, uncertain where to sit or even if I wanted to be there.

"I got us a table." He avoided eye contact until we were seated across from each other, safely separated by a barricade of condiments and sculpted cloth napkins.

"You look well."

"It took a while," he said. His face seemed less full than I remembered —a waning moon—and although it had been less than a year, the streaks of grey in his ginger hair had widened.

The unexpected affection I found in his eyes brought back all the feelings I'd pushed down. Furious with myself, I swallowed hard and tried to think of a joke to hide behind. No luck. I patted my eyes with a napkin, examining the smudges of mascara as if they were part of a Rorschach test that could explain what was going on inside me.

"Sloan tells me you're a mom now."

"A co-mom. Tiffany's the biological mother."

I took a gulp of the Martini the waiter had brought and placed Tony's photo on the tablecloth in front of Ben. As I watched him run his finger over the picture, caressing it, a

242

glint of gold caught my eye. "You're wearing your wedding band."

He fidgeted with the ring, rotating it nervously, darting an embarrassed look past my left ear. "Leslie Ann is as close to being cured as you can be when you have cancer. We decided to try and start over and since she's been wearing her ring again, I put mine on too. We're not living together, not yet. He smiled weakly, confused by his own explanations. Then he turned again to the photo. "What's his name?"

"Tony."

Ben paused, like he always did when searching for the perfect words. "You know, Leslie Ann was the one who didn't want kids. I went along with it to keep the peace."

"Why are you telling me this?"

He leveled a stare at me, as if I were being deliberately dense. "What it means is that now that *this* has happened...now that you have a child...choices about his future will have to be made. That's what you want isn't it?"

I didn't know how to answer that question, or even if I should.

Ben persisted. "The first step is to clear the air, don't you think?"

I nodded warily and when he ordered another drink, declined.

"Jerome said all these things about you, and though I doubted every detail was accurate, it was like all of a sudden—"

"The wool was pulled from your eyes," I volunteered. I left it there, not feeling up to setting him straight.

"I believed what my brother told me because it made everything else make sense, especially the lies I suspected you were telling me but never could get a handle on. What puzzled me was, why be so greedy? Why steal from me when I was perfectly willing to give you everything you needed?"

I wished I hadn't turned down that second drink. "It wasn't me who stole your painting. Once we were together,

243

things were different. Maybe I didn't care to share much about my past. That didn't give you the right to assume the worst about my actions in the present."

Ben reached for my hand. I pulled it out of his reach.

"Maybe I went too far. I'm sorry," he said. "Let's not dwell on all that. This baby could have a great future. Do you know how much it costs to raise a child? Leslie Ann and I have talked it over and we're willing to adopt him. But you and Tiffany would have to be willing to totally disentangle yourself."

As if the bonds of motherhood were pesky cobwebs to be swept out of sight.

"Anthony Kaplan has a nice sound to it, don't you think?" Ben continued, pleading his case.

"His name is Tony Mays-Donovan. Tiff and I hyphenated it when we agreed to co-parent."

"Why not Tony Mays-Doyle?"

"My real name is Donovan. One of the many things you don't know about me. Not that it's entirely your fault. I kept you in the dark about a lot of things."

Ben stayed silent, digesting this information.

"As for your offer, thanks but no thanks." In my fantasies Ben had woken up to the truth and apologized for letting Jerome ruin our relationship. Now all I saw was a man looking over his shoulder for any evidence of dishonesty he might have missed. And even if his suspicions were to magically disappear... I took a deep breath.

"I'm sorry. Tony has all the family he needs and Tiff and I are perfectly capable of supporting him."

His face flushed with disappointment, or was it embarrassment, at his own insensitivity. "Can I visit sometime?"

"Only if you show some respect and to be honest, that's not what happened here today."

I stood up, bumping into the table so that it rocked precariously, and walked fast out of the restaurant and down the street. I had someplace more important to go.

***

The hospice, which was in a Catholic hospital on Eastchester Road in the Bronx, took patients like Frank, who were covered by Medicaid and nothing else. It was a long ride by train and bus, leaving plenty of time to think about what I'd say, none of which felt right.

Frank was waiting for me in his room and told me he was anxious for a change of scenery. It was too cold to sit out on the terrace, so we took the elevator to the atrium. The cacti among the ferns and tropical plants growing under the glass roof ironically reminded me of Tucson. At least the hospital smell couldn't reach us in here.

I pulled up two chairs and we sat facing each other over a flimsy card table in the activity room. Frank's physique had passed the point of gauntness. It was like I was talking with a skeleton.

"Stella told me you ran off with a, how did she put it, 'lowlife grifter?' Why would you do something like that?" This from a man who had raised me to admire rogues.

"You're dealing from a stacked deck, Dad. You've heard a lot about my life and I know almost nothing about yours. Like what happened between you and that woman you moved in with in Tucson?"

He shifted uneasily in his metal folding chair. "Maybe we should stick with the present, since the past is unpleasant and, in my case, there's no future."

"How are they treating you?"

"The nurses are okay. They push painkillers when you need them and faith even if you don't. I'm glad you came, Sandie. It means a lot to me."

"So why did you give up on me when I was fifteen? You weren't sick then." It was a stupid question but I had to ask.

Frank bit his lip, I assumed to hold back a tirade about my youthful indiscretions. After a while, he said, "Actually, Stella was impressed by how you've pulled your life together

245

and are working in the theatre. After you left Gile's party that's all she would talk about, Sandie this and Sandie that. You'd better make sure you invite her to your wedding in the Bahamas."

He waited a second or two before he winked at me. Frank had always been sharp. "Honestly. You should move back in with her."

"Did Stella tell you to say that?"

"What difference does it make? It's a good idea."

I pushed away the memories of my aunt criticizing my every move. "I'll think on it." The lie seemed to reassure him and he let it go.

We talked until Frank's voice faded to a whisper and fatigue drained his already ghost-like complexion of any hint of color. I felt the last of my anger leave me. It was like seeing the back of an unwelcome guest who had stayed far too long. Frank had given me life and I decided to settle for that.

Back in his room, I told him I'd be back in a bit.

"If I'm still here."

No use in denying the truth of that. I kissed the top of his head and he reached out to stroke my cheek before I left.

Three Years Later

Now that we could safely hang out at the Inwood Bar and Grill, Tiffany was making the most of it. "I'm easy but I've got my standards," was her motto. I could tell when she was into a guy by how much she revealed in the first five minutes. If she merely described herself as a native Alaskan who knew how to "dress an elk," she was simply passing the time. But if I overheard the words "Recovery Ranch" or "my three-year-old son," I knew her companion had met the sniff test and I'd be walking back to our apartment alone to pay the babysitter.

Tonight was no different except that the sound of Tiff's key turning in our multiple locks woke me at 1 a.m., way earlier than expected. "Something must have gone wrong," I thought groggily, too exhausted to get out of bed and investigate.

I heard her kick off her stilettos before opening the creaky door to the room she shared with Tony. Then I pulled a pillow over my head to block out the noise I knew she'd make in the kitchen and tried to get some shuteye.

Next thing I knew, the alarm was beeping and I had forty-five minutes to breakfast, shower, and get dressed for an early call at the theatre. Sunday matinees had destroyed my Saturday night prospects but I was a recent hire and grateful for the work. At least La Bohème required less makeup than Aida, otherwise I'd be up earlier than the sun.

It was strange to be working one of the few jobs in existence that would have earned my father's approval. Every Saturday morning up until Mom died, he'd have me switch on the stereo while he opened the windows of our tiny apartment in Yonkers. "Turn it up, kid!" he'd yell, right before setting the thunderous voices of his favorite divas loose on the neighborhood. I'd pictured them as costumed elephants trumpeting their emotions across the rooftops all the way back to Italy. "Opera singers make everyone who hears them feel larger than life," he liked to say. This coming from someone whose chronic unemployment and status as a kept husband had made him feel small.

Frank died last year at the hospice in the Bronx, while I was still working for the DiCapo theatre. I had steady employment as their theatrical makeup artist for almost two years, some kind of record for me, and it was sad that I never got to invite him to a show. He may have deserted me and blown up my adolescence but not before he'd filled my childhood with trips to the beach, tinfoil-hat conspiracy theories, and classical music. During sound checks at the DiCapo—a well-appointed theatre with a 30-piece orchestra that totally out-classed the artsy dump where I work now—I used to lurk in the wings, picturing Frank's face in the audience beyond the dazzling lights.

After the DiCapo closed, I signed on at the low budget McDougal Theatre—only to have it go dark after the first patients were officially diagnosed with Covid-19 in New York. To make matters worse, our Artistic Director, Darragh O'Sullivan, refused to go digital, not in rehearsal or performance.

"If I was meant to be pixilated, I'd have been born wearing spectacles and waving my umbrella in a dangerous manner," O'Sullivan informed anyone who questioned this decision. Eccentric as he was, Darragh had a lot of cred, having worked his way up from roving street busker to the most in-demand tenor-for-hire in Dublin.

The McDougal reopened six weeks ago, just as my unemployment checks were drying up. I was on my way there now and as I approached the subway entrance on St. Nicholas, I noticed several unmasked people hogging the pavement and ambling toward me. I looked for a safe way round and not seeing one, stepped off the curb into the street. A sec later I caught myself and hopped back on the sidewalk. The pandemic was over and although we might all feel nervous as rabbits for the rest of our lives, it was time to let go and live a little. Paradoxically, this also meant no more brightly colored fabrics and slogans like "FU Corona," and "If you can read this you're too close."

Close. The word had a new definition. As did breathing, especially when done by big chested opera singers capable of exhaling high numbers of deadly droplets.

The McDougal was just a few blocks north of Bowery, where the old Amato Opera building still stood, shorn of its lovely, light gray brick façade and fanciful ironwork by some cruel developer. Darragh shared the Amato's vision of "community opera with close ties to the neighborhood." He'd taken over the lease to an old movie theatre and remodeled it. Rumor said a backer was involved, an anonymous angel.

It was a five-minute walk from the Broadway-Lafayette station to the theatre on East Houston. It was our first cast and crew meeting after the reopening and Darragh announced he would be issuing checks for back pay. There was a collective gasp.

"I would have reimbursed you sooner but the government loan came through later than expected," he explained. No one was more amazed than me, since Darragh's assistant had told me the loan fell through.

Darragh's choice of La Bohème to kick off the season had been received with less enthusiasm than his financial generosity. "I know what you're thinking," he told us.

249

"Mimi's tragic story ends in her death from consumption. Sandie, are you here?"

When I waved from the back of the room, Darragh raised his voice to reach me. "I want you to avoid the traditional feverishly haunted look. The audience should see themselves in her. I want them to think, 'there but for the grace of God,' that sort of thing."

Francesca Adeloff, who played the part of Mimi, was waiting for me in the combined greenroom and make-up cubicle. When they remodeled the Oldtime Cinema, someone had the bright idea of providing workspace for the opera company behind the newly constructed stage. This was okay for make-up but even after sound proofing was added, every note of a singer's warmup was audible to anyone gaining early entrance to the house.

Francesca knew her character so well she would have applied her own greasepaint if the union allowed it. We agreed that Mimi should be made up to look fierce, not weak. As Francesca put it, "that woman was much more tormented by jealousy than she was by disease."

I had our *prima donna* ready a solid half-hour before curtain time and was picking up my bag and sweater, when I noticed that underneath Mimi's luminous glow, Francesca was looking nervous. "Where're you going?"

"Don't worry. I've got an errand to run and will be back before you go on," I reassured her. Perspiring under hot lights can melt the most exquisitely made-up face into a Salvador Dali nightmare. If something went awry during performance, someone had to be there to come to the rescue.

On West 4th, the lunch crowd made it difficult to fast-walk to my destination. Where there were hordes of people there were also pickpockets and it amused me to think of the item stashed in the left front pocket of my jeans. They'd never know what they'd missed. Not that they would have appreciated it.

Jeffrey Vega's client had agreed to meet me at noon in Washington Square Park, a half mile north of the theatre. I'd have plenty of time to walk there and back, factoring in a few minutes' conversation.

"His name is Gordon and he'll be wearing a red t-shirt," was all Jeff had said when he delivered the piece yesterday, along with a disclaimer. "This is the best I could do from a photograph."

Jeff still worked as a prop master and had added a lucrative side-business in "antiqued jewelry," as a result of our original, successful collaboration. He liked the creative end but not the footwork. Although working for him had tided me over during the pandemic, now that I was back to work at the McDougal, this would be my last "delivery." When you're co-parenting a child, the only thing worth risking is a bit of vomit on your best blouse.

Right on time, I arrived at the fountain. Through the sparkling curtain of water between us, I spotted a pudgy but taller than average guy with some skin bulging at the bottom of his crimson tee. He responded to my wave by dodging a kid on a skateboard and two bicyclists to reach me in one piece.

"Pleased to meet you Ms. Doyle," he said, using the name I reserved for these events.

He made a move to bump elbows and I dodged, causing him to step back awkwardly.

"Nice to meet you too, Gordon," I offered as compensation for my rudeness.

"No worries. It's the new normal."

Gordon swiveled his gaze around the park. I'd already checked. There was no one within earshot. "Have you got it?"

I showed him the cloth bag with Jeffrey Vega's piece and he led me to a bench off the main walkway where we could have more privacy. Through a loupe, he examined the fake seventeenth century bracelet, made of real but low-carat gold with an emerald mounted in the middle. He took

251

his time, studying Jeff's work so closely you'd think he was a human spectrometer.

"Very nice," he finally said. "I like the inclusion in the gem. Gives a touch of authenticity without being flashy."

He was talking about the imperfection that Jeff had mimicked when he cast the emerald, a tiny fracture that would decrease the value of a diamond but in emeralds are considered to add natural beauty. It also gives the mark the idea they're getting something unique.

"We agreed on six hundred," Gordon said. Most of Jeff's buyers were middlemen who knew exactly what they were getting. They didn't pay top dollar.

"Glad you like the piece," I responded. "But Jeff said seven hundred."

I didn't like his little attempt at subterfuge or his assumption that I'd fall for it. When he gave me the cash I pulled out the badge I carried in my purse.

"You've got to be kidding!" He skittered away from me on the bench, his torso deflated. I could see the muscles in his mouth tightening as he bucked up his courage, waiting for me to tell him he was under arrest.

I slid the badge across the smooth wooden slats so he could have a better look at it. It only took a moment for Gordon to realize he'd been made a fool of and jump to his feet. "Bitch," he muttered.

"Maybe next time you'll remember to ask the buyer if they're a police officer before there's even a hint of a transaction." I addressed these words to Gordon's retreating back while returning Jeff's badge replica to its compartment. What was it Jeff had said when he gave it to me? "Something to have some fun with while teaching the amateurs a lesson."

This was the end of it. On my way back to the McDougal, I felt a spring in my step at the thought of being paid to do what I loved without risking the safety of my loved ones.

ACKNOWLEDGEMENTS

Every book is a unique journey, with many helpers contributing along the way. I'll start by thanking Daniel Willis of D.X. Varos for believing in and publishing *Sandstorm.*

To Larry Cheek, Jane Isenberg, Jeanne Matthews, Pete MacDonald, and Scotty Johnson—without your honest critiques, I might never have found the hidden heart of this book. A shoutout of "thanks!" to my brother Rick for his never-failing encouragement, to my husband, Gary, and our son, Ian, and to my agent, Jo Ann Deck, whose bi-weekly phone calls shored me up during the most challenging hours.

About the Author

Joyce Yarrow was born and raised in the Southeast Bronx. She escaped to Manhattan at an early age, where she wrote poetry while riding the bus through the Lower East Side. When she was seventeen *The Bus Poems* were published and her writing career was launched. Today, she enjoys writing suspense fiction, in which her protagonists use brains rather than brawn to prevail. Joyce is also a Pushcart Prize Nominee and her short stories and essays have appeared in Inkwell Journal, Whistling Shade, Descant, Arabesques, and Weber: The Contemporary West and the Los Angeles Review of Books. Yarrow is a member of the Authors Guild and the Sisters in Crime organization.

Other Exquisite Fiction from
D. X. Varos, Ltd.

CPSIA information can be obtained
at www.ICGtesting.com
Printed in the USA
BVHW071658200721
612415BV00007B/344